Mind Games

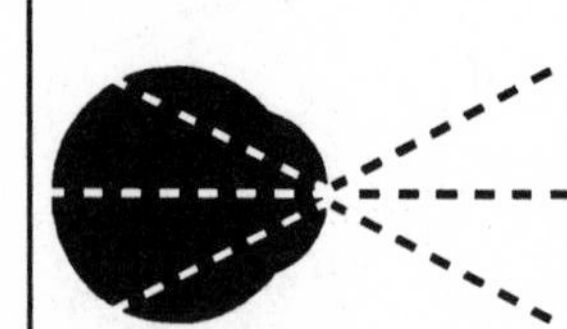

This Large Print Book carries the Seal of Approval of N.A.V.H.

KAELY QUINN PROFILER, BOOK 1

MIND GAMES

NANCY MEHL

THORNDIKE PRESS
A part of Gale, a Cengage Company

Farmington Hills, Mich • San Francisco • New York • Waterville, Maine
Meriden, Conn • Mason, Ohio • Chicago

Thorndike Press, a part of Gale, a Cengage Company.

Thorndike Press® Large Print Christian Mystery.
The text of this Large Print edition is unabridged.
Other aspects of the book may vary from the original edition.
Set in 16 pt. Plantin.

**LIBRARY OF CONGRESS CIP DATA ON FILE.
CATALOGUING IN PUBLICATION FOR THIS BOOK
IS AVAILABLE FROM THE LIBRARY OF CONGRESS**

ISBN-13: 978-1-4328-5859-9 (hardcover)

Published in 2018 by arrangement with Bethany House Publishers, an imprint of Baker Publishing Group

Printed in the United States of America
1 2 3 4 5 6 7 22 21 20 19 18

To God

Thank you for being with me
every step of the way.
You are my heart, my soul, my life.

PROLOGUE

He stood in the middle of his secret room, staring at walls covered with old newspaper clippings. The aroma of aging paper was like a powerful drug, sparking his hate. His fingers clenched and unclenched. Stories full of fear and death. Pictures of people before they became victims of a vile murderer who had ravaged the people of Des Moines twenty years earlier. Women smiling in driver's license photos or family pictures, unaware that they were living on borrowed time. No hint of the horror awaiting them. And no clue that someday soon their pictures would be snapped again by police photographers pretending the carnage was routine. It never was.

He walked up to a picture of the monster who had finally been caged. Ed Oliphant. A husband, a father, a churchgoer. He had a lot in common with Dennis Rader, the infamous BTK Killer who had terrorized

Wichita, Kansas, for so many years. But unlike Dennis, Ed never showed remorse for what he'd done. Of course, many experts dismissed Rader's so-called repentance. They didn't believe he was really sorry for his horrendous acts. He was only sorry he got caught. Unlike Rader, Ed hadn't even bothered to acknowledge the families of his victims.

He pulled the picture of Ed off the wall and stared into his eyes. Eyes full of darkness and evil. He had fourteen official kills to his name. Many experts believed there were more than that. Of course, not all his victims were dead. Quite a few people still lived under the shadow of Ed Oliphant. He spit on Ed's picture and stuck it back on the wall, wiping the extra spittle from his mouth on his pant leg.

The Raggedy Man. Serial killers shouldn't be given nicknames. It only fueled their egos. It wasn't until his seventh murder that investigators began to hear the same thing from friends and family of victims. That the victims had come in contact with a homeless man before they were killed. A young girl who saw Ed approach a woman whose body was found twenty-four hours later called him a "raggedy man." Thus the moniker. He'd originally picked the guise of a homeless person because they were the invisible people. Most citizens liked to pretend they didn't exist, so Ed was able to hide in plain sight. It was a cruel irony that those who actually noticed Ed — those who were kind — became his targets.

Once law enforcement started looking for someone under the guise of a homeless person, Ed changed his MO and began to dress as a police officer. He realized that the frightened citizens of Des Moines were now overly cautious of strangers but gravitated toward the police since they represented safety. Which, of course, Ed Oliphant did not. His plan worked beautifully and made his hunting easier. Even so, The Raggedy Man nickname stuck all the way through his reign of terror and his subsequent trial. Ed was finally stopped by an FBI profiler who narrowed down the search, even guessing that Ed was hiding as a LEO, giving authorities what they needed to finally catch him.

He moved a few steps to his right until he stood in front of a picture of the Oliphant family. Marcie, Ed's wife. Submissive, quiet, kind. She'd insisted she had no idea her husband was a monster. He didn't believe her. Their daughter, Jessica, also claimed to be unaware. He cursed at the thought.

People who knew her portrayed her as a bright, inquisitive girl who excelled in school and made friends easily. How could she have been so clueless? She knew. She just didn't say anything. She let people die.

He stared at her picture. An angelic face framed by curly auburn hair and wide guileless eyes. An incredible smile. But in later pictures, after the truth came out, the look in her dark eyes changed. Innocence had been replaced by shadows. Her smile was gone. The public assumed her childish bliss had been overcome by a determined wariness. He knew better. She was dealing with the weight of what she'd done. She could have stopped him. Lives could have been saved.

After the trial, Marcie took Jessica and her younger brother, Jason, to Nebraska. Eventually, Marcie remarried. He wondered how she could ever trust another man. Did she believe men like Ed were rare? He snorted. Most men had secrets, their families living on borrowed time until the truth came out. Human beings were full of deceit, their hearts scarred by selfishness and hatred. Pretending otherwise was naïve.

Much to her mother's chagrin, after college, Jessica joined the FBI. Then she went to Quantico in Virginia and trained as a behavioral analyst — just like the man who'd been instrumental in capturing her father. Now Jessica was in St. Louis, driven away by the notoriety of her connection with an infamous serial killer. But the FBI didn't dare dismiss her. They needed her. She had a rare talent. She chased after evil. Sought justice — as if such a thing actually existed. She seemed to believe her efforts could undo some of the damage her father had done, but Ed Oliphant and his daughter wouldn't get away that easily.

No one could lessen the carnage he'd visited on the world, and Jessica could never erase the malevolent seeds that had been planted deep inside her heart. No one could live that close to wickedness without being affected. Without being aware of its existence. He was convinced Ed Oliphant's iniquity was alive and flourishing in Jessica. He was certain her quest to dispel darkness was born from her desire to rid herself of guilt. But he had no intention of allowing her that kind of grace. Evil had to be eradicated.

He laughed quietly in the stillness. Jessica wasn't quite as clever as she believed herself to be. He planned to challenge her. Destroy her self-righteous crusade to make things right. The sins of the father were going to be visited on his child. And he was the person delivering that judgment. He couldn't trust God to do it. He and God had parted ways years ago. That door was closed forever.

He sat down at the rickety desk in the middle of the room and opened his notebook. It was all there. The plan, the way to implement it, and the keys to the destruction of Ed Oliphant's daughter. The woman who now called herself Kaely Quinn.

He smiled to himself, a feeling of euphoria overtaking him. It was time. Let the mind games begin.

ONE

As she poured the sparkling red claret into the serial killer's glass, she wondered if it reminded him of blood. She pushed it toward him, but he ignored it. Kaely smiled. Just as she thought.

"You strangle your victims because you don't like blood," she said. "You took food from their refrigerators. You're on a limited budget and saw a way to profit. But you only took cheese, fruit, vegetables, desserts, yogurt . . ." She tapped on the base of the wineglass. "You're a vegetarian, but not vegan."

She pulled the wineglass away and pushed another toward him. This time she filled it with white wine. He reached through the shadows and picked it up.

Kaely riffled through the pages of the file she'd brought with her. Then she leaned back and stared at the chair across from her. He was a white male. Between twenty-five and thirty-five. He worked a menial job. Was shy around people. Probably awkward. Yet he seemed to have a purpose. But what was it? All of his victims were different. A successful black male attorney, a poor Hispanic female artist, and a white male college student. It wasn't something inherent about them, so whatever it was that drove him to punish them was something they did. He was angry with the people he killed, but he didn't enjoy the act of killing. Didn't feel good about it. Strangling them from behind meant he didn't have to look them in the eyes. Afterward, he posed them, their arms folded across their chests. It was a sign of remorse.

"I'm confused," she said. "There's no connection between your victims. Different sexes. Different races. They don't live near each other. You don't seem to have a kill zone."

"You're confused?" he whispered. "That's new for you."

"Hush," she said. "I'll tell you when you can talk." Kaely frowned at him. The rules were very clear. They weren't allowed to speak unless she gave them permission.

A disturbance to her right made her shift her focus to the table nearest her. A chubby, florid-faced man and his haggard-looking wife scowled at her as they addressed the waiter they'd called to their table.

"What kind of place is this?" the man asked loudly. He pointed at Kaely. "You let crazy people in here? You need to remove that woman."

Louis Bertrand, the owner of Restaurant d'Andre, stomped up to the table, his face set and his hands gesturing wildly as if they had a mind of their own. "This is not a crazy woman, monsieur. This is the famous FBI profiler, Kaely Quinn. That is her table, and she is allowed to use it whenever she wants."

"But this is unacceptable," the man said, his face growing even darker. Kaely began to worry about his blood pressure.

"It is acceptable to me, monsieur," Louis stated simply. "But you are not. I will ask you to leave now. No charge for your meal."

The man began to sputter and curse. His wife, seemingly embarrassed about the entire incident, grabbed her purse, stood up, and hightailed it out of the dining room. Her husband continued to protest. He gestured again toward Kaely, his eyes wide with anger and confusion. "But she's talking to herself. There's no one there!"

Kaely felt her cheeks grow hot. She hadn't meant to use her private technique in front of other people. She'd been so focused on the information in the file she'd forgotten she was in public.

"I do not care what she does, monsieur. She is welcome in my restaurant any time." Louis grabbed the man's arm and helped him to his feet. "She caught the man who killed my only son. She cleared my Andre's name, and she will be shown the respect, *n'est-ce pas*? If you cannot do so, then you must leave, *oui*? And please do not cross my door again."

Kaely sighed to herself. She'd been judged and criticized for her process by those she'd worked with. She quickly scanned the room. Other diners stared at her too, although it seemed they wanted nothing more than to avoid Louis's wrath. She hated to embarrass the kind restaurant owner. He'd wanted to do something to thank her for her help in locating his son's murderer last year, but she couldn't allow him to disrupt his business. Tonight would be the last time she'd come here. For Louis's sake.

Kaely gave the restaurant owner a brief smile and turned her attention back to the file as Louis escorted the sputtering man to the front door.

"He's not the only one who thinks you're crazy, is he?" the killer said softly.

"No, he's not, but I'm used to it. Now be still. I can't talk to you anymore."

She was flipping through the file one more time when Louis came up to the table. "I am sorry for that man's rudeness. It will not happen again, *mon cher amie.* What have you decided for dinner tonight?" he asked.

"I'll have the salade niçoise with salmon, Louis," she said.

"Good choice. It is *délicieux.* Iced tea to drink?"

She nodded. Louis used to argue that a little wine wouldn't hurt her. She had nothing against wine, but she didn't like anything that softened her sense of control, including alcohol or drugs of any kind. Her mother had become addicted to pain medication when Kaely was seventeen. Thankfully, she'd kicked it, but watching her mother's struggle had convinced Kaely that pharmaceuticals were something to be avoided, if at all possible. She slowly pulled the glass of water she'd used for her invisible guest's wine back to her side of the table.

"And for . . . ?" He jerked his head toward the seat across from Kaely.

"You don't need to placate me, Louis. I know there's no one there. It's just . . . it's a way I work through information sometimes.

I'm . . . I'm sorry I caused you a problem."

The restaurateur paused a moment before saying, "You could never cause me a problem, *mon amie.* You are my friend and always will be. Everything I have is yours. If it wasn't for you, Andre's death would still be considered a suicide. Proving he was a victim of a serial killer gave my boy back his dignity. You eased his mother's mind — and mine as well. We will always be grateful to you."

"Just doing my job, Louis. That's all."

"It might be just a job to you, *ma chère,* but to me it means more than I can ever say." Louis actually bowed and clicked his heels together before turning around and heading toward the kitchen. Kaely was happy to see how successful Restaurant d'Andre had become. The restaurant had been Louis's salvation. He'd put his heart and soul into it, and somehow it had helped to ease his pain.

Kaely turned back to the file. She stared at the reports and pictures spread out in front of her. The file had been overnighted from Nashville, where three murders had recently occurred. Although Nashville could have asked for assistance from the FBI at Quantico due to the federal serial murder statute, the police chief there had called

Kaely's boss, Special Agent in Charge of the FBI's field office in St. Louis, Solomon Slattery. The chief had asked Solomon to let Kaely peruse it first. He was afraid there would be another killing before the FBI could gather their resources together.

Kaely reread the information. Each person had died in their own home, strangled with something that had been removed from the scene. The medical examiner narrowed the ligature down to some kind of leather strap, but that was as close as he could get. There were no signs of a break-in. Whoever killed them had been given access into the victims' houses or apartments. None of the victims knew each other, and they had nothing in common. The perpetrator had to be someone they felt safe with. He probably dressed as a public employee. Someone from the electric company, the cable company, the water company. But the victims didn't share any of these services. Two of them used the same electric company, but one of the victims lived in a house where all the utilities were paid for by the owner. True, the killer could have changed uniforms, but Kaely didn't think so.

This was an organized killer, but there was also an odd randomness involved. He planned his murders, which showed organization, but it was clear he wasn't certain when people might be home and within his reach. One of the murders happened when a victim had taken the day off to drive his mother to the doctor. It had been a last-minute decision. The killer couldn't have known.

"Your MO is the same, but what is your signature?" she whispered to the man sitting across from her, making sure she couldn't be overheard by others around her. "What is it that drives you to kill?"

There was no response from her dinner companion.

As she carefully flipped through the file page by page, a waitress brought her food. Kaely quickly gathered the pictures together and closed the file so the young woman wouldn't see images that would shock her. When Kaely began training as part of the FBI's Behavioral Analysis Unit, referred to as the BAU, they horrified her too. Now they were just clues to a puzzle. It wasn't that she didn't care about the victims — she did. But this was the only way she could do her job. She worked for the victims. Getting justice was her way of caring. Allowing herself to fall apart wouldn't help anyone. Eventually, she learned how to build a wall of protection around herself and her emotions. Sometimes the wall cracked, but she'd always found a way to repair the breach.

Kaely thanked her waitress and took a bite of the salmon. Delicious, as always. After the waitress left, her companion picked up a soup spoon and began eating, slurping, making a mess.

"You're not refined," she said quietly to him. "Simple, really. Whatever it is that motivates you is simple too. Nothing complicated."

As he continued to gulp his soup, she realized he lived a very basic life. Unpretentious. A small apartment or boardinghouse. He owned an older car but probably kept it clean. Didn't throw trash around. Didn't like mess. She quickly wrote her thoughts down on her notepad. She wanted to stop. Wait until she was home to finish her "interview," but she felt compelled to finish. As if she had no choice but to keep going until she got the answer.

The waitress returned to refill her glass. "Sorry. I won't bother you again for a while. I can see you're working."

"You're fine," Kaely said. "Don't worry about it."

The waitress smiled and walked over to another table. Kaely overheard the woman at the table ask, "Could I have a doggie bag, please?"

"Of course, ma'am," the waitress said as she picked up some of the dishes on the table. "I'll bring it right out."

Kaely started to take another bite of her salmon. But before she could lift her fork, she froze. That was it. She dropped the fork and began looking through the file again. Finding the medical examiner's report, she went through it carefully. Then she reread the crime-scene investigator's notes. Sure enough, it was all there.

Finally, she began to shuffle through all the interviews. Friends, family, neighbors. Little by little, everything became clear. Kaely stared across the table.

A man sat there. Medium build, dumpy, in his early thirties. Blond hair, crooked teeth, wearing a T-shirt with writing on it.

"There you are," Kaely said with a smile.

"It isn't me," the man replied, onion soup dribbling down his T-shirt, which had a picture of a panda and the words *Caring for Animals Isn't What I Do. It's Who I Am.*

"Seriously?" Kaely said with a sigh.

She pulled a cell phone out of her purse. "Solomon?" she said when he answered. "I have something for you on that Nashville case." She listened for a moment. "I'm going to give you the profile, but I'm also going to tell you the name of Nashville's UN-SUB."

Two

Special Agent in Charge of the St. Louis field office Solomon Slattery put the phone down, shaking his head. He should be used to Kaely Quinn by now, but she still took him by surprise. In all his years with the FBI he'd never worked with anyone like her. She was more than incredibly talented. She was born to do what she did. Somehow she was able to see into souls that dwelt inside some of the most evil individuals the world had ever spit forth. But it was more than that. Much more.

He quickly dialed another number. When he heard the voice of his friend in Nashville, he said, "I figured you'd still be in the office."

A deep sigh came over the line. "Still trying to find this guy. You have anything for me?"

"How about a name?"

There was a brief pause. Nashville Police

Chief Phil Thompson said, "A name? I don't understand. I thought you were sending me a profile."

Solomon chuckled. "She thinks she knows who your unidentified subject is."

"I don't believe you."

"That's up to you. I'm just passing the information along, but I wouldn't bet against her."

He hesitated a moment. "Okay, let me have it."

Solomon heard the skepticism in his friend's voice. It made him smile. "Your UNSUB's name could be Charles Morgan."

"Wait a minute. Charles Morgan? The guy we interviewed in the park after the second murder? You're delusional. That guy couldn't kill a fly. Literally. He's some do-good animal lover. Works for a rescue group. No way."

"Kaely profiled your UNSUB as someone committed to rescuing unwanted and mistreated animals. He's a vegetarian. Innocuous, not someone you'd ever suspect or even notice under normal circumstances. If you'll do some checking into Morgan's background, I believe you'll find he was abused by one or both parents, but he had a dog or a cat growing up. His pet became his family. He can't relate to people. Won't have close, enduring relationships. However, he feels connected to animals, and he doesn't understand people who don't own pets. He truly believes they're selfish individuals who are responsible for animals that are never adopted and end up euthanized. He's angry and seeking revenge."

"This is crazy. How in the world . . ."

"First of all, your victims have nothing in common."

"True. We couldn't find any connection."

"Not one of them has a pet," Solomon said matter-of-factly.

"I . . . I'm not sure about that."

"Check it out."

"I will."

"You'll also have to explain the animal hair."

"What animal hair?" Phil asked.

"Animal hair on the victims' clothes. Animal hair in their homes."

"Hardly any. Accidental transfer. Happens all the time. Friends and family bring their pets with them when they visit."

"Maybe, but explain the dog hair on the necks of two victims."

Solomon could hear Phil riffling through papers. "Uh . . . okay."

"They were strangled with a leash. A dog leash."

"But this guy . . . I mean . . ."

"Morgan's strong enough to strangle someone from behind, Phil. If you check the victims' homes, you might find some kind of flyer. You know, trying to raise money for rescue shelters or whatever. He may have used something like that to gain access. Even people who don't own pets have a hard time saying no to someone trying to help abused animals."

This time the silence spoke volumes.

"You already found them, didn't you?"

"Yeah. In two of the victims' residences. We thought they were being passed out in the neighborhoods."

"Nope," Solomon said. "He used them to get in. He seemed harmless, so people opened their doors."

Phil grunted. "Now, wait a minute. The victims were willing to donate to the cause, but that wasn't enough?"

"Not for this guy. Probably thinks they're trying to assuage their guilt with money."

"That's nuts."

"Uh . . . is that a serious comment?"

"No. Okay, we'll pick him up for questioning, and I'll let you know how it turns out."

"Please do. And, hey, this guy doesn't take actual trophies, but you might find empty food wrappers or containers from the victims' homes. You might even discover donations. He may not have sent them in, but if there are any checks . . ."

"We'll look. And Solomon . . ."

"Yeah?"

"Thanks for doing this. Your agent may have kept us from a fourth victim. She's amazing. Never seen anything quite like her."

"I know. And by the way, Phil, Special Agent Quinn is fully aware that you guys are the ones who really solve these crimes. If Morgan's witness statement wasn't with the paperwork, she wouldn't have been able to finger the guy."

A low laugh came across the line. "I know she respects us, Solomon. That's one of the reasons we value her so much. I'm not the least bit offended. I'm just very grateful."

"Just gather the evidence you need to solve this so we can keep Kaely out of it. BAU has a problem with her going rogue. Good-bye, Phil."

"Bye."

Solomon put the phone down and checked the time. Eight-thirty. Past time to head home, but he still wasn't ready. His wife, Joyce, had grown quieter and quieter over the last several months. He knew she missed their son, Austin, who'd left for college a couple of months earlier. Their last child to move away. Their daughter Teresa was in her third year of college, and their other daughter, Hannah, was married and living in Seattle. The house was empty, and Joyce felt abandoned and useless. He'd hoped she'd get involved in other things, develop new interests, but so far, it hadn't happened. She seemed focused on him, looking for more attention than he could give her. By the time he got home, he was physically and emotionally exhausted. Joyce had been begging him to take her on a two-week cruise through the Caribbean. Maybe he'd figure out a way to do it. His Assistant Special Agent in Charge could cover things. Even though Ron hadn't been with them long, he was a great ASAC. So why was Solomon fighting his wife's request? And why was he avoiding their home? He picked up the phone and called Joyce to tell her he was finally on his way. She sounded subdued, and he felt guilty.

Kaely pulled up to the guard shack outside her gated community. Ernie Watts, the security guard, smiled when he saw her and waved her through. Ernie was a retired police officer who now protected the condos where Kaely lived. Although she would rather live in the country, away from people, past threats made protection a necessity.

She drove around to her covered parking spot and got out. Then she jogged to her front door, the biting November wind nipping sharply at her face. Her two-story condo was perfect for her lifestyle now. Low-maintenance and safe, it wasn't much more than a place to sleep and work. Alex used to tell her it was about as inviting as a motel room: austere, everything in its place, nothing that wasn't functional. But that was exactly how Kaely wanted it.

She unlocked the door and went inside, quickly closing it behind her. The light in the kitchen was on so she headed there first. Her friend Georgie stood behind the counter, smiling at her.

"Hi," she said as Kaely came into the room. "Did you forget about Mr. Hoover?"

Kaely sighed. "Thanks for reminding me. I didn't plan to be so late. What would I do without you?"

Georgie grinned, her wavy chestnut hair framing a friendly face. "I have no idea. I hope you don't mind me letting myself in."

"Of course not. You always show up at exactly the right time." Mr. Hoover, her cat, jumped up on the cabinet and sat down. He was a handsome fellow. Exactly the way she'd always envisioned her first pet would look. Gray stripes, a white nose, and four white paws. She smiled as he began to purr loudly.

"Happy you took my advice and added Mr. Hoover to your life?" Georgie asked.

"Yeah. You were right. He's awesome. We weren't allowed to have animals in the house when I was a kid."

"I know. I'm sorry." Her brown eyes were full of compassion.

"Thanks, but I'm okay with it. Especially now that I have this guy."

The big cat purred even more loudly, as if he'd understood what Kaely had said about him. Kaely had grown very fond of him and even named him after the infamous FBI director. With her odd hours and the way she got so involved in her cases, she wasn't sure she'd be a good pet owner. Thankfully, Georgie was around to remind her about Mr. Hoover's needs. Kaely was hopeful this trial run would work out.

Kaely was extremely grateful for Georgie. She was exactly the kind of friend Kaely needed. Someone she could talk to about anything, but who never tried to push past her personal boundaries. She reminded Kaely of her best friend in junior high. One of the many friends she lost after her father was captured.

"So what did you have for dinner?" Georgie asked.

Kaely poured a glass of iced tea. "I had the salade niçoise with salmon. It was delicious, but something went wrong tonight."

Georgie sat down on one of the chairs in front of Kaely's breakfast bar. "What do you mean?"

"I forgot where I was. I was reading a file and I . . ."

"You started talking to someone who wasn't there?"

Kaely nodded. "I can't believe I did it. People at the table next to me complained, and Louis threw them out. It was really embarrassing." Kaely plopped down in the chair next to Georgie. She could feel a tension headache coming on and rubbed her temples. "How could I do that? After what happened at Quantico . . ."

"Oh, honey, it was a mistake. Give yourself a break. You get so intense about your cases, sometimes you forget where you are."

"Normally, I wouldn't, but Solomon wanted me to look at something as soon as possible. Louis insists I show up at least once a month for a meal, so I thought I could kill two birds with one stone. Obviously, that was a bad idea. Trust me. I won't take files out in public again."

Georgie nodded. "Good. Bring them home and go over them here. You have the perfect place for it."

Georgie was referring to Kaely's upstairs bedroom. There was a large dry erase board on one wall with a huge corkboard next to it, which she used to sort evidence. Sometimes it helped her to see connections and patterns that could lead to an effective profile. She called it her war room. It was where she waged war against evil. She'd also placed a small table with two chairs in the corner of the room. Kaely usually conducted her "interviews" there. That room was the only space in the condo that really meant something to her. Except when she was sleeping, she spent most of her time in the war room. Working cases, thinking. Being herself.

"Someday I have to start acting like other agents. No one else does anything *weird* like this."

"Well, you're not everyone else. And your method makes perfect sense given the way you were raised."

"Maybe to you, but not to anyone else. Not at Quantico."

"Forget Quantico. You're in St. Louis now, and SAC Slattery thinks you're wonderful.

Just do your best here. Everything will be okay."

Kaely smiled. "I don't know what I'd do without you, Georgie. You always manage to make me feel better. You know that, right?"

Georgie nodded. "I know, honey. That's what I'm here for, right?" She stared at Kaely for a moment, her forehead creased with concern. "How are you really doing? I mean about Alex leaving?"

Kaely took another swig of tea and shrugged. "It's not a problem. It was his choice."

Georgie laughed lightly. "Okay, now let's try that again. And this time tell me the truth."

Kaely gazed into her friend's eyes. "I miss him," she said softly. "But I had to let him go. He wanted . . . more. I couldn't give it to him. You understand."

"Yes, I do. But someday you'll have to let someone in, you know. It's healthy. I realize you're trying to protect yourself. Keep your job your first priority. But people need love, Kaely. You're thirty-four years old. Don't you want a husband someday? Kids?"

"I don't know. I'm not really missing out on anything." She smiled at Georgie. "I have you and Richard. That's enough for me."

"It's *not* enough, Kaely, and you know it."

Kaely drained the rest of her tea and stood. "No, I don't. Richard moved all the way out here from Des Moines so I wouldn't be alone. He's the father I never had. That means more than I can say."

"Well, that creepy reporter followed you from Des Moines too. He certainly hasn't helped you."

"Richard isn't Jerry Acosta. You know better than that."

Dr. Richard Barton was a longtime friend of the family. He and his wife, Bella, had been close to Kaely's mother and father. When her father was exposed as The Raggedy Man, it had devastated them, especially since Richard was a family therapist. He blamed himself for not seeing past the mask her father wore. After Bella died, Richard followed Kaely to Virginia so she would have someone to support her. Then after she had to transfer to St. Louis, he moved again. He and Georgie were the only people Kaely completely trusted. Whenever she needed a compassionate ear or an encouraging word, Richard was there for her. She truly didn't know what she'd do without him. And Georgie was her sounding board for things she couldn't even tell Richard.

"I love Richard too, but he's almost sixty.

Not really your type." Georgie laughed. "You've never been in love, sweetie. Wouldn't you like to find out what that's like?"

"Not every woman needs a man to feel whole, Georgie." Kaely pointed at the door. "I love you, but go home. I need some sleep."

Although Georgie always left when Kaely was ready to be alone, for some reason she didn't budge.

"What's wrong?" Kaely asked.

"Do you remember when we talked about . . . a feeling? That feeling that something's wrong somewhere? Like something bad is getting ready to happen?"

Kaely grinned at her. "You mean 'a tremor in the force'?" It was a joke they shared based on their love of *Star Wars.*

Georgie stood up and faced Kaely, but she wasn't smiling. "Something's coming, Kaely. I don't know what it is, but I feel it. Don't you?"

Kaely didn't say anything as Georgie left, but the truth was, she'd felt the same thing for days now. A shiver ran down her spine. She turned off the lights and stood in the dark, trying to shake away a sense of danger. Something lurking in the shadows. Something with eyes trained directly on her.

THREE

Solomon had just finished his second cup of coffee when his administrative assistant walked into his office with an odd look on her face.

"What's going on, Grace?" he asked.

"Sorry, Solomon. It's that reporter from the *St. Louis Journal* again."

He felt a flash of irritation. "I told you I didn't want to talk to him. Send him to our media coordinator."

"I tried, but he says you have to talk to him. That Kaely Quinn's life is at stake."

"Oh, come on. He's caused her nothing but trouble. Now he's at it again. Tell him to get lost and not to come back."

Jerry Acosta had been trying to get an interview with Kaely for the last year. He was a pest who'd followed her from Virginia to St. Louis. Acosta was obsessed, determined to write a book about the daughter of a monster who now fought monsters for a living.

Back at Quantico, Kaely had been instrumental in giving law enforcement clues that led to catching quite a few dangerous criminals. Acosta heard about the talented profiler and planned to write a story about her. Then someone tipped him off about her background. When he contacted her, Kaely met with him. Tried to get him to back off. Acosta refused unless she granted him an in-depth interview for his book. She'd said no, unwilling to give him that much power in her life.

When the article came out, revealing that Kaely was the daughter of The Raggedy Man, the head of the Behavioral Analysis Unit made the decision to transfer her. The Bureau picked St. Louis, and they'd accepted her. Kaely was told by the powers-that-be at Quantico that they weren't sending her away because they didn't want her. They were transferring her to keep any distractions away from their team — and to protect her from people who blamed her for her father's twisted deeds.

Although Kaely assumed Acosta had gotten what he wanted and would leave her alone, he showed up in St. Louis. He'd already written several articles about Kaely for the *St. Louis Journal.*

Solomon sighed. It had been hard for Kaely, but they'd weathered it. Or so he thought. But somehow Acosta discovered Kaely's odd process of profiling. To this day, Solomon wasn't certain where he got that information, but it had to be from one of her fellow trainees in the Behavioral Analysis Unit at Quantico. She admitted to Solomon that she'd revealed it to another agent she thought was a friend, and the female agent had told others. One of them must have leaked it to Acosta. Solomon swore softly. No wonder Kaely didn't trust many people.

He realized he was clenching the sides of his chair so tightly his arms hurt. He willed his body to relax, but it was difficult. They'd gone to great lengths to keep Kaely out of the public eye, but Acosta was relentless, as if this was some kind of personal mission. Calls to the newspaper had finally stopped the extraneous columns about her. But even though the stories had disappeared, people hadn't forgotten. His office constantly had to contend with writers, reporters, and even other LEOs who wanted to hear about the incredible Kaely Quinn and her highly unusual background.

Solomon decided from the outset that he would keep Kaely and ignore the distractions. Slowly, things started to improve. But now Acosta was at it again. Solomon had no intention of helping him write his book.

"Like I said, send him to Jacqueline Cross, Grace. I don't have time to deal with him today."

"He says he has a letter. Something . . . disturbing. A threat against Agent Quinn. He seems convinced that if you don't see him, it will put her life in danger."

"Grace . . ."

She stood her ground and stared at him, her eyes narrowed to slits. Solomon knew that look. It meant Grace had already decided he should see the guy.

He sighed again, this time much louder. "Five minutes, Grace. I mean it."

"Yes, Solomon," she said soothingly. He could hear a slight hint of victory in her voice, but he decided to ignore it.

Solomon reached for his coffee and took a sip. Cold. It only added to his irritation. Acosta was a pushy liar who would do anything for the story he wanted. Solomon had no idea what his ploy would be today, but he was convinced this was just another way of trying to manipulate the Bureau into giving him the interview he so desperately wanted.

A couple of minutes later, Jerry Acosta stepped into Solomon's office. Today he seemed a little different. The ingratiating smile was gone from his face, and he looked a little nervous.

"Okay, Acosta. What is it this time? No matter what, you're not going to talk to Special Agent Quinn."

Acosta slid into one of the chairs in front of Solomon's desk even though Solomon hadn't invited him to sit. "I'm not here about that. This is . . . something else. I felt you should see it right away." He reached into his tattered briefcase and pulled out a plastic Ziploc bag. Solomon noticed a letter inside. What was this about?

"This came in the morning mail. I put the letter and the envelope in this bag to protect them. I mean, in case there are fingerprints. I . . . I touched the letter when I opened it, so my prints will be on it. Sorry. I didn't know what it was at first."

Solomon took the bag from the reporter's hand and carefully placed it on his desk.

Block letters on cheap yellow-lined notebook paper. Easy to obtain. The envelope was also economical. Nothing special. Self-adhesive. Probably no DNA. No return address. Postmarked from St. Louis. A closer look at the letter revealed it was a poem.

SEVEN LITTLE ELEPHANTS
A EULOGY FOR KAELY QUINN

Seven little elephants walking in the forest
One hit his head and fell down dead.
Six little elephants called it a day.
They packed up their trunks and they all
ran away.

Six little elephants swimming in the lake
One was slaughtered and went underwater.
Five little elephants called it a day.
They packed up their trunks and they all
ran away.

Five little elephants playing on the swings
One grabbed a rope and ended up choked.
Four little elephants called it a day.
They packed up their trunks and they all
ran away.

Four little elephants playing with matches
One built a pyre and set himself on fire.
Three little elephants called it a day.
They packed up their trunks and they all
ran away.

Three little elephants sat down for a meal
One took a bite and then said good night.
Two little elephants called it a day.

They packed up their trunks and they all
ran away.

Two little elephants playing all alone
One knew the truth and told it to the sleuth.
One little elephant called it a day.
She packed up her trunk and ran far away.

One last elephant facing final judgment
She was found guilty and given no pity.
Jessica Oliphant called it a day.
She picked up a gun and blew herself
away.

Tell Jessica the elephant hunt will begin
soon.
Watch for me.

Solomon dropped the bag like it was on fire. He cursed loudly and jumped up from his chair. "What kind of sick game are you playing?" he shouted at Acosta. "Did you think this would get you access to Agent Quinn? Well, it won't. Now get out of here."

The subdued reporter remained in his seat. "Look, Agent Slattery, I assure you this isn't a game. I . . . I really did get this in the mail. I thought about taking it straight to my editor, but I brought it to you first. If you turn it over, you'll see a note to me from the writer."

Grunting in disgust, Solomon flipped the bag over and read:

> Acosta,
>
> Deliver this personally to Solomon Slattery at the FBI if you want to hear from me again. If you don't do as I ask, you'll not only lose the story of a lifetime, you'll lose your life as well.

Solomon felt his gut turn. Would even a slimeball like Jerry Acosta go this far? Somehow, he didn't think so.

"I'm not asking for an interview with Agent Quinn," Acosta continued. "I just . . . I think this might be real. Please take it seriously." He picked up his briefcase. "I have a copy of the letter, and I have to see my editor now." He gulped. "I . . . I had to follow the instructions. For Special Agent Quinn's sake."

His fingers nervously tapped on his briefcase. "You do whatever you need to, but I truly believe her life has been threatened. Maybe it's just some crazy person, but I get a weird vibe from it. Please don't just dismiss it out of hand because of the way you feel about me." He paused for a moment. "I know you won't believe this, but I never meant any harm to Agent Quinn. Even in Virginia. It was just a story. I really don't want to see her hurt." He started to stand up, but Solomon stopped him.

"We need your fingerprints for comparison so we can eliminate them from the envelope and the letter." Solomon picked up his phone and punched in a number. When Grace answered, he asked her to get someone from ERT to escort Acosta to a processing room.

When she acknowledged his request, Solomon put the phone down. "Please wait out there," he said, gesturing toward the outer office. "An agent will be by soon to escort you."

"I'm in a pretty big hurry," Acosta said, frowning.

"Listen, Acosta," Solomon growled, "you brought this to us. Now you're going to cooperate so we can see if there's anything to it."

"All right, all right. But your people need to speed it up. I can't stay here all day." With that, Acosta left Solomon's office, pulling the door closed behind him.

Solomon stared down at the poem on his desk. Was this just another trick, or was someone actually planning to kill Kaely Quinn? Even as he asked himself the question, down deep inside, he was pretty sure he knew the answer.

Four

Solomon stared at the letter, trying to decide what to do next. After a few seconds, he pushed a button on his phone. "Grace, send Special Agent Noah Hunter in here."

"Yes, boss."

Solomon hung up and then sat down. His chair squeaked comfortably under his weight. Grace had suggested more than once that the maintenance guy oil it, but Solomon liked it the way it was. For some reason the noise calmed him. This was going to be tricky. Kaely Quinn needed protection. Someone to keep an eye on her until they could determine if this threat was real. She would hate it, and so would any agent he assigned to her. She'd worked closely with Agent Alex Cartwright since she'd arrived in St. Louis a year earlier. He'd come to understand Kaely, trusted her. Unfortunately, Alex crossed the line and fell in love. Kaely wasn't the kind of person you got romantic toward. She lived and breathed her job — and nothing else. Solomon had warned Cartwright from the beginning, but in the end, he'd given in to his feelings. Now he was gone.

Solomon pulled Noah's file closer. He hadn't been with them long, but he was perfect. A member of their SWAT team. No-nonsense. Totally dedicated to his job. Pragmatic and dedicated. He'd been married, but his wife had died. According to the agents who knew him, Noah had no interest in getting involved with anyone. Solomon hated to use Noah's pain as a way to protect Kaely, but she was too important to him to take chances.

A loud knock at the door interrupted his thoughts. "Come in," he called out.

The door opened, and Special Agent Noah Hunter walked in. Tall, with dark wavy hair, he was the epitome of a professional FBI agent. He rarely smiled. Looking at him you got the feeling he was wound tight, ready to tackle anything or anyone that got in the way of his doing his job successfully. He actually made Solomon a little tense, and although that sounded negative, it wasn't. The last thing he needed now was a laid-back agent. He wanted a fighter. A warrior.

"Have a seat, Noah," Solomon said.
"Yes, sir." Noah slid into the chair recently vacated by Acosta.
Solomon tossed him a quick smile. "You're doing a great job. You helped us shut down that intrastate drug cartel. Your supervisor has nothing but praise for you."
Noah's bluish-gray eyes widened slightly. "Thank you, sir. It was a privilege to work on that task force."
"You can call me Solomon. We're not big on titles around here."
"Thank you, sir. I mean . . . Solomon."
Solomon nodded. "I have a new assignment for you, Noah, one I feel you're uniquely qualified for. I want you to know I wouldn't give this to just anyone." He pushed the plastic bag toward Noah. "Jerry Acosta from the *St. Louis Journal* brought this in. It was sent to him in the mail. I'm not sure where this is going, but I think we need to take it seriously."
Noah picked up the bag and read the letter inside. He looked up, surprise etched on his face. "It's a threat against one of our agents?"
Solomon nodded. "I want you to investigate. I'm making you lead agent."
Noah straightened up in his chair. Obviously, he thought he was getting an impor-

tant mission. He was right.

"And I'm assigning Special Agent Kaely Quinn as your co-case agent."

Noah's jaw clenched, and his complexion paled. "Agent Quinn? Because she's the object of the threat?"

Solomon frowned at him. "No, not completely. She's one of the best agents I have, and we need her help. You'll appreciate her abilities once you spend some time with her."

Noah stared at him as if trying to gauge his next words. "Okay. I . . . I mean, what would be her role?"

"As I said, she will be co-case agent. Kaely is focused and pays great attention to detail. She'll pick up things most agents would miss. Her specialty will be helping you create a profile. I realize this letter isn't much to go on, but you'll be surprised at what she can come up with on nothing more than this. Hopefully, we'll get more information as time goes on. Then she can write up a real profile. Something that will lead you to your UNSUB."

Solomon pointed at the letter. "For now, I want you both to tear this poem apart. See if you can find something we can use to catch this guy. We need to start a chain-of-evidence log: from Acosta to me, then from me to you. Once I turn it over to you, you'll send it on to the lab at Quantico. You need to have them look for prints, DNA . . . you know the drill. I sent Acosta to the processing room to get his fingerprints for elimination." He locked his gaze on Noah. "Send the letter to BAU for comparison with other threats in their threat database. This seems to be written specifically for Special Agent Quinn, but still, it wouldn't hurt to make sure. Might want to also send a copy to the Secret Service. Have them check their database as well."

He looked away from Noah for a moment, trying to gather his thoughts. Had he forgotten anything? Nothing came to mind. He turned his attention back to Noah. "As far as Agent Quinn, you will partner with her. Stay with her until we can assess the situation completely." He studied his agent closely. Noah looked nervous and a little disturbed. It didn't make any difference. He was a trained agent. He'd do what he was told. "I want to make certain she stays safe, but she's not to know I've asked you to watch her. Like I said, she won't like it. Frankly, I don't blame her."

Noah didn't argue, but Solomon noticed the pulse in his neck throb. Finally, Noah said, "All right. When do I start?"

Solomon tapped his fingers on the desk as he thought. "I want to bring Agent Quinn up to speed myself. Then I'll turn this letter over to you. After that, the two of you can get started. I'll also call your SWAT team leader and tell him about your new assignment."

"Yes, sir."

This time Noah didn't correct himself. Solomon pushed away a pang of annoyance. What was it with these agents who held such a low opinion of Kaely Quinn? He wanted to read them the riot act but knew that would only make things worse. He still believed Noah was the right person to pair with Kaely.

"You'll find that Kaely is an incredible agent, Noah. If you've heard anything else, you need to forget it. Judging her without knowing her is a mistake." He tented his fingers and leaned forward. "Besides, I'm not asking you to like her. I'm asking you to work with her. Do you understand?"

"Yeah, Solomon. I get it."

Solomon fought back a smile. Noah looked like a man suffering an attack of acute indigestion. He actually felt a little sorry for his agent, but he had no plans to change his mind. In his estimation, Kaely Quinn was one of the most important assets the FBI possessed, and he'd do anything to keep her safe.

"I'll call you after I've talked to her. We'll get Special Agent Walker from our Evidence Response Team to take this to the lab at Quantico. You need to stay here and work with Kaely. I'll have Walker get with you so we can note the chain-of-evidence log. It might take a day or two to get the report back from Quantico, although I know it will be given high priority since lives may be at stake."

Noah nodded and stood up, striding quickly to the door and pulling it shut behind him.

Solomon picked up his phone and called Kaely, asking her to join him in his office. A few minutes later, there was a knock on his door.

"Come in, Kaely," he called out.

Kaely Quinn walked into the room. Her curly auburn hair was pulled into a messy bun, soft tendrils framing her delicate face. Confusing her slight build with weakness would be a mistake. Kaely Quinn was one of the toughest human beings he'd ever known. "Is this about Nashville?" she asked as she sat down.

Solomon shook his head. "No, something else. I need you to look at this." He pushed the plastic bag toward her.

As she read, her expression hardened.

"Jerry Acosta brought it in," Solomon said. "There's a note to him on the back."

Kaely flipped it over and frowned. Then she carefully pushed the plastic bag back toward Solomon. "Acosta received this in the mail?"

"Yeah, this morning."

She shook her head. "Why not send it directly to me?"

Solomon knew the question was rhetorical. Kaely didn't expect him to have an answer.

She looked at him. "You're waiting for me to explain this to you."

Solomon ran a hand through his salt-and-pepper hair. "Don't read my body language, Agent Quinn. You know I don't like it."

"Sorry," she said. "Second nature." She paused a moment. "It's clear the writer isn't just threatening me," she said finally. "He plans to kill innocent people to prove some kind of sick point. Send me a message."

"I find this poem very disturbing. Whoever wrote it appears to be obsessed with you."

"True," Kaely said. "Something's set him off. Some kind of defining moment. Whatever it was, he believes he's free now to take revenge through something he's planned.

This feels very organized. This guy is a budding serial killer."

"It appears you're the final objective."

She nodded, her dark eyes narrowed, her expression intense. "He's challenging me to catch him. If he makes it through his list, I'm his final target."

"But why not just come after you first?" Solomon asked. "Why threaten other people?"

Kaely shrugged. "This UNSUB seems to have a personal grudge against me. He feels that if he gets away with these other murders, it will prove I'm not good at my job. That he's smarter than me. He wants to defeat me completely. Professionally and personally."

"You need to go through past cases, Kaely," Solomon said. "Maybe he's angry about something you've been involved with."

"Yeah, probably."

Solomon studied her closely. He might not be able to read people like she could, but he noticed the muscle over her left eye twitch. She was more concerned about this threat than she let on.

"I assume the *Journal* intends to print it?" Kaely asked.

"I'm sure they do, but we'll ask them to

hold it for a few days. We need some time to figure out if this threat is real or not."

"Yeah. I don't think sharing it with the public will help us. It's not like the Unabomber's manifesto. This was written for this specific situation. I doubt there's anything here friends or relatives would recognize."

"I agree," Solomon said. "Kaely, I've assigned Agent Noah Hunter to oversee this situation. You're on as co-case agent." He cleared his throat and immediately realized his mistake. It was a giveaway. Showed his nervousness. That he was hiding something.

Kaely's face flushed. "You want him to look out for me. Why? I don't need protection. I'm a trained agent."

"Don't give me attitude, Special Agent Quinn. I'm not going to argue about this. I only put you on as co-case agent because the threat is about you, and you're the best person to figure out who's behind it." He studied her for a moment. "I can't give you the lead, Kaely. Not when you're a target."

"I realize that. But this Hunter guy's only been here a few months. Why him?"

"He's good. Focused. I think he's the best man for the job." Solomon locked his gaze on her. "He lost his wife a while back. I'm not pairing the two of you because of it, but

I think his circumstances might keep him from going down the same road Alex did."

Kaely didn't respond. Just waited. The pulse in her smooth neck pumped with emotion-fueled adrenaline. Her eyes bore into his, but he held his ground against her.

"What do you want me to do now?" she asked finally.

"Tell me everything you can about our letter writer before anyone gets hurt. Hopefully, this is nothing. A nut who wants attention. Or even a new scheme from Acosta." He frowned. "I can't stand that guy, but what he told me feels . . . real. He seemed truly rattled."

Kaely snorted. "Not sure Acosta has *true* emotions."

"You could be right. Everything he does is for himself. I don't completely trust him."

Kaely stood up. "We'll find out who sent this. I'm not worried."

"I'm glad you're not, but there's something . . . creepy about this poem."

Kaely gave him what passed for a smile. Not something she did much. "All the people we deal with are creepy, Solomon."

He sighed in acknowledgment.

She pulled her cell phone out of her pocket and took several pictures of the letter, back and front. "You're sending it to the lab, right?"

"Yeah. Special Agent Walker will fly it over there. I want Noah to stay here and work the case with you."

Kaely nodded. "I doubt the lab will find any fingerprints or DNA. This guy's too smart for that."

"How smart can he be if he sends his *threat* to Jerry Acosta?"

"Actually, it was a brilliant move. If we'd gotten it directly, we certainly wouldn't have notified the media. Our UNSUB knew exactly who to use. Someone who wanted contact with me. A man who wouldn't dare allow this opportunity to get past him. We've been notified of our UNSUB's intentions — and so has the press. We need to get on this right away. I'm not sure we have a lot of time. We also have to inform local authorities about the letter." She got up and headed toward Solomon's door. "I'll start pulling past cases right away, see if I can narrow down the possibilities."

"I'll call SLMPD and bring them up to speed. Ask them to watch out for this guy. And Kaely?"

"Yeah?"

"*You both* will get started. Noah's in charge. Don't force me to remind you again." Although he tried to sound tough, he knew she wasn't afraid of him. She showed him respect, but she also knew he cared about her.

She didn't answer, just shot Solomon a look that made him shake his head. As she closed the door behind her, he prayed she'd not only find a way to work with Noah Hunter but also that she'd stay safe. Although he wasn't her parent, Solomon felt a strong connection to her. She was a well-trained agent with an incredible talent. But there was something about her that concerned him. Fear wasn't always an enemy. A lack of self-preservation could get her killed if circumstances got out of control.

And that was exactly what he was afraid might happen.

Five

When the call from Solomon came a couple of hours later, Noah Hunter got up from his desk and quickly walked down the hallway. He should have gone straight to Solomon's office, but instead he headed for the bathroom. He was grateful to find it empty. He walked up to one of the sinks and stared into the mirror that hung over it. How could he wind up with this assignment? Big brother to an agent with possible mental problems. Someone who shares meals with serial killers. He shook his head. Rumor was that Special Agent Cartwright had fled the city just to get away from her.

In Noah's wildest dreams it would have never occurred to him that he would be the next agent assigned to her. Most of the other agents snickered behind her back, calling her Jessica Elephant. Not just because they knew her history and her real name but also because once she saw a crime scene she seemed able to recall everything — even down to the smallest detail. Maybe she had some all-consuming desire to rid the world of killers like her father, but that wasn't Noah's problem.

"So now what?" he asked his image in the mirror. He didn't really know Kaely Quinn. Had nothing against her personally. He'd come from Quantico ready to use what he'd learned to make the world better. Now he was nothing more than a glorified babysitter. He swore softly. Then he turned on the cold water and slapped some on his face, hoping he'd wake up and find he'd imagined all of this. But of course, he hadn't.

As he continued to gaze at himself, he considered his options. Was there a way out? Maybe Special Agent Quinn would reject him. It was possible, but how would Solomon react? He was tough but fair. Would he have mercy? Or would he be angry? A voice from somewhere deep inside answered his question. When Solomon gave an order, he expected it to be followed. Period. Noah shook his head. Maybe this would be over quickly. They'd find out the threat wasn't real. But somewhere in his gut, he knew differently. There was something about that strange poem. The anger behind it was palpable. Frightening.

Noah closed his eyes for a moment. Then he let out a breath to steady himself. There was only one thing to do. Obey his orders. Track down the letter writer. Bring this threat to a conclusion. He could already hear the teasing comments he'd get from his SWAT team members. He had no choice. He'd have to hang on and ride this out.

He stood up, straightened his shoulders, and used a paper towel to pat his face dry. Then he walked out of the bathroom and headed to Solomon's office. Nathan Walker was waiting in the outer office. He stood up when Noah walked in and nodded at him.

"Go on in," Grace said. "He's expecting the two of you."

Noah knocked on Solomon's door before opening it. Solomon waved them in. In front of them, Solomon signed a chain-of-evidence log, then pushed it toward Noah, who signed it and gave it to Walker. Every time the letter changed hands, the log would be signed, which helped to keep track of important evidence. At Quantico, when the letter went to someone who was charged with testing it, the log would be signed again. The Bureau would keep a record of every single person who came in contact with the letter.

"Keep me updated," Noah told Walker.

"I will," Walker said. He took the letter, put it into a special briefcase he'd brought with him, and left the room.

"Kaely's waiting for you in the conference room," Solomon told him.

He nodded and left the office. The conference room was around the corner. The door was shut, so he knocked lightly. From inside, a voice said, "Come in."

When he pushed the door open, he saw Kaely Quinn sitting at the conference table, a pile of folders in front of her. It was difficult to believe she was an FBI agent. Kaely was small. At first glance, you'd think she was a teenager, not in her mid-thirties. She'd taken off her jacket and wore a sleeveless blouse with her black slacks. The muscles in her arms were clearly defined. She was in tip-top shape. Curly auburn-hued hair had been tugged into a bun. Several strands had successfully fought to escape captivity.

As she tilted her head up to look at him, he noticed her pert nose and soft, full lips. He'd never really studied her closely, but he suddenly felt as if the breath was sucked out of his body. Her eyes captured his attention. Deep, dark pools full of something that grabbed you and tried to pull you in.

For a brief second, when she'd first looked at him, he'd noticed something. A flash of vulnerability.

In that moment, he was suddenly transported back to his childhood. His father had taken him hunting with his buddies. A rite of passage. Noah had been excited to be a part of the group, but when the moment came and he stared into the eyes of the deer he was supposed to kill, he couldn't do it. Sensing his hesitation, one of the other men brought it down. Although Noah laughed it off at the time, playing along with the men who were celebrating their "kill," he cried himself to sleep that night. The next day, his father told Noah he'd decided he'd had enough of hunting and wondered if they could do something else together — maybe hiking. His father never acknowledged his son's reaction to his one and only hunting experience, but they spent many happy days hiking in the hills of Colorado where Noah had grown up. He suspected his father was a little confused when his son joined the FBI, yet hunting criminals didn't bother Noah. Pursuing bad guys was completely different than stalking innocent animals.

He slowed his breathing and tried to calm his pounding pulse. "Special Agent Noah Hunter," he said. "Looks like we're going to be working together."

"I know who you are, Special Agent Hunter," Quinn said in a light, almost musical voice. "Please, have a seat."

Noah slid into a chair across the table from her. He waited for her to say something, but she seemed engrossed in a file open on the table. Her long, slender fingers tucked back a wild tuft of hair that had fallen across her smooth forehead. When she finally looked up, she appeared to study him. The sense of vulnerability was gone. Her eyes seemed to look straight through him, making him feel exposed and uncomfortable. What was it about this woman? Something else was brewing behind the façade. Something he couldn't put his finger on. She had a no-nonsense reputation. From what other agents had told him, Quinn lived for her job — and nothing else. They insisted there wasn't anything to her besides her obsessive commitment to the Bureau.

"You've been put in charge of this investigation," she said, pushing a piece of paper toward him. Noah looked down and found a copy of the letter he'd seen in Solomon's office. "I took a picture with my phone and made a copy so we'd have something to work with."

He nodded. "Good. I understand Solomon believes this is a direct threat against you."

"Well, actually, I think we need to focus on a potential serial killer who is about to hunt down people in St. Louis. I think that's the most important thing, don't you?"

Instead of answering her, he pointed at the files on the table. "What are you looking for?"

"Going through past cases. Seeing who might have something against me." She shook her head. "I'm afraid the list is rather long, but as you probably know, behavioral analysts only help narrow down the field of possible UNSUBs. People associated with our victims or our perpetrators wouldn't usually know anything about me."

"What about the articles written by that reporter? Acosta?"

"That certainly could be the link. Acosta made it sound as if I single-handedly brought down every serial killer, arsonist, rapist, and terrorist over the past few years. It's ridiculous."

"So that opens it up to lots of possibilities," Noah mused.

"We have a lot of work to do," Kaely said simply. "And you would rather do anything else, right?"

He frowned at her. "No, of course not. If this is a serious threat . . ."

She slapped the file shut, cutting him off. "A partnership won't work if you lie to me, Agent Hunter."

Her response angered him. What did this woman want? He was doing the best he could under the circumstances. "I don't see how you can possibly know how I feel, Agent Quinn."

She leaned back in her chair. "I can tell by your body language. First of all, look at your feet."

Surprised, he stared down at his shoes. What was she talking about?

"They're pointed toward the door. You want nothing more than to get out of here. Also, you picked a chair as far away from me as you could. You've adjusted your collar twice since you sat down. That's a pacifying gesture. You're trying to soothe yourself. You've pursed your lips three times, and you're pressing so hard on the arms of your chair, the tips of your fingers are white."

"Are you profiling me?"

"No. That's not profiling. That's just reading people. Being observant." She nodded toward the files in front of her. "Behavioral analysis allows us to identify some of the most evil people on this planet. That's why

I joined the Bureau. What about you? I'm pretty sure it isn't because you get to wear those nice dark suits and those ties you hate so much."

For a split second he thought about asking her how she knew he hated ties, but he didn't. Most men felt the same way. Didn't take any special insight to come to that conclusion.

"So, if watching physical reactions isn't profiling, how is it used?" Although his intent was to get her off of reading him and on to something else, he found he really was interested in her answer.

"When law enforcement interviews witnesses or suspects, watching how they react can indicate if they're telling us the truth. We all have certain behaviors that show what we're really thinking. It doesn't work all the time. It's not an exact science. The way someone holds their mouth isn't something we can take to court. We still need evidence, but the ability to know what someone is thinking can still be very valuable. I once determined that the suspect we had in a series of bombings in DC wasn't our guy by reading his reactions to our questions. Although he came across as mostly truthful, I could tell he knew *something.* Sure enough, he led us to our bomber, even though he had nothing to do with actually setting off the explosions. Seems he helped make the bombs our terrorist wanted to use to kill thousands of American citizens."

She folded her hands and fixed her gaze on him. "I believe it's our job to use all the weapons in our arsenal to catch the monsters, Agent Hunter. And that's what I do. I chase monsters. While we're working together, I'd be happy to teach you a few things you might not know. But you're in charge. However we work together is up to you." She scooted forward in her chair and sought his eyes. "One thing I want to make clear: I don't need a babysitter."

Noah blinked several times and immediately wondered if he'd just sent another signal. This was going to be harder than he'd thought. "So you know Solomon is worried about your safety?"

She made a noise that was close to an actual laugh. "Reading people, remember?" She sighed and leaned back in her chair. "Solomon Slattery is an incredible SAC. I'm honored to work under him. But he has two daughters, and he's identifying me with them. He started not long after I arrived here. I've talked to him about it, and he denies it, but I know I'm right." She waved her hand toward Noah. "I can't change him. That's just who he is." She frowned. "Look, I really want to work with you on this case, but if you can't do a good job because you're distracted by me, I'll ask Solomon to assign someone else. He might listen."

Relief flooded through him. She'd just offered him a way out. He opened his mouth to accept her offer, but it was like someone else took over his words. "I . . . I guess I'd like to know more."

"About?"

"About you. About what you do."

It was the truth, but he hadn't realized it until that moment. What would she say? He was surprised to see the corners of her mouth twitch.

"Okay, I'll give you the same deal I gave Alex. You can ask me three questions. Anything you want. No limits. But after I answer them, you decide to commit to this, or I'll ask Solomon to pick someone else to work with you. Do you agree?"

"I do."

"Don't hold back. You won't get another chance."

"I understand." He hesitated. "What did Agent Cartwright ask?"

"Is that your first question?"

"No."

"Then let's move on." She tapped her fingers on the table. "Before you start, I'd like to ask *you* something. Do you mind?"

"No, I guess not."

Kaely riffled through the pile of folders and pulled one out. She opened it and took out a stack of pictures. She laid each one on the table in front of her, one right next to the other. Then she spun her chair toward the wall. "Please pick one picture. Keep it in your mind."

"Is this some kind of trick?"

"No. You said you want to understand what I do. It's an example of how to interpret physical actions and reactions. Our job is to find the truth. We need all the tools we can get to catch the bad guys."

"Okay," he said slowly, drawing out the word. He picked a picture. "I've chosen one."

"When I turn around, please don't be staring at the pictures. Look away."

"Sure." He swung his eyes toward a photo of the director of the FBI hanging on the wall.

Kaely's chair swiveled in an arc until she faced him again. She gathered the pictures together and put them to her side. "I'll come back to this later. Now you can ask your first question."

Noah stared at her for a few moments, trying to decide what he really wanted to know. At the last second, he decided to be bold. After all, what did he have to lose?

Six

Cindy Linthicum stopped a moment to catch her breath. The afternoon air was invigorating, and the vibrant reds, yellows, and oranges of the leaves on the trees in Forest Park were magnificent. She breathed in the fall air and began to jog in place, getting ready to finish her journey through St. Louis's premier park. The sky above her had been filling with clouds that promised rain, so she needed to complete her run before the weather got bad. She took off her glasses and wiped them on her sweatshirt. Then she put them back on and pulled the woolen cap covering her short dark hair a little tighter. When she got home, she'd drink coffee and work on her blog. She enjoyed sharing her love of Amish fiction, scrapbooking, and collecting cookbooks with online friends. Life was good.

She left the regular running trail and headed toward the art museum, her favorite building in Forest Park. She liked to sit on the steps for a few minutes at the end of her run and enjoy a magnificent view of the Grand Basin, an incredible water feature created on the other side of Art Hill, which was situated between the two famous sites. The trees along the avenue in front of the grand structure glowed red as if they were on fire. As she ran toward the front of the building, she noticed someone lying on a park bench to her right. At first she thought he was asleep. As she jogged past she noticed he was wearing a nice suit but his shoes were gone. His hands were folded oddly across his chest. She stopped, turned around, and jogged over to check on him.

When she approached the bench, she called out, but there was no response. When she got a closer look, Cindy Linthicum began to scream.

Solomon slammed his phone down and cursed under his breath. Then he got up and hurried past Grace, who looked surprised to see her boss doing anything outside of his tightly controlled schedule. He pulled open the door of the conference room and interrupted Noah and Kaely, who appeared to be deep in conversation.

"He's already struck," he said. "His first

murder was carried out before we got the poem."

Kaely looked surprised. "How do you know it's our guy?"

"The killer pinned an outline of an elephant on the dead guy's chest with the number 1 drawn inside of it. The chief of police just called to let me know. If we hadn't alerted him about the letter, it might have been a while before we were able to link this to our UNSUB."

"Has the crime scene been cleared yet?" Kaely asked.

"No. The body's been removed and the scene is intact, but it's starting to rain. They're doing everything they can to protect the evidence. I think you need to stay here, Kaely. You go, Noah."

Kaely shook her head. "We're a team, Solomon. We both go or I want out." She looked at him through narrowed eyes. "Look, let's get this out into the open. I know you're worried about my safety, but our UNSUB isn't going to move against me yet. He has a long-range plan. It's a game. Taking me out now would ruin the fun." She glanced quickly at Noah before saying, "Besides, you need my eyes there. I could pick up something others might miss."

"You mean me?" Noah asked sharply.

"No, I mean the police. They have an excellent crime lab, but I trust our training above theirs."

Solomon frowned at her. "I don't know."

Kaely stood up. "Solomon, I'm a professional, capable agent. You made me co-case agent on this. Let me do my job."

Solomon fixed his gaze on Noah. "All right. But I want you to keep a close eye on her. Understand?"

When Kaely started to say something, he waved her comment away. "I'm not going to argue with you about this, Special Agent Quinn. I respect you, and I respect your training. But if I feel one of my agents is in danger, whatever I decide to do, I expect you to accept it. I'm still in charge, I think." He had no plans to argue with her. Right or wrong, he had a feeling. Warning bells going off inside. He'd felt them before during his career and had learned to trust them. "Do you have any problems with that?"

Kaely's face flushed, but she shook her head. "No, sir."

"What about you, Special Agent Hunter?"

"No, sir," he said. "Not a problem."

"Then head to the art museum in Forest Park," he said. "Both of you. We really don't need an invitation when one of our agents is threatened, but let's play it like we do.

Thank the police chief and treat him with deference. He's always been willing to work with us. I don't want to make him feel like we're taking over . . . yet. We're going to need his help down the road."

"Okay," Noah said. "We'll be respectful."

"So can we call in ERT to go over the crime scene?" Kaely asked.

"If the chief says it's okay. I know you have more confidence in our people, but St. Louis has great crime scene investigators who don't miss much. If the chief doesn't want our team in there, don't argue with him."

Kaely closed the files and stood up.

"Leave them," Solomon said. "This room is yours now."

"Thanks, Solomon," Noah said. He nodded at Kaely. "Are you ready?" he asked.

"Absolutely."

They left the room and hurried down the hallway. Solomon stared at the door as it closed behind them. This could be the most valuable team he'd ever put together. As long as being human didn't get in the way.

Noah pulled into the entrance of Forest Park and drove toward the art museum. Warm afternoon rain mixed with frosty November air, causing an eerie mist to cover the area. Police lights sliced through the fog, revealing their location. Noah followed the road to where a crime-scene van was parked. Crime technicians were gathered around a bench near a line of trees.

The bench wasn't far from the impressive building that housed the museum. The statues that lined the top of the museum appeared to be looking down on them, staring with horror at the scene of death that didn't belong in view of the idyllic structure. The statues, acquired through the 1904 World's Fair, symbolized six great periods of art: Egyptian, Classic, Gothic, Oriental, Renaissance, and Modern. But the crowd that gathered to stare at the work of a killer wasn't there to appreciate works of beauty. They had assembled to examine a study in horror.

Noah stopped in front of the museum, not wanting to get in the way of law enforcement officers or crime-scene techs. Kaely started to get out of the car, but he stopped her.

"I think you should stay here," he said. "This could be a setup."

"Our UNSUB has written a play with seven acts. This is only the first one. I'm perfectly safe."

Noah looked at her pointedly. "You're going to do this my way. I'm in charge. At least wait until I scope out the area."

"Our car doesn't have bulletproof glass, you know. He could take me out while I'm sitting here if he wanted to. You're just afraid of letting Solomon down."

Noah raised an eyebrow. "You read me wrong this time. Believe it or not, I really don't want to see you die. Too much paperwork to fill out."

Kaely looked away, but not before Noah saw the hint of a smile on her face. She didn't say anything but finally nodded her assent.

Noah got out and walked around the car. Except for some people standing back by the road that led to the park, no one seemed suspicious. Frankly, he felt Solomon had been right to question whether Kaely should come to the crime scene. However, it seemed she got her way when she pushed. Noah went back to the car, opened the trunk, and took out two hooded jackets. When he opened Kaely's door, he handed her one, which she took. Once they put them on, they began walking toward the spot where the police had gathered.

"I need to see your credentials, sir," an officer said to Noah as they approached the area protected by bright yellow tape. Even though they wore jackets with *FBI* emblazoned across the back and front, this was a crime scene and protocol had to be followed.

Noah and Kaely took out their creds. "Chief Harper called us to look the situation over."

The officer nodded. "I was told you were coming. Sorry, I had to check."

Noah nodded. "Not a problem. We understand."

"Notice anyone suspicious hanging around, officer?" Kaely asked. "Anyone who seems a little too interested?"

The young cop frowned. "Actually, yeah. See that man over there? The guy with the red hair and the beard? Says he's a newspaper reporter."

Noah and Kaely turned at the same time. Jerry Acosta watched them from behind the crime-scene tape. He had on a raincoat, but his head was uncovered, and he didn't have an umbrella. His shoes were covered in mud. He looked like a drowned rat. Noah could tell he had something under his raincoat. Probably a camera.

"Oh great," Kaely said. She turned back and smiled widely at the officer, surprising Noah. "Yeah, he is, but he's not someone you want to talk to. Please don't give him any information. Let's wait for the chief to release a statement."

The cop returned Kaely's smile. He was clearly charmed by her. "The chief already told us not to give any information to the press. Everyone else has been cooperating, but that guy's really pushy. We found him hiding behind the trees over there, taking pictures. We made him move behind the tape."

"We've run into him before," Kaely said. "He's a real pain. I don't trust him."

The young officer nodded. "Thanks for the heads-up. I'll keep an eye on him."

Noah thanked the officer. As they walked away, he said, "So you *can* smile."

"When it's necessary to get what I want."

"I'll remember that."

Kaely grunted. "You're a pain, you know that?"

Noah grinned. "I've been told."

As they drew closer, Noah recognized Chief of Police Dan Harper. Short and muscular, he had a reputation for being tough, but he was great at getting results. The chief noticed them and walked over to greet them. When he nodded at them, a trickle of water ran down the top of his hat and dribbled onto his poncho.

"Figured this would be something you'd

be interested in," he said. "Seems to be connected to that poem you sent us this morning. Anything you can do to shed some light would be appreciated. This is certainly a weird one."

"Thanks for calling us, chief," Noah said. "I'm Special Agent Noah Hunter, and this is Special Agent Kaely Quinn." He flashed his badge but noticed Kaely didn't do the same.

The chief smiled. "I know Agent Quinn. She's helped us many times." He held his hand out first to Kaely. "Good to see you again," he said as they shook hands enthusiastically. Then he extended his hand to Noah, but only after looking him up and down. "Where's Special Agent Cartwright?"

"Transferred to Detroit," Kaely said quickly. "He has family there."

The chief nodded. "Too bad for St. Louis. Good man."

Kaely nodded. "Yes, he is."

"Well, nice to meet you, Agent Hunter. Too bad the circumstances are so tragic."

"What have you got here, chief?" Kaely asked.

The chief and Kaely began walking toward the area where other LEOs were already gathered. For a moment, Noah felt like a third wheel, but he reminded himself that this was what it was going to be like hanging around Kaely Quinn. She was the rock star. He was the roadie, even if he was in charge of the investigation. He wondered if he needed to say or do something to establish his authority. But was it really that important? For now, finding the person who wrote the poem was their top priority. Noah decided he could handle any slights that might come from being teamed with Kaely. Truthfully, he was intrigued. This was shaping up to be the most interesting day he'd had as an FBI agent. He wasn't ready to leave the adrenaline rush behind . . . yet.

The body was gone, and the forensic team was scouring the area for evidence, anything that might lead them to their unknown subject. Gathering clues and evidence was the key to turning the unknown into the known.

"Any idea who the victim is, chief?" Kaely asked.

He shook his head. "No ID on him. His clothes weren't right for running. And he wasn't wearing shoes. Of course, it's possible our UNSUB took them. Or maybe a homeless person saw a chance for an upgrade. We're checking the park to see if we can locate them."

"What about house keys?"

"Nope," the chief said.

"Either your UNSUB is taking trophies, or he's trying to make it hard for you to identify the victim."

"You're right." Chief Harper called out to a woman taking pictures. She came over to where they waited.

"Agent Quinn, do you remember our crime-scene photographer, Officer Glans?"

"Yes, I do. Hello, Patsy. How are you? This is Special Agent Noah Hunter."

"I'm fine, thanks for asking. Nice to meet you." Officer Glans looked Noah up and down. Then she grinned at Kaely. "You sure have a knack for getting paired with good-looking partners, Agent Quinn."

Noah was surprised to see Kaely blush. "Not on purpose. Agent Hunter is one of the best we have."

Glans winked at Kaely. "Sure, honey. If you say so."

Chief Harper cleared his throat. "*Officer* Glans," he said, emphasizing the word *officer,* "would you show these agents the pictures of our victim?"

Glans immediately lost her smile and seemed to remember she was standing next to the chief of police. "Yes, sir," she said. She held up her camera, which was wrapped in plastic, and pulled the LCD panel to the side, careful to shield it from the rain. She pressed a button and began to review the pictures she'd taken. Suddenly, she stopped. "Here he is," she said. Kaely leaned closer to Glans and Noah stood over her. He could clearly see the image of a man lying on the park bench, staring up at the sky with sightless eyes. He was dressed in a nice blue suit. Tie. No shoes, just black socks.

Officer Glans clicked to another picture, this time giving them a closer look at the man's head. "Medical examiner said he was killed this morning. Blunt force trauma," she said. "Strange-shaped weapon though. Not sure what it was."

"Left-handed putter," Kaely said in a whisper only Noah could hear.

He glanced at her, trying to see if she was kidding. How in the world could she know something like that?

Chief Harper, who had walked away for a moment to talk to another officer, came back. "You need to see this," he said, handing Kaely something in an evidence bag. She took it carefully as if she expected it to explode. Noah peered over her shoulder. It was the piece of paper with the drawing of an elephant on it. Inside the elephant was the number 1. "Good thing we got here before it started raining. This image might have been washed away."

"Yes, it is," Kaely said. She stared at the chief. "Is it possible for us to see your evidence? Crime-scene photos, forensics, everything?"

The chief frowned at her. "Sure. Can you tell me what's going on, Agent Quinn?"

Kaely rubbed her hands together as if trying to warm them up. "We've got the makings of a serial killer on our hands, chief. I think this is going to be a bad one."

Seven

Jerry Acosta knocked on his editor's door and waited for permission to enter. Gilbert Banner ran the *St. Louis Journal* like it was his personal possession and no one else had a right to an opinion. Jerry hated the man but was at his mercy. He had no choice but to kowtow to him any time Banner deigned to acknowledge Jerry's existence.

When he called to speak to Banner, he'd been instructed by Banner's administrative assistant to go to his own editor. When Jerry insisted, she coldly informed him that if he angered the editor-in-chief, Jerry's days at the *Journal* would be numbered. Although her intention was to intimidate him, he was willing to take the chance. After what he'd seen today, he was convinced he was sitting on a story that would change his life. He could finally see a way to finish the book he'd started years ago. Now he was part of the story. Maybe Kaely Quinn, aka Jessica

Oliphant, would finally agree to an interview about her famous father. With her help, he could become famous too.

He opened the door and walked in. Although he tried to look confident, Banner had a way of making him feel like he'd forgotten to dress this morning.

"What do you want, Acosta?" Banner barked out. He glared at his reporter like an ill-tempered bulldog whose bone had just been snatched away.

"I got a letter in the mail you need to see, boss," he said. "It's important."

"You're bothering me about some letter?" Banner said. His chubby face turned red. "Are you kidding me? Maybe you've heard that I've got a paper to get out."

"It . . . it's not just a letter," Jerry said. He hated the way his voice sounded. High and squeaky. Full of fear. He cleared his throat and tried to calm his nerves. A sudden spark of anger pushed back the terror, and Jerry took a step closer to Banner's desk. "I got a note . . . well, a poem, from someone who claims he's going to kill six people. Including that FBI agent . . . you know, the profiler?"

"The woman you've been badgering?" Banner snorted. "So you've written some kind of poem, hoping the Feds will think it's from a serial killer? You think this will get you an interview with Quinn? The FBI's not that dumb, Acosta, and neither am I. Now get out of here. And pick up your final check on the way out."

"Now, wait a minute," Jerry said, annoyance igniting rage. "I didn't write this. It's from a killer. His first victim showed up a little while ago in Forest Park. They've pulled Kaely Quinn in on it. I just came from the scene." He shook his head. "But I guess if I'm fired, I can take it to the *Kirkwood Dispatch.* It's a smaller circulation . . . until they print this, that is. Should shoot their subscriptions through the roof." He turned and headed toward the door.

"Hold up, Acosta," Banner said loudly. "Let me see what you've got."

Jerry had half a mind to do exactly what he'd threatened, but he needed his job at the *Journal.* The *Kirkwood Dispatch* couldn't begin to pay him what he made now. After pausing a few seconds for effect, Jerry slowly turned around, hoping to make it seem to Banner that now he was hesitant to share his story. He wanted the editor to pay for his insolence. After playing the moment for all he could, Jerry finally placed his copy of the poem on Banner's desk.

"It arrived this morning. Wasn't sure it

was real at first, but it bothered me. And then . . . well, the first elephant is dead."

Banner's eyes widened as he read the poem. Then he picked up his phone. "Dixon, come to my office now." He slammed the phone down and read the poem again. "Why would someone send this to you?" he asked. "You're nobody. It doesn't make sense."

Jerry took a quick breath and choked back a snide response. Then he said, "I'm assuming it's because of the articles I wrote about Agent Quinn."

"When you outed her in Virginia, or when you announced she was in St. Louis?"

"Look, people have the right to know when a serial killer's daughter is living in their town."

Banner scowled at Jerry through thick gray eyebrows that framed his bloodshot eyes. "Yeah, I'm sure your intentions were purely altruistic."

Jerry started to defend himself, but Banner waved his response away. "Forget it," he said. "A good journalist goes after the truth. We'll let the do-gooders out there decide what's right or wrong. That's not our job. We . . ."

A sudden knock on the door interrupted Banner's next comments. The door swung open, and John Dixon strode into the office.

"You need to see me, Gilbert?" he asked. His gaze locked on Jerry. Dixon looked nervous, and Jerry understood why. Many times, being called into Banner's office resulted in all your belongings stuffed in a cardboard box and a security escort from the building.

"You're writing about the death in the park this morning?" Banner asked.

"Yes?" John's eyes darted back and forth between his editor and Jerry. It was obvious he was confused.

"Tell me what you know."

"Not much yet. It was a man between twenty-five and thirty. No identification on the body. He was definitely murdered, blunt force trauma to the head. He was found on a park bench."

"Anything else?"

"Well, yeah, but the cops don't know what to make of it." Dixon shook his head. "You'll think this is nuts, but there was a drawing with the body. An outline of an elephant. Someone wrote the number 1 on it. The police don't want that released, but I was going to include it anyway. I got this from the woman who found the body."

"Hold up on your story," Banner said.

"We may have a new lead."

"Okay," John said slowly. Dixon was clearly suspicious, no doubt wondering why his story had been pulled. It was obvious he suspected Jerry was involved somehow.

"I'll get back to you," Banner said. "You can go."

John glared at Jerry, then left the room. The door slammed behind him with so much force the windows rattled. Banner seemed not to notice and turned his attention back to Jerry.

"You say your profiler was there? Looking over the crime scene?"

Jerry nodded. "That's right."

"You get pictures?"

"Yeah. Lots."

Banner picked up the paper again and perused the poem. "The first murder was in Forest Park," he said softly to himself. Jerry could tell he wasn't expecting an answer, so he stayed quiet. "Have the Feds seen this?" This time his comment was directed to Jerry.

"Yeah. I took them the original this morning. If you'll read the note on the back, you'll see that whoever sent it left me a message. If I want to hear from him again, I had to personally deliver the poem to Solomon Slattery. It took some effort, but I finally got in to see him." Jerry laughed humorlessly. "I also wanted to see their reaction. Find out if they took it seriously."

"And?"

"They did. And if they sent Kaely Quinn to the park . . ."

"Then this is the real deal."

"Yeah."

"I suppose they want us to withhold this?"

Jerry smiled at him. "I didn't ask. I just gave them the letter and left."

"Good." Banner tapped his fingers on the paper for a few seconds, his forehead wrinkled in thought. "Get to work on this," he said finally. "I want this story out as soon as possible." He pointed his finger at Jerry. "You make sure all your ducks are in a row. This better be the best story you've ever written, understand?"

Jerry nodded. "Do you want me to call the Feds and tell them we're going to run the story?"

"Nah. Let's surprise them. After all, it's our job to let the good people of St. Louis know a killer's on the loose, right?"

"Right, boss."

"And Acosta?"

"Yeah?"

Banner waved the poem at Jerry. "I take it you have other copies?"

"I do. You can keep that one."

"Good. Now get going and write me a great story, Jerry."

This was the first time Banner had ever called him by his first name. Acosta was floating on air. "I will, Gilbert. Don't worry."

Jerry hurried out of Banner's office before the cranky editor changed his mind. He almost ran into Dixon, who stood in the hallway.

"You got the story?" he asked.

Jerry nodded at him. "Sorry. I actually started on it this morning. I really wasn't trying to take it from you."

"You're a lying scumbag, Acosta. We only found out about the murder this afternoon. I'll remember this, don't you worry."

Jerry smiled at him. "After this story, I don't think you'll be able to touch me, John. You have no idea what this is really all about, but it's big. A career maker."

Jerry turned his back and walked down the hall, John cursing him all the way. This was the best day of Jerry's life, and he was determined to enjoy it.

Eight

On the ride back to headquarters, Kaely was quiet. It was obvious Noah wanted to talk about what they'd seen, but she needed time to process. He finally fell silent. He didn't seem offended, so she hoped he understood.

She couldn't help but wish Alex was with her now. He knew her. Knew how to help her. She still couldn't believe he'd left. She'd made it clear from the moment they started working together that she was all about the job. Nothing more. That there couldn't be anything else. Not until she learned how to trust people. Until she could look at someone and really see inside them. Even with the skills she'd developed, she still didn't have that ability. Some people were skilled liars. They lied so much they believed their lies to be the truth. These people were the hardest to see through.

She couldn't take the chance of turning

out like her mother. Believing in a man who didn't really exist, who was someone else behind the mask. It was too big a risk. One she wasn't ready to accept now — or maybe ever. At this point in her life, all she wanted to do was rid the world of men like her father. It was the reason she got up in the morning. The reason she breathed. There wasn't room for anything else. Kaely suddenly realized she was a little angry with Alex. Angry because he was weak. Angry because he'd given in to his feelings.

She tried to shake off the rush of emotion that caused her to feel her heart thump in her chest. She glanced over at Noah. Jaw set, eyes narrowed, looking straight ahead, both hands on the steering wheel. There wasn't any real pressure in his grasp, and his face displayed concentration, not annoyance. He was thinking. Good. Probably processing what they'd seen at the crime scene. She thought about telling him his ruminations were a waste of time, but you never knew. Sometimes people came up with things she hadn't thought of. Another perspective. Yet this was different. She knew exactly what they were facing, even if she had no idea who was behind it. The truth was, it frightened her, and fear was an emotion she wasn't comfortable with. In fact, she battled it diligently. She was able to keep it at bay during the day, but at night, silently and without warning, it would slip inside her. In the dark, where she couldn't see its face until it showed up in her nightmares.

"When will ERT get to the park?" Noah asked, breaking the silence.

Their Evidence Response Team was exemplary. If the police missed anything, ERT would find it. Kaely was grateful Chief Harper had agreed to let them look over the crime scene. "I'm sure they've already arrived." She sighed. "I know they'll carefully walk the grid, but I'm not sure they'll be able to determine what belongs to our guy and what doesn't. A public park is the perfect place for a murder. Hundreds of people through there every day. Lots of trace evidence. And with the rain . . ."

"It's getting late," Noah said softly. "Should we pick up something to eat and take it back to the office?"

Food. She'd forgotten. She could go all day without eating, but she realized other people expected three meals a day. Alex used to chide her about food. *"If I only ate when you thought of it, I'd turn to dust and blow away,"* he used to say.

"Sure," she said. "That's a good idea."

"What do you want?"

"I really don't care. Anything's fine. You pick."

He turned and smiled at her. "Are you sure?"

His bluish-gray eyes reminded her of storm clouds. Appropriate. She felt as if there were something brewing behind them. She just wasn't sure what it was, and not knowing made her feel unsettled.

"Absolutely. I'm not picky."

A few minutes later, he turned into a fast-food Chinese place.

"I'm surprised," she said. "I figured we'd be scarfing down greasy burgers and fries."

He laughed lightly. "There's a time for that, but this is my favorite place. I hope you like Chinese."

"You might not believe this, but I eat here three or four times a week."

Noah's jaw dropped, and he turned to look at her. "You're kidding. Hey, maybe I'm the one who can really read people."

Amused, she nodded at him. "Maybe so."

He ordered orange chicken and Beijing beef with fried rice, while Kaely got string bean chicken breast with vegetables. She found it funny that even though Chinese food was healthier than burgers, Noah still gravitated toward the fried choices. It wasn't all that far removed from greasy red meat.

"Crab Rangoon?" he asked.

"I'll take one," Kaely said.

Noah got the small order. Two for him. One for her.

Kaely handed him a twenty, but he pushed her hand away. "Hey, first time we've worked together. It's on me." He paid the cashier at the window and slid the change into his pocket.

"Thanks," Kaely said. "I'll get it next time."

"So, how long do you think it will take for us to get what we need from ERT?" he asked as they waited for their food.

"By the time we eat our supper, I expect we'll have crime-scene photos, a list of evidence they collected, a video of the crowd, and the ME's report."

"We're lucky the local police department's willing to work with us," Noah said. "Not all of them are so helpful."

"Most of the time we work well together. It's silly, really. It's not about territory. It should be about finding the truth."

Noah chuckled. "Yeah, you're right. It should be, but some people are looking for glory. I guess we all want to be the one who catches the bad guy."

"Is that what you want?" she asked. "Glory?"

He turned his head to look at her, and she saw something in his face that made her want to take the question back. He wasn't offended. He seemed hurt.

"No," he said softly. "I don't want glory. I guess I want . . . justice."

"Not a lot of justice in the world."

"I know, but I still want it."

She nodded. "Good. Me too. Truth and justice."

He laughed. "Sounds like a line from a bad movie. I suddenly feel like a member of the Justice League."

She frowned at him. "What's the Justice League?" The look of confusion on his face made her smile. "I'm really not that clueless, Noah. But I think we're more like the X-Men. You know, superpowers. Able to do things no one else can."

"Maybe. In your case anyway." He appeared to study her for a moment. "I'm amazed by what you do, by the way. I've never seen anything quite like it."

"I haven't really gotten started yet."

"I know. But I'm still impressed."

"It's not an exact science. Sometimes I'm wrong."

"If you didn't miss it once in a while, you'd scare me."

The drive-through window suddenly

popped open, and the woman inside handed them their orders. Noah took the bag and gave it to Kaely. When the aroma of the food hit her, she salivated a little. She was hungrier than she thought.

It took them about ten minutes to get back to work. When they got inside the building, Kaely headed for the conference room, with Noah following behind her. They each grabbed a chair and pulled their carryout containers, napkins, and forks from the sacks.

"I'll get us something to drink from the pop machine. What do you want?"

"Just water, thanks."

After he left, Kaely prayed over her food and poured a packet of soy sauce on her green beans and chicken. Before she had a chance to take a bite, someone knocked on the door and then pushed it open. It was Grace.

"This just came for you. Chief Harper had it delivered." She put a large manila envelope on the table.

Kaely thanked her, and Grace left. Kaely opened the envelope from Chief Harper and pulled out the crime-scene photos. She really appreciated the chief's willingness to share information. Usually, in cases like this, it took three murders for the FBI to get involved in helping local law enforcement if they requested their assistance. Because Chief Harper wasn't territorial, he welcomed their help. Of course, since a federal agent had been threatened, the Bureau had every right to take over. Thankfully, cooperation between the FBI and the local police meant both agencies could concentrate on finding a killer instead of trying to stake their claim to the case.

A lot of agents viewed digital pictures on their laptops, but Kaely liked to hold the actual photos in her hands. She was glad the chief had sent hard copies. When she'd worked with him before, he'd confessed to her that he felt the same way.

She stared again at the body found in the park. The feeling of déjà vu was overpowering. This wasn't the first time she'd seen this crime scene or this victim. Someone was sending a message. And the message was specifically for her.

Nine

Solomon slammed his phone down in anger. Grace had asked him more than once to be gentle with it, but today he was too upset to remember her reprimand. His media coordinator, Jacqueline Cross, had spent almost an hour on the phone with Jerry Acosta, asking him to wait to print the poem. Jerry had given her the runaround. Jackie had no idea if she'd gotten through to him. The last thing the Bureau wanted was to tip off the killer. They needed time to go over the evidence and develop a strategy to catch him.

"Jerry's slippery, Sol. I did my best, but I'm just not sure. I don't trust him or the slimy editor he works for."

"Thanks for trying, Jackie. We'd better plan for the worst."

They both knew that when the story hit the papers, especially after the death in Forest Park, every Tom, Dick, and Harry would be certain his neighbor was a serial killer. Women would turn in their ex-husbands, husbands would point at their ex-wives. It would be a mess. Press coverage could also push the UNSUB to change his game plan. Something they didn't need.

He checked his watch. It was late. He should have left long ago. Jackie should be at home too, instead of writing up a report about her conversation with Acosta. He'd told her that, but she'd ignored him.

"Working late again, boss?" Jackie had countered.

"Yes," he'd responded gruffly. "Is that something I need to clear through you?"

"No, but I worry about you."

"It's not your job to take care of me. I'm a grown man."

Jackie had laughed. "Grown men. They're the biggest babies on the planet. Go home, boss."

He wanted to be irritated with her, but it was hard to get angry at people who cared about you. A mild heart attack last year had made his agents think they needed to mother him. They didn't. His doctor had given him a clean bill of health. He was fine.

He shuffled through the papers on his desk, not really seeing them, debating with himself about telling Noah and Kaely about the article. He didn't want to distract them, but at the same time he didn't want them to feel ambushed. He decided he had no choice but to warn them.

He hated working with the press. The previous editor at the *Journal* had been much more accommodating, but this guy, Banner, had ink running through his veins and sales figures for brains. Jackie had experienced problems with him many times before. Once in a great while, he'd consent to hold back a story when it helped them close a case, usually only after the promise of an exclusive story down the road, but those instances were happening less and less. Any time someone in the media put their headlines above the safety of citizens and law enforcement, it made Solomon furious.

During a previous case, they'd contacted the owner of the paper. That got them nowhere. He was an out-of-touch businessman who left all management decisions to Banner. Talking to the owner was like trying to have a conversation with a brick wall.

His phone jingled, and he picked it up.

"Sol, Unit Chief Donald Reinhardt . . ."

"I don't have time to talk to him now," Solomon said, interrupting her. "It's late. Tell him I'm —"

"Uh, Sol? He's not on the phone. He's here. In the building."

Solomon froze. What was Reinhardt doing here all the way from Quantico? He sighed. "This can't be good," he said. "When are you leaving, Grace?"

"When you do."

"I might be working late tonight."

A long drawn-out sigh came over the receiver. "Joyce is dealing with empty-nest syndrome, Sol. She doesn't need her husband to abandon her too."

Solomon snorted. "I'm not abandoning her."

"Then get Reinhardt out of here and go home. I'll walk you out." With that, she hung up.

Solomon shook his head. This was the second time someone had encouraged him to leave. Grace was a good friend and wasn't afraid to challenge him when he needed it. Maybe she was right. He'd get rid of Reinhardt as quickly as he could and head home. Evenings had grown quiet, he and Joyce finally ending up in front of the TV. Usually, he fell asleep and when he woke up, he'd find himself alone on the couch. He wished he knew what to do. How to talk to her.

He hung up the phone more gently this

time. Today wasn't a good day for a visit from Quantico. Reinhardt was a unit chief within the FBI's Critical Incident Response Group, called CIRG, which included the Behavioral Analysis Units, Kaely's specialty. Reinhardt was the one behind Kaely's transfer from Quantico after the article written by Acosta revealed the FBI had a special agent who was the daughter of a serial killer. *Don't embarrass the FBI* was a motto not touted to the public but was front and center within the Bureau. Although Reinhardt had been instrumental in Kaely's training, now it seemed he had a problem with her.

Not long after the first article that revealed Kaely's past, Acosta published another one that detailed her strange profiling process. Although it was something Kaely usually kept private, someone at the FBI leaked the story. Reinhardt had come unglued. He wanted profilers who played it by the book, and that wasn't Kaely Quinn. He believed she was a lone wolf who didn't follow the policies and procedures he and others in the unit prescribed. He pressured the powers-that-be at Quantico to kick Kaely out. Eventually, they gave in and sent her to St. Louis. Solomon had decided to ignore Reinhardt's warnings about Special Agent

Quinn. He had no authority over the St. Louis field office. Frankly, Solomon didn't care if Kaely dressed in a clown suit and stood on her head when she worked a profile — if it got results. If she wanted to use a unique method to help them catch criminals, so be it. Besides, Solomon was certain Reinhardt had been intimidated by Kaely when she was at Quantico. If she'd stayed, she might have been a unit chief by now.

He sighed. Why did Reinhardt have to show up today? Just when this new case had popped up? When the *Journal* was ready to push Kaely into the spotlight again? He pushed his chair back and waited. Finally, the phone buzzed again. He picked it up.

"Unit Chief Reinhardt to see you, sir."

"Send him in."

Solomon stood up and waited, his body rigid with resentment. The door swung open, and Reinhardt stepped inside. He was an imposing figure. Tall and distinguished-looking with a full head of silver hair, black-framed glasses that made his blue eyes look larger than they were, manicured nails, his dark suit pressed and perfect, and his tie straight even though he'd probably just flown from Virginia to St. Louis. He looked like a man who knew what he was doing.

And he did. But the parameters he used to judge himself and others were narrow, and not many people fit them.

Solomon stuck out his hand. "Hey, Don. Good to see you. You should have told me you were coming."

"It was a quick decision, Sol," he said, grasping Solomon's hand and shaking it firmly. "Didn't have much time to notify anyone."

Solomon gestured toward one of the chairs in front of his desk. "Sit down. Coffee?"

"That sounds great. Thanks."

Solomon called Grace and asked her to get Reinhardt a cup of coffee. He covered the mouthpiece with his hand. "You take it black, don't you, Don?"

"Yes. I'm surprised you remembered."

After telling Grace what he needed, he hung up. "I remember the conversation we had once about froufrou coffee at Quantico."

Reinhardt grinned. "I recall that too. I believe we decided real men drink their coffee black."

"Yeah, and then an attractive waitress at a local restaurant encouraged us to try their new . . . what was it?"

"Special Christmas mocha peppermint latte."

"And we both ordered it like a couple of whipped puppies."

They both laughed at the memory. Solomon had almost forgotten that he and Reinhardt weren't always adversarial with each other. He actually missed those days.

"So how can I help you today, Don?" Solomon asked.

Reinhardt's expression immediately shifted, and any trace of humor vanished. "Heard something about your new case, Sol. Came to offer our help."

Solomon pushed back a powerful surge of annoyance that fought for expression. He resisted giving it a voice and smiled. "My goodness, this thing is still fresh. How in the world did you guys get hold of it already?"

"I have friends at the SLMPD."

At that moment, Solomon would have given a thousand dollars to know exactly what nincompoop with the St. Louis Metro Police Department contacted Reinhardt. Probably some rookie cop hoping to be accepted into the FBI's training program. Reinhardt must have jumped on the next plane to St. Louis and come straight to Solomon's office.

"Actually, this case still belongs to the local PD," Solomon said, hoping to deflect his offer of assistance. "We're only offering support."

Reinhardt frowned at him. "When one of our agents is threatened, we can get involved without being asked. And if the murder is connected . . ."

Reinhardt wore his professional face. Solomon recognized it immediately. It meant *You're really not up to this, and I'm here to save the day.* Solomon prepared himself, and he wasn't disappointed.

"We feel you're going to need assistance," Reinhardt continued. "Especially from BAU. Kaely Quinn isn't . . . well, she shouldn't be working this case, not when she's personally involved. There's a definite threat to her, and a promise of more killings to come. You have a serial on your hands. You know that, right?"

The door to his office opened, and Grace came in with two cups of coffee. She studied her boss for a moment and seemed to pick up on the tension. She put the cups down and quickly left the room.

"We're not sure if it's a serial yet. As I said, this is still new. I have confidence in the St. Louis Police Department. They'll probably capture the UNSUB before it goes any further." He paused. "Or maybe he's a one-hit wonder. We just might never hear from him again."

Solomon stood, hoping Reinhardt would follow his lead. Right now, he wanted this smug so-and-so out of his office. "I appreciate your offer, but let's see what we've got first. If we need your help, we'll contact you immediately."

Even though Reinhardt had no authority to tell him what to do, he could stir up trouble. For now, Solomon just wanted to placate him until he could figure out how to put him in his place. Unfortunately, Reinhardt didn't take the hint and stayed right where he was.

"I'll go in a minute," he said in a low voice. "But Quinn needs to stay out of it. I mean that, Solomon."

"I'm sorry you feel that way, Don. I don't want to fight with you, but I believe in Kaely Quinn. She has expertise, training . . . and something else. Call it a gift or a mission. I can't explain it. No matter what you say or do, I'll back her all the way."

Reinhardt scowled. "The FBI doesn't need psychics or people who think God speaks to them. . . ."

"Agent Quinn has never claimed to be psychic — or a mouthpiece for God. And you know that."

"I don't care. Perception is reality. We have trained behavioral analysts who rely on facts and evidence. Those are the people I respect . . . and trust. Not some unbalanced young woman who thinks she's the Joan of Arc of the FBI."

Solomon could feel his temper rising past his ability to control it. If Reinhardt didn't leave right away, they could have a problem that might not be easily solved. "Special Agent Quinn respects facts and evidence, Don. She's pointed us to the right UNSUB more times than I can count. She's completely qualified. You should know that. You trained her." He waved his hand toward Reinhardt as if trying to dispel a bad smell. "I don't want to talk about this anymore. Let's stop before one of us says something we're going to regret."

Finally, Reinhardt stood up. "I can't tell you what to do, but I think you should keep Quinn in check. If you don't, you may be sorry." He turned on his heel and strode toward the office door. But before he left, he turned back and stared at Solomon through narrowed eyes. "I'm doing what I feel is best for the Bureau. I think you know that." He hesitated for a moment. Then he said, "Your UNSUB's no one-hit wonder.

He's in for the long haul, Sol. More people are going to die." With that, he pushed the office door open and left.

Solomon slumped down in his chair. Whatever Reinhardt's faults, one fact was irrefutable. He was great at his job. He had talent and instinct. In his heart of hearts, Solomon knew Don was right about their UNSUB. Unless they found a way to stop him, more people were definitely going to die.

Ten

Noah returned to the conference room, holding a bottle of water and a can of pop. He handed Kaely the water. When he closed the door, she gestured toward the chair he'd sat in earlier. He was still unsettled by the weird poem and the murder in the park, but Kaely seemed completely calm and collected.

"I'm sorry," she said. "I guess your three questions will have to wait."

Noah frowned at her. "Hold it. I may need to ask other questions . . . you know, about the case. You can't suddenly tell me I've used up all my questions."

"Okay. How about you call them your *special* questions? I won't hold anything else you ask against you."

"Agreed."

Kaely stared at him with raised eyebrows. "So, you've decided to hang in there? Keep me as your co-case agent?"

"I'd answer you, but you probably already know what I'm thinking, right? What would be the point?"

She nodded. "You're right."

"Is there some way you could stop trying to read my mind? It's annoying."

Kaely looked past him for a moment. "Fair request," she said finally. "I'll try, but I can't promise anything." When she swung her gaze back his way, she actually gave him a subtle smile. "Solomon says the same thing. It's so automatic I don't realize I'm doing it."

"I'll take that deal. Thanks." Relieved, he sat down. "So now what?"

"We start building a profile."

"From the murder?"

"Yeah, although since he's imitating someone else, it will be a little challenging. Let's start with the letter." She handed him their copy of the poem. "Tell me about our UNSUB."

Noah shook his head. "I'm not you, Kaely. I mean, we're all trained in behavioral analysis, but it's never been my forte. I don't think I can do what you ask."

"Actually, you're wrong."

He looked at her in surprise. "I don't understand."

"Okay. Tell me about . . . me."

Noah instantly felt uncomfortable. "I can't . . . I mean, we just met. There's no way . . ."

"Nonsense." She spit the word out like a bullet looking for a target. "You have instincts. We all do. Tell me what you see in me. No holds barred." She fixed her gaze on him, her dark eyes unreadable. "If we're going to be working closely together, you need to know who I am. It's how we build trust."

Noah squirmed in his chair. "Now wait a minute. I still have a personal life outside of this place. I don't intend to give you access to everything about me."

Kaely looked down at her notebook and drew a strange squiggle. Then she shot him a look of caution. "Anything you hide from me is potentially dangerous. I have to know how you will react in any given situation. Especially one like this. This UNSUB is coming for me — and you'll be close, Agent Hunter. Too close. If you do something I haven't anticipated, it could end badly for both of us. Your life is in danger too, you know. I can't force you to open up completely, but I urge you to think about what I'm saying before one of us ends up dead."

"Okay, I'll consider it."

"Good. Now profile me. Don't think

about it. Just say the first thing that comes to your mind and don't sugarcoat it."

Noah collected himself, squaring his shoulders. This was crazy, but if she really wanted to hear what he thought, he'd tell her. "Okay. Your life was shaped by what your father did. You're trying to make up for his evil. Your whole existence revolves around that. You live, eat, and sleep your job." An image of that look he saw in her eyes when he first entered the conference room flashed in his mind. "But there is someone vulnerable inside you. You keep it hidden because you're afraid of it." The words that came out of his mouth surprised him. Kaely Quinn, afraid? He saw her jaw clench momentarily. He'd hit a nerve. "You *are* afraid, Kaely. But not of serial killers. Of other people. And yourself. You don't have any real friends. You don't trust your own emotions." Although her expression didn't change, he felt a sudden connection with the woman who now met his gaze without hesitation.

"Anything else?" she asked.

"You're incredible at what you do, and you've given up a lot to become as good as you are. It's impressive."

"Very good," she said briskly. She crossed her arms and leaned back in her chair.

"You're right, Noah. About all of it. Except for one thing."

"What's that?"

"Friends. I have a couple."

"I'm glad."

"Yeah, me too. I can't live inside my head all the time. No one can. I may be all those things you said, but I'm human too."

"Good. Perfection is highly overrated." He studied her for a moment. "What about your family, Kaely? Do you ever see them?"

It was as if a shadow crossed her features. Noah not only saw it, he felt it.

"My mother lives in Nebraska. She remarried, and we don't talk much. She's avoiding me. She didn't want me to join the Bureau. She thinks I'm drawn to law enforcement because I feel it's my duty to pay for what my father did." She looked away. "I also think I remind her of him."

Noah found that hard to believe. He'd seen pictures of Ed Oliphant, and he was not a good-looking man. Kaely was beautiful. She looked nothing like him. He wondered what it was her mother saw when she looked at her daughter.

"And my younger brother . . ." Her voice trailed off. "I don't know where he is. We lost touch years ago. I . . . I don't think he wants anything to do with me either. He needed a new life." She tried to sound nonchalant, but Noah could hear the hurt in her voice. "He's angry. When he got older, he convinced himself that my mother and I knew something was wrong with my father but we didn't try to stop him. A lot of people believe that, but it isn't true."

"It is a little hard to accept that he never did anything to cause suspicion."

She didn't seem offended by his comment. "I realize that. In fact, I wonder about my mother. How could she have been so clueless? I was just a kid. I mean, your father's . . . your father, you know? The idea that he might be a serial killer never really enters your mind."

Noah nodded. "Yeah. As kids we revere our parents. Until we get to be teenagers, and then we decide they don't know anything."

"I never made it that far. I go over it and over it in my mind. What did I miss? I keep trying to uncover that clue, you know? The comment that might have shown me who he really was. I just can't find it." She hesitated for a moment. "Except . . ."

"Except what?" Noah asked when she paused.

"Nothing, never mind," she said dismissively. "It's just a weird nightmare I have sometimes, but my father isn't in it. I'm not sure what it means."

"One other question. Not a special one, but I think it applies to our conversation."

"And that is?"

"Why did Alex Cartwright leave?"

"That's almost a special question."

"No. No, it's not. I'm stepping into a partnership with you. I want to know the truth. Why did he transfer?"

She stared down at the notebook in front of her. "Because he got too close. He began to care more about the woman than he did the agent. Don't do that and we'll be fine."

"Caring about people is natural, Kaely. What you're asking . . ."

"You don't understand. You can care. That's fine. But my professional side must come first. Not my personal side." Her eyes sought his. "Solomon told me something about you that made both of us decide you and I would be a good fit for this assignment. I mean, besides the fact that you're a great agent, someone who can do this job." She hesitated, then said, "He told me about your wife."

If Kaely Quinn had thrown a knife at his chest, it wouldn't have affected him as deeply as the words she spoke. He stood up, barely even realizing he was on his feet.

"That doesn't enter into this. If it does, I want out. Now."

"Sit down, Noah," she said soothingly. "Let me explain."

"I'll stand, thanks." He turned a bit. "You notice my feet really are pointed toward the door now?"

Kaely clasped her hands together and sighed. "It's important because we know you're not looking for a girlfriend — which is something I'll never be. And that's it. You have my word."

Although he still didn't like Solomon and Kaely discussing Tracy, as he felt his resentment lessen a little, he realized what she said actually made some sense. He slowly sat down again. "I won't fall in love with you, and you'll leave my wife out of our relationship. Okay?"

She nodded. "Okay. Now let's get to work."

Eleven

Noah finished off his supper while looking at crime-scene photos. Not the best way to aid digestion. He picked up his empty carry-out box and took it over to the trash can. As she pored through files of past cases, Kaely picked at her meal. She ate like a bird. Noah felt an urge to persuade her to eat, like she was a child and he needed to take care of her. He recognized the impulse was one that could get him into trouble and decided to ignore it.

Kaely Quinn didn't need a babysitter, even though that was what he was originally worried about. She was smart, competent, and tough. He had to treat her like an equal. Show her respect and try not to see himself as her protector, even though the instinct was there. They were partners. Being certain of his role in her life would keep him from having to transfer to another city — like Alex Cartwright.

As he was walking back toward his chair, the door swung open and Solomon came in, looking upset.

"What's wrong?" Kaely asked as soon as she saw him.

Solomon rubbed his face with his hand. "Nothing. Just tired. Why are you two still here?"

Noah slipped back into his chair. "We're just now getting a chance to look at the evidence." He glanced quickly at Kaely. "I'd like both of us to stay and work for a while, if it's okay with Kaely."

"I'm good," Kaely said. "I'm looking through past cases, trying to see if our UNSUB might be connected somehow. I think I recognize the killing in the park, but I want to be certain." She pulled a large stack of files toward her. "This might take a couple of days. We need to get a jump on it."

"That's fine," Solomon said. "You find anything yet?"

She shook her head. "Not really. We need to figure out how I'm connected to our UNSUB. I've obviously done something that's angered him. We have to find out what it was. He seems to have knowledge about me. About my work."

Solomon grunted. "Acosta. He wrote about several cases you were associated with. It would be easy for friends or family to read his articles and blame you for putting their loved one behind bars."

"That's true, but we have to remember that his news stories might not have anything to do with our killer at all. We're flying blind here. That's why we need to go through everything. Carefully."

"Okay," Solomon said, "but tell me about Acosta. What specific cases did he talk about in his articles?"

"There were six of them. Four of them simply wouldn't fit this scenario. Two serial killers in other states without any family support or friends. No one who is upset they're behind bars. A bomber who hid out for years. Again, no family or friends. And a guy with ties to terrorism who shot himself not long before he was captured. His 'friends' are overseas — and they couldn't care less about me. They have a larger agenda."

"And the other two?" Solomon asked.

"A serial rapist in Virginia, and that guy I profiled here. You know, the male nurse who was killing people in a local hospital?"

Solomon nodded. "Michael Edmonds. He murdered four people before he was arrested. You gave the police a profile that helped them to nail him."

"Same thing happened in Virginia."

"Why do you think these cases are possibilities?" Noah asked.

"Because in both cases, there are family members or friends who insist we got it wrong, that their loved ones weren't capable of what they were charged with. The rapist in Virginia came from a nice family. Parents and a brother who insist he's innocent. They're still fighting for him." Kaely rolled her eyes. "He's guilty, by the way. And Michael Edmonds has a girlfriend who insists Michael didn't kill anyone and claims some other nurse was behind the murders."

"And is he guilty too?"

Kaely frowned at him. "I have no idea. I only worked the profile in that case. The police took it from there. But the way Acosta wrote the story, you'd think I single-handedly tracked down and arrested the guy. It was ridiculous."

"It was a profile we didn't have to do, by the way," Solomon said. "Chief Harper asked us to look at it, so we did."

"So, now we delve into the cases I mentioned, along with all the rest I've had anything to do with. We don't have a choice." She exhaled softly. "But as far as the cases Acosta wrote about, I have my doubts."

"Why?" Solomon asked.

"Well, the family of the rapist —" she pulled a file near her and opened it — "Archie Mason . . . They're just not the kind of people to do something like this. They're solid citizens. The truth is, they simply can't accept that they raised a son who became a serial rapist."

"And the nurse?"

"I don't see it. Edmonds convinced himself he was helping people. An 'angel of mercy' thing. Seeking revenge toward me just doesn't fit."

"Well, check them all out anyway," Solomon said. "Whatever it takes to go through all of this. Don't worry about food. I'll send it in. Just do your best."

Kaely studied Solomon for a moment. "Okay, what's going on? Something's obviously bothering you."

"You mean besides stopping a potential serial killer?"

"Yeah."

Noah watched the struggle on Solomon's face. He didn't need Kaely's talents to see their boss was conflicted. What now?

"Reinhardt's in town," Solomon said quickly, as if he were pulling off a Band-Aid and wanted to get past the pain.

Kaely blinked several times and leaned

back in her chair. "What does he want?"

"Donald Reinhardt?" Noah asked. "From Quantico?"

Solomon nodded.

"He'd just become unit chief when I left."

"Reinhardt helped train me," Kaely said. "He also made sure I was kicked out of Quantico."

Noah frowned. "He was behind that?"

She nodded. "The reputation of the Bureau comes first."

Although he didn't say anything, Noah was struck by how unfair it was that Kaely was judged for something her father did. Something she had no control over.

"Well, he's concerned about the case," Solomon said, rubbing his hands together. "He's offering their assistance."

"That's good," Kaely said. "We could use the help. We're going to need them."

"With Reinhardt here, things could get . . . complicated."

"I know that, but we need to find this guy, Solomon. Using every tool we have is the right thing to do. This isn't about Reinhardt . . . or me."

"I told him the police may solve this on their own. But if they don't, or there's another killing . . ."

"I say we bring them in now," Kaely said

matter-of-factly. She shifted her gaze to Noah. "I'm sorry," she said quickly. "This is your call. I didn't mean to overstep."

"You're not," Noah said. "I agree with you. Whatever we can get from NCAVC should bring us closer to the truth." He knew that input from the National Center for the Analysis of Violent Crime at Quantico could bring them closer to their quarry, and he was relieved that Kaely didn't have a problem using the FBI as a resource, even after the way she'd been treated.

"At some point, you'll need to set up a command post," Solomon said. "Invite the local PD to join us. I'll have our liaison contact Crisis Management and ask them to find and set up a location."

"What about Reinhardt?" Noah asked. "He won't hijack our investigation, will he?"

"He can't remove you. If he oversteps his authority, I'll take care of it. I'm still in charge here."

"Then we need to get busy," Kaely said. Her voice had taken on a hard edge. Noah could see she was determined to get some traction on this case.

He nodded at Solomon. "We'll do our best."

"Never occurred to me you wouldn't." He hesitated a moment.

"Something else?" Kaely said.

"The *Journal* might be printing the poem in tomorrow's paper. We argued, but I doubt we won. Just wanted you to be prepared."

"But we need some time to work on this before it goes public," Noah said.

"I realize that, but Acosta and his boss don't care," Solomon said, weariness in his voice. "They're only concerned with selling newspapers."

Noah and Kaely were silent. What was there to say? They'd just have to find a way to deal with it.

"Good night." With that, Solomon shoved the door open and walked quickly down the hall.

Kaely pushed the file they'd gotten from the police toward Noah. He could almost feel a wave of intensity emanating from her.

"So what do we have?" he asked her.

She cradled her head in her hands and stared down at the table for a moment. Finally, she said, "What we have is George Anderson."

He blinked several times, trying to comprehend what she was saying. "I . . . I don't understand. George Anderson? The serial killer from Georgia?"

She turned her incredible eyes toward him. "Yes. Do you remember the case?"

"Anderson killed thirteen men. Men he felt had things in life he didn't. Men he decided didn't deserve what they had."

"Do you recall any other details?"

"Just that you caught him."

Kaely's eyes widened, and she took a quick intake of air. "No, Noah. *I* didn't catch him. Just like I didn't catch Michael Edmonds. Profilers help to point the way to those investigating a crime or crimes, but we never, ever *catch them.* Facts and evidence catch criminals. And that's it. I never take credit for a capture. All of that goes to the people who do the real work. The hard work."

"I realize that. Sorry." He smiled at her. She obviously had no desire for celebrity. "I think your attitude's admirable."

"Not admirable, Special Agent Hunter," she fired back in sharp staccato. "The truth."

"Okay," he said. "Am I to understand that when you call me *Special Agent Hunter,* I'm in trouble? Like when my mother called me *Noah Robert Hunter,* I knew I was about to get grounded?"

The corners of her mouth turned up. "Yeah, I guess that's what it means."

"Okay. Point taken." He pulled a file toward him and opened it. "So you're saying this guy was killed in the same manner Anderson handled his victims?"

"No, not in the same manner. *Exactly* like Anderson." She got up. "Let me get something from my filing cabinet. I'll be right back."

She hurried from the room while Noah looked through the file of the day's crime scene. He pulled out one of the photos and stared at it. Although he'd seen the picture at the scene, he could make out more detail now. The victim looked to be around thirty. Brown hair. A face that wouldn't be noticed in a crowd. Average height. Average weight. Blue suit. Expensive watch. His feet were clad in black socks. Blood on the side of his head where he'd been hit.

Noah carefully perused the photos of the area where the body had been found. Not far from the museum, near a grove of trees. Posed on a bench. His hands were folded across his chest as if he were sleeping. His ankles were crossed. If it hadn't been for the discoloration on the side of his face, and the blood, Noah would have thought the guy was taking a nap. Of course, most of the people who sleep in the park don't wear thousand-dollar suits.

The door suddenly opened, and Kaely dumped a large file on the table. "My personal file from the Anderson case."

"Wow. Don't you use your computer for anything?"

"I like paper files. Real pictures. Some of this came from digital documents I copied." She looked down at the materials. "I keep information from all my cases — and others that interest me."

Noah stood up. "You're a strange person, Kaely Quinn. So let's see what you've got."

"First I want you to look at this."

She began shuffling through the file's contents. Finally, she pulled out a manila envelope labeled *Photos.* She opened it and flicked through the stack of glossy eight-by-tens until she found the one she wanted. She walked over and slapped it down on the table next to the original picture. "What do you see?" she asked.

He moved over so he could view the photos. As he leaned down, his face near her hair, he could smell a faint hint of strawberries. At that moment, she reached up and tucked her hair behind her ear. For the first time, he noticed a long, light-colored scar that ran down the side of her face, right next to her hairline. Even though the scar was faint, it had obviously been a serious injury. He wondered what had happened but didn't feel they were close enough yet for him to ask her about it. He forced himself to concentrate on the picture she wanted him to see. When he realized what he was looking at, his mouth dropped open.

"They're the same," he said. "Exactly the same."

The photo from the Anderson file showed a man lying on a bench, near a row of trees, dressed in a suit. He had brown hair, an expensive watch, and he was wearing a blue suit. And like their vic from this morning, no shoes. His arms were folded across his chest, and his ankles were crossed. Blood had crusted on the side of his head. Noah couldn't believe what he was seeing.

"Why did Anderson dress his victims like this?"

"You tell me," Kaely said.

Noah stared at the picture for a moment. "Anderson dressed them in expensive suits and killed them with golf clubs because he saw these things as something connected to the kind of men he hated. Rich men."

"Yes. He wanted to send a message that even with their wealth, they weren't safe from him. They couldn't save themselves. He wanted them to be victims so he wouldn't feel like one."

Noah frowned. "Why did he take their shoes?"

"You tell me," she said again.

He scowled at her. "I take it this is going to be a habit? Answering my questions with a question?"

Kaely almost smiled. "I'm trying to show you that you know more than you think you do. Can't you tell me why he took their shoes?"

Noah sighed loudly. Finally, he said, "Well, this is out of left field, but you asked for it. Shoes are for walking. Going somewhere. If he takes their shoes, not only does he have a trophy, but he's saying their journey is over. They're not going anywhere else."

"And you would be absolutely right," Kaely said.

"Okay. Why a left-handed putter? And don't ask me to tell you why. I have no earthly idea."

Kaely shrugged. "Anderson was left-handed. Police found the putter in his home with traces of blood from the victims on it."

"You set me up."

"I think you did that on your own."

Noah laughed. Maybe Kaely Quinn was different, but she had a sense of humor. Maybe working with her wasn't going to be that bad after all.

"You understand the body," Kaely said

softly. "Now look at his surroundings."

"It's like it was taken in the same spot. There's a row of trees behind him. What's that building?" He pointed at a large structure not far from the body.

"That's the High Museum of Art in Atlanta. It's different than our museum — very modern. But the killer doesn't care about that. He's only concerned that it's a museum and that the body was found on a bench next to a row of trees."

Noah leaned over the table, staring down at the back of Kaely's head. "I don't get it."

When Kaely straightened up and turned, she was just inches from Noah's face. "I'm convinced the weapon used to kill the man in the park was a left-handed putter. Just like this murder." She jabbed the photo with her finger. "We have a potential serial killer who may be imitating other killers. Someone who thinks this is a game. Someone wearing a mask. We're not seeing him directly, we're glimpsing him through the eyes of other serials."

"How could the UNSUB know this many details of the crime scene?"

"It wouldn't be that difficult. The case got a lot of publicity. Besides the media, there's the trial. Anyone attending would have picked up the particulars. Of course, LEOs would be able to access the facts of the case too."

"One of us?"

"I find that hard to believe," Kaely said. "But at this point, there's no way to narrow it down."

"Great," he said with a long, drawn-out sigh. "I was going to contact Quantico, ask them to run this crime scene through ViCAP, but if our UNSUB is copying this crime . . ."

"Do it anyway," Kaely said, interrupting him. "And have them run the poem too. We need to make sure we've covered all our bases, even if we don't think we'll learn anything new."

He nodded. "So now what?"

She grabbed their copy of the poem. "The first killing follows the pattern. *Seven little elephants walking in the forest. One hit his head and fell down dead. Six little elephants called it a day. They packed up their trunks and they all ran away.*" She pointed to the paper. "Now we have to prepare for the UNSUB's next move."

"Read it," Noah said.

"Six little elephants swimming in the lake. One was slaughtered and went underwater. Five little elephants called it a day. They packed up their trunks and they all ran away."

"Well, the forest turned out to be Forest Park — so it wasn't just a forest. That means we can't take the clue literally."

"Maybe . . ." she said slowly. "We also can't send agents out to every lake in Missouri." Kaely took a drink of water and then licked her lips. "We need to be on top of this. Ahead of him. Watching for something that doesn't seem right."

"What do you mean?" Noah asked.

"Anyone overly interested in this case. Media. Police officers. This guy's watching us, I'm sure of it."

"Doesn't that bring us back to Jerry Acosta?"

"He was at the crime scene this morning." Kaely stared closely at one of the pictures. "But I don't think he was at Forest Park at the time of the murder. I suspect he was here, talking to Solomon, when our victim was killed."

"He could be working with someone. Could he get access to Anderson's files?" Noah asked.

"Not the files, but, as I said, most of this came out at trial. It would be fairly easy for a reporter to get details of the case."

Noah's forehead crinkled at her comment. "I think we need to keep him on our list of possible suspects. I don't trust him."

Kaely nodded. “Okay.”

“I wonder how long the *Journal* will wait to print this poem.”

“They’ll definitely publish it,” Kaely said. “I hope they wait a while, but I wouldn’t count on it.”

“When it comes out . . .”

“People will go crazy. It will be a mess.”

“Maybe someone will recognize the poem.”

“I seriously doubt that,” Kaely said. “I think our UNSUB is too smart for that.” She pushed back a strand of unruly hair that had escaped her bun. “I’m truly afraid more people will die before we catch this guy, Noah.”

Twelve

"Do you see anything here that helps us?" Noah asked after they looked through everything the police had sent over.

"Not really," Kaely said. "So now we search through all these old files. Then we give Solomon whatever we can."

She could not stop looking at the two photos. The one from today, and the one from four years ago. She wanted to find something wrong. A difference. Something the UNSUB had missed. Finally, she saw it. She pointed at the photo with the recent victim. "Different time of the year," she said. "The leaves show fall colors here." She moved her finger to the old photo. "Green in this shot. It's raining, but it looks like summer. This man was killed in . . ." She started to grab the file again but stopped and closed her eyes. She thought for a moment. "July. July 19, 2014."

"You remember the date?" Noah asked, a

hint of surprise in his voice.

"Yes." She looked up at him. "Isn't that why you all call me Jessica Elephant behind my back?"

She was gratified to see him blush. Although the name didn't bother her as a tribute to her memory, she hated being called anything that reminded her of her father.

"So what does that mean?" he asked quickly, obviously trying to move the conversation away from the mention of her uncomfortable nickname.

"It means he wanted to re-create this particular killing even though there are differences he couldn't control. Like the time of year. This murder was important to him."

"Why?"

"I don't know. I guess he just wanted an old case I'd worked. Look, we're dealing with something different here. This guy is after me personally. Challenging me. There isn't any modus operandi here, but there's a definite signature."

"I thought MO and signature were pretty much the same thing."

Kaely turned her chair toward his. "A lot of people in law enforcement think that, but it's not true. MO is the *way* someone kills. *Signature* is the emotional reason he kills.

What he needs to fulfill himself. Our killer has a very specific signature."

"His hatred of you?"

"That's part of it. He wants to defeat me. Prove he's smarter than I am. More powerful. His final play is to see me dead. It's a game to him, and he intends to win. But we also need to look at the poem. The picture of the elephant left with the body. He gets satisfaction from these things."

"So his need to beat you is just part of his signature?"

"That's right. A very important part, but it also goes to motive. He's angry. To go to all this trouble means the wound is deep. Maybe he lost someone and blames me for it."

"What could you have done that caused a death?"

Kaely rested her chin on her hand as she thought. "Maybe my profile was wrong and it took longer to catch a killer. Perhaps the delay led to other murders. Maybe one of the victims was a friend or family member."

"Have you ever given a wrong profile?"

"Not wrong per se, but not entirely accurate." She leaned forward and studied him. "Profiles are just educated guesses, Noah. Of course I'm not always right. No one is."

Noah chuckled. "Well, your reputation hasn't been tarnished. People are impressed by you."

"I don't want that. I really don't. No one can live up to the expectations of others. You have to be true to yourself."

Noah was silent for a moment. "Maybe we should be looking for someone connected to a perp you put away. That's a pretty big list."

Kaely reached up and released her hair from its messy bun. Then she ran her fingers through her curls. It felt good to free her hair from the tight band that usually kept it under control. "Right now, all we know for sure is that we're looking for someone who has a grudge against me and was privy to details of this crime." She thought for a moment. "We'll learn a lot from the next killing. Does he have information about other crimes? Or is this the only one? After all, there are seven little elephants. He has at least six more murders planned." She frowned and grabbed their copy of the poem. "Actually, I guess it's five more murders."

"What do you mean?"

"Well, look at the last two stanzas. *Two little elephants playing all alone. One knew the truth and told it to the sleuth. One little elephant called it a day. She packed up her trunk and ran far away. One last elephant facing final judgment. She was found guilty and given no pity. Jessica Oliphant called it a day. She picked up a gun and blew herself away.*"

"The second elephant doesn't die?" Noah said.

"Doesn't sound like it." She jabbed the paper with her finger. "This is important. We need to figure this out. And try to determine who the sleuth is."

Noah lifted his hand and motioned toward the rooms outside. "Kind of hard to find one sleuth when you're surrounded by FBI agents."

"And what is the truth? I don't have any *truth* to tell anyone. It doesn't make sense."

"Maybe he was just trying to find words that rhymed."

Kaely shook her head. "No, every word means something. He worked on this very carefully. We've got to understand what he's trying to say."

Noah rubbed his temples. "This is incredibly frustrating."

"Welcome to my world."

"Can you profile him at all now? I mean, beyond what you've already told me?"

She continued to stare at the photos for several seconds, then she said, "He's very,

very organized. He's been planning this for a while, and I believe he's already picked out his victims. Unlike many serial killers, this guy moves easily around in public. He's smart. Creative. And completely dedicated to his quest. I would say that whatever he does, he's successful at it, although he may have recently taken a leave of absence or quit his job. He seems to have lots of time to work on this . . . mission." She shook her head. "He's a psychopath. He doesn't care at all about these victims. He hates me so much he believes sacrificing them is okay. They're only a means to an important end." She reached down deep inside herself, trying to draw on her instincts. "I think he has a nice car, dresses well, and will be someone no one suspects. When we catch him, we'll be surprised."

She paused for a moment before continuing. "Probably a white male, only because statistically most serial killers are white males. Also, the writing is confrontational, forceful. More male than female. I'm not sure of his age. Thirties? Forties? Could be older but not so old he can't overpower his victims. His planning and meticulous attention to detail makes him seem more mature." She paused, then said, "Something happened to him. A stressor that set him off. He may have held this grudge a long time, but when this happened, it sent him over the edge. The loss of a job or someone close to him. Whatever it was impacted him greatly."

"That's pretty good."

"Not good enough." Kaely still couldn't see him. This killer wasn't like anyone she'd ever faced before. She felt confusion, something she almost never experienced. She had the feeling the UNSUB was trying to keep her off balance. Make her look in the wrong direction. She wasn't confident that what she'd just told Noah was right. She wasn't completely relying on her training. She was going with her gut.

"Can you do that . . . you know, that thing you do?" Noah's face flushed. He was obviously embarrassed.

"No, I don't think so. Not yet. I need more info before I do that . . . *thing.*"

Noah scooted a bit closer to her. "I'm sorry. I don't mean to be disrespectful. I mean, if I knew more about it, I suppose I'd understand."

She arched an eyebrow as she stared at him. She remembered the first time Alex brought up her process. He was just as uncomfortable as Noah was now.

"Do I sense a question coming on?" she asked.

Noah took a deep breath and said, "Yes. My first *special* question. Why do you pretend to eat with an UNSUB? You know people make fun of you, right? Forgive me, but it doesn't seem very professional."

Kaely snorted. "So being *professional* means doing it by the book? It isn't measured by results?"

"I thought I was the one asking the question."

"Fair enough."

She leaned back in her chair and stared at him without saying anything. What secrets was she willing to share with Noah Hunter? Would he betray her like so many others had?

Thirteen

"I want to make one thing clear," Kaely said in a voice so low Noah almost didn't hear her. "I don't talk about my father. I mean, if I bring him up it's all right. But it's not okay for you to mention his name. Understand?"

Noah hesitated a moment before saying, "Unless it has something to do with the three questions you gave me? You said . . . no limits."

"You're right." She shook her head and mumbled something he didn't catch. "The whole thing started in my head. Where most of the things we do begin. Think about something long enough and you'll find yourself acting it out." She grabbed her water bottle. After taking a drink, she said, "For example, you're getting ready for bed and suddenly you think about that chocolate almond ice cream in the freezer."

Noah almost jumped out of his chair.

How did she know chocolate almond ice cream was his favorite? And that he had some in his freezer right now? He tried not to react. Not give her the satisfaction of letting her know she had guessed his favorite dessert. Obviously, it was a fluke. He struggled to calm his jangled emotions. He needed to stay focused.

"If you keep thinking about it, you'll get a bowl," she continued. "Even though you shouldn't eat before bed. It's because the thought becomes real in your mind. It translates into action. Exactly the way serial killers think. Every single one of them. They fantasize about their kills first. Until they feel compelled to carry them out."

"That's interesting," Noah said, "but how does that relate to my question?"

Kaely slapped her hand on the table. "If you interrupt me, I'll count it as a question. I mean it."

The tone of her voice made it clear she was serious. Even though it angered him slightly, he really wanted to hear her response, so he just nodded. Obviously talking about this was difficult for her. She could shut down if challenged.

Kaely straightened up in her chair, her body taut with tension. "My father wasn't the kind of man you could have a conversation with, but at supper, my brother and I were expected to talk. To share what had happened during the day. It was the only time my father really spoke to us. Frankly, it was the one time we really communicated as a family. Later, when I was introduced to the methods of behavioral analysis, I started evaluating those supper conversations. What had I missed? What did he say that could have revealed the truth? I was just a kid, so I wasn't looking for clues to prove he was a monster. But I ran those conversations over and over in my mind.

"Then, in my thoughts, I started having conversations with my father. Asking him about things he'd said. Trying to make him admit the truth. After a while, I started doing the same thing with the UNSUBs we were chasing. Of course, at Quantico, something like that didn't fly, but I couldn't get it out of my head. I'd sit down at home and pretend to share a meal with an UNSUB. Just like I had with my dad. It started working. I began to *see* the UNSUBs. They began to take shape.

"Then I made a mistake. I told someone at Quantico about it. Someone I thought was a friend. She pretended to be, anyway. Instead of keeping my secret, she told other agents in our training group. It got back to my instructors. To Reinhardt. It was humiliating. Then someone leaked the story to Jerry Acosta, a local reporter. An article appeared in a small local paper where Acosta worked at the time. The story grew legs, spread on social media, and made the Bureau uncomfortable. That's what got me transferred here. After I arrived, at Solomon's insistence, I shared the technique with him. He didn't make me feel crazy. He actually saw value in it."

She sighed, and all the tension seemed to drain out of her body. "To be honest, I don't use it as much now as I used to. It seems to be something that helped me link my experiences with my father to my training. The training side has grown stronger, so I don't need the process like I did when I first started profiling."

"Now that you explained it, it doesn't sound nuts at all."

Kaely wrapped her arms around herself as if she were cold. "I had a lapse in public last night. I was having dinner at Restaurant d'Andre. Not long after I arrived in St. Louis, the owner approached me when he found out I was with the FBI. His son had died in a fire in New Orleans. Authorities said he started it himself. Called it suicide."

Noah frowned. "Not many people commit suicide by fire. It's a terrible way to die."

Kaely nodded. "Louis asked me to look into it, and I did. The NOPD allowed me to look at their evidence. I found a pattern that pointed to a serial arsonist. Andre didn't commit suicide. He was murdered."

"That's great work. But you said you had a lapse?"

"Louis insists I come to his restaurant at least once a month for a free meal, you know, out of gratitude for finding out the truth about Andre's death. I went there last night, and I made the mistake of taking along a file Solomon gave me. Somehow, I forgot I was in public. Started talking to my UNSUB. Caused quite a stir in the restaurant."

Noah fought back a grin but lost the battle.

"It really wasn't funny," Kaely said grimly.

"It kind of is."

She glared at him. "You have a strange sense of humor. You may not think what I do is professional, but to me, being professional means you get results, no matter what you have to do to get them. Even pretending to talk to people who aren't there." She sighed heavily. "A lot of people use the same technique. Attorneys will pretend to argue a case with an opposing attorney just to prepare themselves for any possibility in court. Politicians do the same thing before a public debate. They try to anticipate their opponent's arguments before they're presented. How many men rehearse a proposal before they actually pop the question? My technique isn't really that unusual. People just make a big deal out of it because of the people I pretend to talk to."

Before he could ask his next question, Kaely suddenly picked up the stack of pictures she'd had him look at earlier. She quickly shuffled through them and then pulled one out. A photograph of a thirty-something balding man in a blue shirt.

"This is the picture you chose earlier," she said. "Is it your father or your brother who had cancer?"

Noah could feel the hairs on the back of his neck stand up. "My father had cancer," he said softly. "But he made it. He's okay. How did you know? And that's *not* one of my three questions."

"Okay. I accept that. After seeing these pictures, you touched your hair twice . . . as if you needed to assure yourself you weren't going bald. I can clearly see there's no sign of male-pattern baldness, therefore someone you know is having a problem with his hair. Has to be someone in your family or you wouldn't be worried about it. I suspected your brother or father had cancer. Either it took a long time for his hair to get back to normal, or perhaps it never did. You're concerned you might lose your hair too. What if it wasn't the chemo that caused your dad's hair loss? What if there's a family trait that causes some of the men to go bald?"

"That's incredible," Noah said softly.

Kaely shrugged it off. "Like I told you, being able to read people helps us sort out the lies from the truth." She waved a hand toward him. "Next question?"

Noah was convinced she had not intended to bring up the picture now but had grabbed it because she needed a way to change the subject. Things had gotten too personal for her, made her uncomfortable. But it was okay. He had gotten the answer he wanted. He glanced at his watch. "I'll save it, thanks. It's after nine. I think we need to wrap it up for tonight."

Kaely's eyes widened, and she glanced up at the clock on the wall. "I had no idea. . . ."

Noah could tell he was going to have many long days working with Kaely Quinn. "Hey, one other quick question — *not* a special question. Your name? I mean, *Kaely* is kind of unusual."

"Not a big mystery. I changed my name when I turned eighteen. Picked Jessie Rogers. Kept a version of my first name and used my mother's maiden name as a surname. After Jerry Acosta wrote his article, I changed it again. For all the good it did me." She leaned back in her chair. "I got into genealogy while I was at Quantico. I wanted . . ." She swallowed hard. "I wanted to know if my father's traits had shown up anywhere else in my family. You know, if . . ."

"If you could turn out to be a serial killer?" Noah said, astonished she would worry about something like that.

"Don't look so shocked," she said. "We don't understand everything about genetics."

He shook his head and chuckled. "Well, I know you'll never be a serial killer, so I guess that puts me ahead in the game."

Her eyes crinkled around the edges and the sides of her mouth turned up. "Well, thank you. I appreciate that. Anyway, as I looked through our family tree, I found my great-great-grandmother, Kaely Quinn. My mother had some old papers and family journals packed away in storage, and I found a diary Kaely had kept. She was quite a woman. Seems people would come to her with problems because they thought she had *second sight.*"

"You mean like ESP?"

"I don't believe in ESP, and she didn't either. She believed God gave her a gift. A gift of discernment."

"So you decided you two were alike and took her name?"

"Yeah, but I also looked up the meaning of Kaely. It means *keeper of the keys.*"

"Keeper of the keys," Noah repeated softly. "I like that. You hold the keys to the minds of monsters."

"Well, I'm not sure that's entirely true, but I like to think of it that way."

"It's hard to look into the heart of evil every day." Noah was not just talking about Kaely. It was an observation he had made at Quantico as they taught agents about the kind of real monsters that roamed the earth. It was hard for him to deal with at first. Truth was, he still had problems handling the depths of depravity people were capable of sinking into.

" 'Whoever fights monsters should see to it that in the process he does not become a monster. And if you gaze long enough into an abyss, the abyss will gaze back into you,' " Kaely said softly.

"Friedrich Nietzsche."

Kaely nodded.

As Noah looked down at the silver cross Kaely wore around her neck, he knew what his next question would be.

But that would have to wait for another day.

Fourteen

Kaely and Noah spent the next two days carefully going through every single case she had been involved with since she started with the FBI. They finally finished late Thursday night, but they had not found anything helpful. Four days since the first murder, and they weren't any closer to stopping this madman.

The lab sent Walker back with the letter, but he didn't have anything interesting to tell them. No DNA, no fingerprints except Acosta's and a few identified postal workers. Although there were cases of criminals copying other murderers, this was the first person to duplicate George Anderson. Kaely was frustrated. They had to find a way to anticipate and stop this guy.

By the time she swung by the store to pick up a few things and finally got home, it was almost ten o'clock. She was fairly certain Noah had followed her to the entrance of her condo complex, just as he had the past two nights. Although she was partially annoyed by his determination to watch her, in another sense, she found it rather comforting. It was something Alex would have done. The thought of him caused an odd prick of pain.

She grabbed her grocery bags. She had to quit thinking about Alex. It wasn't doing any good. He wasn't coming back. She'd learned that dwelling on things she couldn't change was counterproductive. A huge waste of time and energy.

She grabbed her groceries, climbed the stairs, and unlocked the door to her condo. After stepping inside, she quickly locked up. She dropped her groceries on the kitchen counter. She'd picked up a roasted chicken, some macaroni salad, and some staples she needed. She put everything away except the chicken and salad. Then she sat down at her breakfast bar, pulled some pieces off the chicken, and dug into the macaroni salad with a spoon. When she was finished, she put the remainder in the fridge. The entire time she was thinking about the person who'd killed the man in the park. He had finally been identified. He was thirty-six years old and an attorney. Just like George Anderson's victim. The killer would have had to search for someone like him, then stalk him, looking for an opportunity. This degree of organization was impressive.

The second verse of the poem kept running through her mind: *Six little elephants swimming in the lake. One was slaughtered and went underwater. Five little elephants called it a day. They packed up their trunks and they all ran away.*

Over the past couple of days, she'd reviewed quite a few past cases that involved water. Unfortunately, there were a lot of them. The Arkansas River Strangler. The Green River Killer. The East River was a favorite spot to dump bodies. The Everglades. The Louisiana swamps. The poem could mean anything. One thing that stuck in her head was that the first killing mentioned the *word* forest, but the writer was referring to something else. Was the second clue going to follow the same pattern? If so, that made it even harder. The word *lake* was used for towns, streets, subdivisions. . . . It was almost impossible to narrow it down.

She'd started toward her bedroom when she remembered Mr. Hoover. She should have fed him by now. She turned back toward the kitchen, where he sat in one of her chairs and stared at her. "Hang in there," she told him. "I'll get this right. I really will."

She checked the front door one more time before heading upstairs. She opened the door to her workroom to drop off some papers and crime-scene photos. She switched on the light and stepped inside. Anyone else might see chaos, but Kaely knew exactly where everything was — and what it meant. The boards on the walls, the notes posted everywhere, the papers pinned up . . . they all held important information that helped her to more clearly see the evidence in whatever case she was working. Not all of the cases she studied were actually assigned to her, but she was interested in them anyway. Sometimes she sent police departments anonymous tips, and more than once her tips had led to the capture of some very dangerous criminals. She'd rather not have to work that way, but for now, it was all she could do. At least she didn't have to hide who she really was from Solomon. He listened to her. Really listened. Other agents at the Bureau might not like her special relationship with the SAC, but she really didn't care. She wasn't trying to be popular. Her life was about chasing evil, not making friends.

After depositing her papers on the table in the corner, she left the room and went downstairs to her bedroom. She grabbed her sweats and T-shirt, took a quick shower, and climbed into bed, praying that tonight the nightmares would stay away. They'd started when she was a child. Since finding God, she'd prayed He'd take them away, but so far she still dealt with them from time to time. She knew He heard her prayers. Knew He wanted the best for her. He had delivered her from so many things. But when she asked Him why they persisted, she felt strongly there was something she needed to see. Something she didn't yet understand. She couldn't help but wonder if she'd noticed something about her father. Even sensed his true nature. Maybe her nightmares were trying to resolve whatever it was that had frightened her when she was young. But try as she might, she couldn't bring up a memory to explain them.

Her mother had grown weary of waking Kaely up during the night when she screamed out in fear, and she'd seen the relief on her face when Kaely finally left home. Her mother had wanted nothing more than to distance herself from the real-life nightmare her husband had created for his family.

"Lord," Kaely prayed out loud, "please show me whatever it is I need to see. Deliver me from these awful dreams. And give me insight into whoever wrote that poem. Help us to stop him before he kills again. Thanks."

She rolled over on her side and looked at the clock next to her bed. Twelve-thirty. She'd only get a few hours' sleep, so she needed it to be uneventful. But as soon as her eyes closed, one particular nightmare she'd had over and over made an encore.

Kaely ran down a dimly lit hallway, calling for help. Something dark, heavy, and malevolent slithered after her, whispering her name. Whatever it was entered the wall. She could hear it rustling behind the drywall, trying to keep up with her. No matter where she ran, she couldn't get away from it, until finally, the hallway ended. There was a small door in the wall, and she ran toward it, trying to secure it so whatever was after her couldn't get out. But it was as if she were moving through molasses, and the harder she struggled to reach the door, the slower she became. In the end, she knew the door would open and the darkness would pour out. Then suddenly everything turned red, and she couldn't see. Although she kept fighting, trying to close the door, she couldn't find it. Her fingers grasped frantically as she fought to hold back the evil, but instead she woke up, screaming.

Kaely sat up and swung her legs over the bed, gasping for breath. Had the neighbors heard her? A young couple lived next door. They'd never said anything, but she'd caught them looking at her strangely more than once. Her heart thundered in her chest. She put her hands up to cover it, trying to slow her breathing and pull herself together. This was getting ridiculous.

"Lord, I wish you'd hurry up and show me whatever it is I need to see," she whispered in the dark, her voice trembling. "I hate feeling so afraid."

Finally, she got up, drank a glass of cold water, and went back to bed. After staring at the ceiling for a while, she finally fell into a restless sleep.

Fifteen

The next morning when she woke up, Kaely called Richard. When he answered, she said, "I had the dream again."

"I'll meet you in the park at seven, okay?"

"Okay. Thanks, Richard."

Kaely hung up the phone, grateful for Richard, who'd volunteered to fill the spot vacated by Kaely's mother and father. He'd helped her through so much. She dressed quickly and headed to Forest Park. She drove straight to the Grand Basin. She loved it here. It was so peaceful. She and Richard liked to sit and watch the fountains glisten in the morning sun while they ate breakfast from a local bakery. Hot apple fritters and coffee. Kaely was aware of the art museum behind them. It had always been one of her very favorite buildings, but this morning, it felt like she was sitting in death's shadow. Would this special place ever feel the same?

She hoped so. It was a convenient spot to

meet since Richard lived near the park, and it was on Kaely's way to work. They used to get together once a week, but lately, Kaely had been so busy that she'd had to cancel several times. She felt a little guilty about it since Richard had moved to St. Louis just to be near her, but he never got upset. He always understood. His total acceptance made her feel loved, something she'd never experienced with her own family.

When she parked her car, she saw him already waiting. She hurried over to the steps near the water and sat down next to him.

"We may have to move to the coffee shop soon," she said, trying not to let her teeth chatter in the cold. Sitting by the water made it even chillier.

Richard grinned at her and handed her a cup of coffee. "Either that or we could build a fire."

Kaely laughed and took the cup from him, then accepted the wrapped fritter he gave her, the warmth seeping through the waxed paper. "I don't understand how you always get these here while they're still hot."

"It's just one of my many talents," he said. "Along with asking Davis, the owner, to nuke them a bit before I leave."

Kaely took a sip of her coffee and then

put it on the ground next to her, unwrapping part of her fritter and taking a bite. Apples, cinnamon, sugar, and pastry melted together in her mouth, making her sigh with pleasure. "Nothing better than this," she mumbled.

Richard pulled his dark blue stocking cap down tighter over his graying hair. Kaely liked his face. It was friendly. Hazel eyes framed by smile lines. A large nose that perfectly matched his wide mouth. Richard's smile always made her feel better. He'd been through a lot in his life. The loss of his wife. The realization that his close friend was a serial killer, and the end of his practice, although that decision was one he'd made on his own. Thankfully, he'd earned quite a bit of money and squirreled it away so he didn't have to work. Originally, the savings were supposed to be for himself and Bella. They'd planned to travel when he retired. Now he was alone — except for Kaely. Recently, he'd started doing some volunteer work at a suicide prevention hotline directed toward teens. She could tell it had reignited his passion for helping people, and she was grateful he'd taken the step to dust off his counseling skills.

"So, how are you?" Kaely asked.

Richard nodded. "Good. I just got back

from Des Moines."

"I had no idea you'd gone."

"I would have called to tell you, but I just wanted to visit Bella's grave. Make sure she had fresh flowers. I left Monday morning and got back last night."

"Did you fly?"

"Yeah. And I hated every minute of it."

Richard had a thing about flying. Kaely was surprised he'd stepped foot on a plane. "It's only about a five-and-a-half-hour drive, you know."

He nodded. "I know, but the old gray mare ain't what she used to be."

"Oh, Richard. You need to sell that car. It's falling apart."

"I know. I will . . . someday."

Richard had held on to his old, dark green 1997 Ford Explorer because Bella had loved it. He'd spent so much money on repairs, he could have bought a brand new vehicle by now. He said he could still smell Bella's perfume in the car.

Kaely reached over and put her hand on his arm. "I'm sorry, Richard."

He smiled and patted her hand. "I know. I sure miss her."

"I do too."

"The flowers you sent were beautiful."

Kaely sighed. "I'm sure by now they

weren't *beautiful.* It's been about three months since I ordered them." She tried to send flowers at least twice a year to decorate Bella's grave.

"I could tell they were gorgeous when they were put out. Thank you for doing that."

"I loved her too."

"I know you did." He sighed and gazed out at the fountains. "I don't think I told you that her sister Doreen passed away a few months ago."

"Did I ever meet her?"

"No, I don't believe so. She and Bella were very close though. After the funeral, Doreen's daughter gave me a box of letters and cards that Bella and Doreen had sent to each other. She didn't have time to go through them, but she hated to throw them away. She thought I might like them."

"That's nice."

"Yes, it was. I feel as if I have a little more of Bella with me now."

"I worry about you. I know you feel the need to watch over me, but I really want you to have your own life, Richard. Maybe you should go back to Des Moines. For good, I mean."

"There's nothing for me there, Kaely. But here . . . well, I feel like someone needs me. And I need to be needed."

His sad smile touched Kaely's heart. "How about coming over for supper one night next week?" she said. "I promise it will be warmer in my condo than it is here."

Richard nodded. "Sounds great. I miss our evenings together."

"I do too. Forgive me for not being a better friend."

Richard shook his head. "If anyone understands how important your job is and how unpredictable your schedule is, it's me. Don't ever worry about that." Richard took a drink of coffee and then set it down next to him. "So you had the dream again?" he said. "Did something happen that triggered it?"

Kaely took another bite of her fritter and chewed as she thought about what she should tell him. When she didn't say anything, he reached over and picked up a copy of the morning paper that he had next to him and handed it to her. She unfolded it. The *St. Louis Journal.* Front page. The headline read *FBI Profiler Targeted by a Potential Serial Killer.*

Solomon was downing his first cup of coffee when Joyce walked into the kitchen after getting the newspaper from the front porch. Solomon liked to read a real newspaper, not get his news online. He wasn't sure how much longer he'd have a choice, but for now, he looked forward to his morning paper and coffee. He could tell by looking at Joyce's face that something was wrong.

"What?" he asked, his stomach tightening with apprehension.

"Promise not to get upset."

Solomon could see the fear in his wife's eyes. His heart attack had put it there. With the kids gone, she was afraid he'd leave her too.

"I promise. Show me." He could already guess what it was. Banner had published the story. God help them. Joyce slid the paper in front of him. When he read the headline, he cursed under his breath.

"Don't swear in the house," Joyce said softly.

"Sorry." He picked up the paper and quickly scanned the article written by Jerry Acosta. Everything was there. The poem, how Acosta got it, that he'd taken the original to the FBI, and the murder in Forest Park, which he tied to the poem. He ended the article with "Now it's up to the authorities to track down what may be the city's first serial killer since Maury Travis. Will the daughter of a serial killer be the answer to catching him? Or will this be the last case for Special Agent Kaely Quinn?"

Solomon started to curse again but caught himself and clamped his lips into a tight thin line. He got up from the table, got his phone from the counter where it was charging, and called Kaely. Her phone rang several times before she picked up.

"Quinn," she said.

"Where are you?" Solomon asked.

"In the park having breakfast with a friend. I've seen the paper."

"I hoped he'd hold the story for a while longer, but obviously that was a pipe dream."

There was a long pause. Then Kaely said, "We'd better prepare ourselves."

"We're just going to have to weather the storm. You and Noah stay on the case. I'll handle the fallout."

"You can always move me, Sol. Transfer me out."

Solomon felt a sudden rush of emotion. It was a combination of the fondness he felt for Kaely and his fury toward the editor and reporter who had carelessly released a story that could destroy a career and lead to more deaths.

"You're not going anywhere, Special Agent Quinn. Period."

"Sir . . ."

"I won't discuss it. I'll get to the office as soon as I can. We'll talk more."

"Yes, sir."

Kaely disconnected the call, and Solomon looked up to find Joyce watching him. "Are you sure keeping her here is the right thing to do?" she asked. "Is that the best thing for Kaely?"

He ran his index finger around the rim of his coffee cup. "The Bureau can't keep pushing her around because it's uncomfortable. Kaely isn't responsible for her father's sins. At some point, we have to dig our heels in and stand with our agent." He gazed into his wife's soft hazel eyes. "I won't abandon her, Joyce. I just won't."

Joyce walked over to where Solomon sat and leaned down, kissing the top of his head. "You're a good man, Sol. I wouldn't expect you to turn your back on anyone." She playfully ruffled his hair. "Just make sure you do what's best for Kaely. Not for yourself."

Solomon reached over and grabbed his wife's hand. "I'll be careful, but you keep an eye on me, okay? There's no opinion I value more than yours."

Joyce squeezed his hand and then went over to the stove. She used a spatula to remove eggs and bacon from two different skillets, placed the food on a plate, and took the plate to Solomon. "Eat this before you leave. I mean it."

He looked down at the scrambled egg whites and turkey bacon his wife had made for him, trying to keep him healthy. Usually, he nibbled on them, moved them around the plate, and then threw them out when she wasn't looking. But today he picked up his fork and ate every bite because he knew she needed him to.

Sixteen

"I'm very concerned about you," Richard said. "You have to protect yourself. Get away from here."

The sun cast a reddish glow over the park as it climbed into the sky. Kaely loved autumn in Forest Park. The park was a retreat. A place to go when she wanted to be alone. To think. To pray. Or to seek Richard's advice. Now the specter of death hung over this special place, like an invisible noxious gas hovering above the incredible beauty that surrounded her. "I can't do that, Richard. I won't. Maybe at some point I'll be forced to leave, I don't know. But I have to do everything I can to stop this guy. He's killing people because of me."

"He's calling you out, Kaely. *A Eulogy for Kaely Quinn?* I'm truly worried."

She twisted around to face him. "What's your take on him? You know almost everything there is to know about me, and you're a trained therapist. Is this someone who believes I wronged them in my capacity as an FBI agent? Or is it something else?"

Richard stared down at the paper again and sighed. "I honestly don't know. It's . . . confusing."

She heard the hesitation in his voice and noticed he wasn't looking directly at her. From his body language, it was obvious he was thinking something. Something he wasn't sharing with her.

"You've got an idea," she said simply. "Tell me."

Richard took a drink of his coffee. "Please hear me out before you say anything. It's probably someone you encountered through your job but . . ." He paused as if trying to pull strength up from somewhere inside himself. "I spoke to Jason the other day."

Kaely almost dropped her Styrofoam cup. "You talked to my brother? How? I mean, even I don't know where he is."

"You never tried to find him, did you?"

She shook her head. "He said he didn't want me in his life, so I gave him what he asked for. Besides, I wouldn't use FBI databases for personal use." She frowned at him. "How did you figure out where he was?"

"I didn't, Kaely." Richard looked down at

his feet. "I hope you won't be angry or feel betrayed, but Jason contacted me. He's done it a few times. Not a lot. Just from time to time."

He raised his head and met her eyes. Kaely could see compassion in his expression. "I cared for both of you kids, you know. When your father was arrested, I promised . . ." Richard's eyes widened, and he looked away. "I promised myself I'd look after you since your father couldn't."

Kaely felt a shiver of revulsion move through her body. "You're lying. What did you promise, Richard? And don't lie again. You know I can tell when you do."

Richard stared off into the distance as the glitter of sunlight spread slowly throughout the park. "Look, Kaely, just because you think one way, it doesn't necessarily mean everyone else agrees with you. You need to allow the people in your life to have their own opinions. You can't make us into your own image. We won't be able to help you if you do that."

"What did you promise, Richard?" she asked again, dread giving way to cold fury.

His voice broke as he said, "I promised your father I'd watch over you kids. Make sure you were okay." He inhaled deeply and then quickly blew air out, his breath looking like smoke in the frosty air. "I didn't do it for him, Kaely. I did it for you and your brother. And before you ask, no. I've never contacted him since he went to prison. Not once. I knew you wouldn't want me to."

"How could you say anything to him about us?" Kaely fought back angry tears. "He doesn't care about us. He never did. There's no humanity in him."

"I'm not saying there is," Richard said softly. "I'm just telling you what happened. It was right after he was arrested. When we believed they had the wrong man. Once I knew the truth, I cut off all communication."

Kaely could feel the surge of resentment she'd felt at Richard's revelation diminish some. "Don't you ever tell him anything about me. I mean it."

"I won't. Like I said, I've never contacted him."

"Has he tried to communicate with you since he's been in prison?"

Richard nodded. "Once. Not long after he went away. He sent me a letter. I didn't even open it. Just threw it away."

Kaely pointed at the newspaper. "Richard, are you telling me you think Jason might be behind this?"

Richard clasped his hands together so

tightly his knuckles turned white. "No, I mean . . . I don't think so. His anger toward you and your mother has escalated for some reason. Most of it is directed at you. He says the nightmares you had since you were a kid prove you knew something was going on with your dad. He's younger than you, you know. I think he feels you should have protected him."

"Being angry and suspicious doesn't make someone a serial killer, Richard."

He nodded. "You're probably right. Sorry. I guess our phone conversation shook me a bit. I tried to reason with him, but he wouldn't listen to me. Told me he wasn't going to contact me again. That he was getting rid of the phone he had so I couldn't call him back." Richard sighed. "I hope he changes his mind at some point, but I don't know if he will." He gave Kaely a stiff smile. "Forget I said anything. I'm just worried about him." He reached over and took her hand. "I love you, Jessie. If Bella and I had been blessed with a daughter, we'd have wanted her to be just like you. If anything ever happened to you . . ."

Kaely didn't correct his use of the name he'd called her as a child. She understood the lapse. Instead, she put her other hand over his. "I know. Thank you."

"So why did you want to see me this morning?" he asked, changing the subject. "Is it because of your nightmare?"

Kaely turned to gaze out at the Basin. "I want them to stop, Richard. I haven't had that particular one for a while. Does it mean something that it comes now?"

"Of course it does," he said softly. "And you know it. Every time you take on a new case, that dream resurfaces. It's trying to tell you something. Something you're not ready to see."

"You told me when I understand it, it will go away."

"It will. But you have to be ready first. Once you are, and you face the message in the dream, I think the other nightmares will eventually cease."

"Like the one where I'm tied up and all the serial killers I've written profiles for are murdering me with the techniques they used on their victims?"

"Kaely." Richard shook his head and looked away. "I wish you'd chosen some other line of work." He pulled his hand away from hers and waved it at her before she had a chance to respond. "I know, I know. You feel called to do what you do. But now you're the target of a very clever killer."

Kaely could see the tension in his face.

She knew he was afraid for her, but there wasn't anything she could say to take away his fear.

"I just want you to be happy. Free of the past," he continued. "I have a bad feeling about this one. Promise me you'll be careful."

A tickle of fear ran through her at his words. Georgie had said almost the same thing. As she tried to reassure Richard, her friend's words echoed in her head. *"Something's coming, Kaely. I don't know what it is, but I feel it. Don't you?"*

SEVENTEEN

Kaely left Richard sitting on the steps by the Basin and drove to the office. She was shaken by the knowledge that he'd promised her father he'd watch over her. Knowing her father acted as if he cared anything about his children infuriated her. She was certain he'd said it because he thought he was supposed to — not because he meant it. Her father was a typical psychopath. Incapable of real empathy. He'd learned to mimic the emotions of other people, and he used those examples when he felt they were appropriate. Narcissistic and selfish, he saw himself as more important than any other human being.

Worst of all, he'd used his family to hide his depravity — something Kaely had a hard time forgiving. Forgiveness was a slow process that God was walking her through. She was thankful He was so patient with her. Someday, she wanted to release all the anger she felt toward her father, if for no other reason than to get the last vestiges of Ed Oliphant out of her head.

She'd initially dismissed Richard's concerns about Jason, but after she parked her car, she sat there for a while, wondering if there could be anything to it. She knew he'd had a hard time believing she and her mother didn't have some kind of hint about what was going on, but would he really resort to something like this? Jason had been such a sweet kid. A good kid. Yes, he was angry about what happened, but his nature couldn't have changed that much, could it? The sister in her said no, but the trained behavioral analyst knew she couldn't ignore the possibility. She'd have to tell Noah about Jason, and they'd have to add him to their list of suspects. Kaely shivered as she sat in her warm car. She felt like a traitor.

She got out and hurried into the building, aware of the stares from other agents as she walked by. Obviously, they'd seen the paper too. She hadn't made any real friends at work since coming to St. Louis, except for Alex. Part of her ached to partake in the camaraderie she saw between the agents, but it wasn't going to happen. She was *Crazy Kaely* to them. She'd never fit in.

She shook off the unhelpful thoughts and

refocused on the challenge in front of her. Although Solomon had promised to keep her in St. Louis, she couldn't help but wonder if he'd stick to what he'd said. They'd said the same thing at Quantico when Jerry Acosta's first article came out.

She felt a rush of irritation. Why was this guy following her? Why was he so determined to mess up her life? It was as if he had a vendetta against her.

She walked into the outer office where Grace sat, typing on her computer. "Go on in, Kaely. He's waiting for you," she said with a sympathetic smile.

"Thanks, Grace." Kaely slowly opened the door to Solomon's office. He was on the phone.

"It's not going to happen," he was saying. "You don't have the authority to make that decision." When he looked up and saw Kaely, he held up a finger. "I have to go. You're welcome to come down here and talk to me about it, but I won't change my mind." Without saying good-bye, he put the phone down. "Sit down, Kaely," he said, his tone serious. Frankly, Solomon looked a little shell-shocked. She was certain the newspaper article had caused problems.

"Was that Reinhardt on the phone?" she asked.

Solomon scooted back in his chair and crossed his arms over his chest. Typical protective gestures. "He thinks you should be moved to protect you and those around you. He says he's worried about collateral damage."

"No, he's not. He wants me out of the Bureau."

"I know that." Solomon dredged up a tentative smile. "He doesn't have the authority to override a SAC, Kaely. You're physically able to serve, and your mental acuity is intact."

Kaely's mouth twitched. "Many people would disagree with you about that last statement."

"Well, I know you well enough to be convinced you're more than capable of assisting Noah. Don't worry about Reinhardt." He rubbed the back of his neck, groaning softly as if kneading his neck muscles caused pain. He fixed his gaze on her. "I know you'd rather be back at Quantico. It's not impossible. . . . Hopefully someday. You should be where we can use your talents to the utmost."

Kaely's eyes widened in surprise. They'd never talked about her desire to return to Quantico. It was something she didn't bring up since she was pretty sure it would never happen. "I don't think they'll take me back. Besides, I like it here."

"You may feel safe, but this isn't the best place for you and you know it," Solomon said. "You've been here a year. In another year you can be considered again as an official behavioral analyst. I intend to help you in any way I can."

"Why are you bringing this up now?" Kaely asked, her stomach knotting. "Are you sending me away?"

Solomon's eyebrows shot up, and he sat forward in his chair. "No, Kaely. Absolutely not." He shook his head. "I was *trying* to encourage you. Seems I stink at motivational speeches."

In spite of herself, Kaely laughed. "Yeah, it might not be your thing. But thanks. I mean that. Sure, I'd like to go back to Quantico. It was my dream. But I thank God every day I found you — and this field office. I don't know what I would have done without . . ." She was horrified to feel a sudden rush of emotion wash over her. She breathed in quickly, trying to regain control. "Sorry," she whispered.

Solomon chuckled. "It's okay. Real people get emotional, you know. You really are one of us — even if you don't think you are."

"Thank you. I know I'm a real person.

Now, can we get back to the situation at hand?"

"Sure," he said, grinning. "I wouldn't want you to get carried away." He pushed the newspaper toward her. "Have you read the whole thing?"

"No, I haven't," she responded. "The headline told me everything I wanted to know."

"Read it."

While Solomon watched her, Kaely quickly scanned the complete article. Acosta had written one entire section about her father, citing his crimes. Then he moved on to Kaely. Her procedure to identify serial killers and how accurate she'd been in the past. It wasn't a bad article, but it certainly wouldn't endear her to some people.

She shoved it back toward him. "So now St. Louis knows they may have a serial killer — and it's all my fault. Mine and my father's."

"Stupid people might blame you, but anyone with a brain will point the finger at the person behind this. The UNSUB. We need to find him as quickly as possible." When he scooted back in his chair, it squeaked loudly, but he acted as if he hadn't heard it. "So where are you and Noah? Have you discovered anything helpful?"

"We've been through all the files. Couldn't find anything that points to our UNSUB. The only cases that raise red flags are the ones I mentioned at the outset. Michael Edmonds and Archie Mason, but I still don't see a connection that points us in the right direction."

"What have you figured out about our UNSUB?"

"Very organized killer. Been planning this for a long time. Trust me, his next targets have already been chosen. I think he copied George Anderson because I was involved with that case. His next kill will also be a copycat. I think he presents well. Educated. Good dresser. Articulate. Nice car. Not someone you'd pick as a serial killer." She sighed. "Can't do much with modus operandi since he modeled himself after another killer. But he is probably picking killers he doesn't mind copying. For example, I doubt he'll choose Dennis Rader or Jack the Ripper. Too revolting for him."

"It's not as if we have a long list of *nice* serial killers."

"I realize that. I'd love to know where he's getting his details. From confidential files? Was he connected to the case somehow? Did he read books? There are quite a few from some of the top folks in BAU."

"No reason they shouldn't tell their story once the perps are in prison."

"You're right. Wish we could keep some details to ourselves though. You know, for situations just like this."

Solomon nodded his agreement. "What's your next step?"

"Well, Noah's the lead agent, so it's up to him, but I believe we need to start thinking ahead. Get a jump on this guy before the next killing. If it's not already too late." She frowned at him. "Did ERT find anything that might help us?"

"No. The police did a great job of processing the crime scene. They're still interviewing everyone who worked at the park that day. If they find anything helpful, I'm certain the chief will let us know. What else do you need?" Solomon asked.

"What about a CP?"

He nodded. "CIRG's Logistics Unit has found a closed print shop not far from here that should make a great command post. The windows are covered up so no one can see inside. It's being set up now. You can move in Monday morning. And BAU is waiting to get information from you so they can assist."

"Good. We really need help from our Critical Incident Response Group. I think we'll need to use ViCAP too." Kaely hoped that the FBI's Violent Criminal Apprehension Program would pick up past crimes their UNSUB was copying so they could get a jump on him. "Maybe we can anticipate what he's got planned."

Solomon grunted. "Sounds good."

Kaely frowned. "I'm certain they're searching words from the poem. I'm hoping they find something from the term *lake.* Not sure how much we can narrow the list on our own, but we'll try."

Solomon stared at her for a moment without saying anything, which started to make her nervous. "Kaely, take some time off this weekend," he said finally. "I mean it. I'll put other people on the case. You and Noah can start in again on Monday."

"I feel like we should keep working, Sol. Get a jump on this guy."

Solomon sighed. "You know how it works. I can't let you burn out. We need you fresh. I have a feeling no matter what I say you'll do nothing but work this case when you're not here. I realize telling you not to obsess is useless, but be careful, okay?"

Kaely nodded and stood up. She appreciated Solomon's concern for her, but she doubted they'd get any real time off. She had a bad feeling they were already too late to save the next victim.

EIGHTEEN

Noah had several files sitting open in front of him when Kaely walked into the conference room. "Sorry I'm late," she said. "Had to stop by Solomon's office."

"I saw the paper," Noah said. "What did he say?"

Kaely dropped down into the chair next to Noah. "He was very supportive, but when I went into his office he was talking on the phone to Reinhardt. He's not happy about the situation."

"I hate to say something dismissive like 'don't worry about it,' but we need to find this creep — not get distracted by some dumb newspaper reporter." Noah pushed away the file in front of him. "Just what is it with that guy, Kaely? What does he want?"

Kaely ran her hand through her hair, hoping her curls weren't totally out of control. "He wants to write a book about my father. There have been a few, but not by anyone who really knew him. I mean, he didn't get close to people. Me, my mom, my brother, Richard and his wife, Bella, who died not long after my father was arrested, were the only people in his life. He was an usher in our church, but he didn't spend time with those people. Not outside of church functions, I mean."

"So Jerry Acosta thinks making your life miserable will encourage you to give him what he needs for his book? That's nuts."

"People are really interested in serial killers. The book would probably sell a lot of copies. Make Acosta rich."

"Maybe so," Noah said. "Sorry about him."

Kaely offered him a small smile. "Not your fault. You don't need to apologize."

"I know. I just hate that you have to deal with this now. We have enough on our plates."

"We need to make some progress." She reached into a stack of papers in the middle of the table and pulled one out. "I suggest we go over the poem again. See if we can figure out where this guy will strike next."

"I've been busy on the leads we have," Noah said. "I looked up Edmonds' girlfriend, wondering what she was up to now."

"And?"

"She's actually married. To someone else, of course. They moved to California a couple of months ago. She's a teacher in Los Angeles, and she hasn't missed any work lately."

"So she's out."

"I've sent information about the family in Virginia to the Richmond office. I asked an agent there to check them out." He turned the screen of his laptop toward her. "I've also been looking online at *lake* references."

"Wow," she said. "That's a lot of lakes."

"Too many." Noah rubbed his hands together. "It could be Lake Street or Lake Park or . . ."

"Well, there has to be swimming," Kaely said. "I mean, if he's being literal at all . . ."

"Yeah, you're right." He picked up a pen lying on the table and began to tap it on the table. Finally, he said, "Let's go over the killers who dumped their victims in water. Who pops to mind first?"

"The Green River Killer — Gary Ridgway — started by throwing bodies in the river, and Wayne Williams ended up tossing victims in water to hide evidence." She thought for a moment. "There's Joel David Rifkin. He used the East River in New York as a dumping site."

Noah looked at her through narrowed

eyes. "Should it bother me that you can pull that kind of information up so easily?"

"Not really. Just part of the job."

Noah looked away from her and cleared his throat.

"What?" Kaely asked. "It's obvious something's bothering you. Spit it out."

"Because I cleared my throat?"

"Shows you're lying or you're uncomfortable with what you're getting ready to say."

"Well, I'm not lying," Noah said, "so I guess it's the latter choice. I'm afraid it's my second question, but I don't think we have time for it."

"We can take a couple of minutes," she said. "Why don't you toss it at me, and I'll answer it if I can."

"You're a Christian, right?" Noah blurted out.

"Yes, I am."

He swiveled around and stared directly at her, an odd look on his face. "How can you see this kind of evil" — he waved his hand toward the files spread out on the table, all the pictures of destruction and death lying in front of them — "and know all the stuff you do . . . I mean, how can you believe in a good and just God when you know this happens?"

Kaely put her head down for a moment

before replying. When she looked up, she said, "Some other time I'll tell you how I found God, but that will have to wait. As far as how I can do this, someone has to, Noah. Why do you think it has to be nonbelievers?" She shook her head. "Those who know God *should* be the ones to confront the darkness, to chase evil. We have the weapons. Those who don't know Him have only themselves. And trust me, it's not enough. Not if you want to make it out in one piece."

She frowned. "After I first found God, I joined a church near my condo. Good people. Felt pretty comfortable there. But when they found out what I did, things got awkward. Seems they felt the way you do. *Nice* Christians don't chase killers." She pointed at the files. "Good Christians don't put this kind of stuff in their minds. I left. Now I go to a church that accepts what I do. In fact, they pray for me. I don't go as often as I should, but when I do show up, they always make me feel welcome."

"Have you made friends there?" Noah asked.

Kaely smiled sadly. "How would I relate? I can't share this life with them. They understand the generality of what I do. But the details? No. I think that's why most of us don't have a lot of friends outside the Bureau."

"But that's my point. How could God want you to get involved in this kind of depravity? Doesn't He care about what it does to you?"

"Yes, of course He does. I believe I'm called to do this, Noah. It's why I'm good at it. And if the day comes where I can't do it anymore, I'm sure He'll tell me." She took a sip of her coffee before continuing. "I'm human. I've had nights when all I could do was roll up into a ball and cry. I have nightmares, Noah. Everyone who does this kind of work knows the emotional toll it can take. But I know with God's help I can get through it. He's never abandoned me. Never let me down." She swallowed hard, trying to rein in her emotions. "It's funny, you know? People asking me how I can believe in God. When you see evil firsthand, you begin to realize there has to be good. There has to be a God."

"But how can you be sure?" Noah asked.

Kaely stared into her coffee cup, trying to find the right words. "I mean, when you know someone, you know them, right? I know God. Better than I know you. It's weird. Tell some Christians God speaks to you, and they freak out. Yet the Bible is full of stories of God talking to people." She shook her head. "There is no one on the face of the earth who could convince me God isn't real. You see, we're friends. He answers me when I pray. He talks to me. And best of all, He accepts me just the way I am. That doesn't mean we're not working on things. He knows there are places in my life . . . in my mind . . . that need healing. But He does it little by little, when I'm ready. No one knows me the way He does." She reached over and put her hand on Noah's arm. "Your wife knew Him too, didn't she?"

Noah yanked his arm away, and his expression turned dark. "I told you I don't want to talk about her."

Kaely pulled her hand back. "I'm sorry. I didn't mean to upset you. Let's get back to work, okay?"

He nodded but didn't say anything.

Kaely stared at the computer screen, looking over Noah's search results. She frowned as she stared at all the listings. "You know, he *should* be giving us more clues to find him."

"What do you mean?"

"He's playing this like a game. Remember the Zodiac Killer?"

Noah nodded. "He used his codes as

clues. He liked playing mind games with the police."

"Right. Besides the poem, are we missing something? Is he trying to give us clues that we're missing?"

"If he is, I haven't picked up on them."

Kaely rested her chin on her closed fist, thinking. "Our only chance to get ahead of him is to pick the right serial killer from the list of possibilities. If we can figure out who our guy is going to emulate, we might have a chance. Slim . . . but a chance."

"Do you have any ideas?"

Kaely pulled over a legal-sized pad of paper and picked up a pen. "Okay, the first killer he picked was George Anderson."

Noah nodded. "Why did he pick Anderson?"

Kaely pointed her pen at Noah. "*That's* the question we need to ask ourselves. Why Anderson? What was it about this guy that appealed to our killer? If we can understand his choice, we might be able to predict his next move. And that could help us stop him."

"Okay," Noah said. "You mentioned three people: Ridgway, Williams, and Rifkin."

"But all three of them dumped the bodies into rivers. Not lakes."

Noah took a breath and blew it out quickly

in frustration. “So this doesn’t help us at all?”

Something jumped into Kaely’s mind. A memory. She stood to her feet. “I’ve got it,” she said. “I know what’s coming next.”

Nineteen

Noah watched as Kaely hurried out of the room. What was she doing? Was he supposed to follow her? He decided to wait where he was. He began to pick up the files scattered across the table. He inserted reports and pictures that had fallen out and started putting the folders in a pile. Going through the files was tough. He wished he could wash his brain of the images he'd seen. He still couldn't grasp how Kaely handled all this horror, no matter what she'd said.

Part of him wished he could accept this God stuff. Kaely was right. His wife, Tracy, had believed in God. He'd even gone to church with her. When she got sick, she was convinced God would heal her. But she died. If anyone should have lived, it was Tracy. She was the best person he'd ever met. Kind, generous to a fault, and always so positive. Why would God let her die and leave all the really rotten people behind? What about these serial killers? Why were they alive while Tracy's life had been snuffed out? It made no sense. No. This was just another one of Kaely Quinn's imaginary devices to make it through life.

He was putting the last file on the stack when the door to the conference room burst open with so much force it made him jump.

"Not all serial killers are famous, you know," Kaely said. "You knew about George Anderson because the FBI was involved in bringing him down. But most people wouldn't recognize his name."

"You've thought of someone else?"

"Exactly." She came over and slapped a file down in front of him.

"More files from your office?" Noah asked.

"Yeah." She opened the file she'd tossed in front of him. "Barton Kennedy. I helped on this case while I was at Quantico."

"And you assisted on George Anderson?"

"Yes. I've been involved in lots of serial killer cases since I joined the Bureau. Most people have no idea how many serial murderers there really are. They don't all get national attention."

"So who is Barton Kennedy?" Noah asked.

Kaely slid into the chair next to him and pointed at the folder she'd brought with her. "Kennedy was an abused kid who decided to take out his bad childhood on other people, especially people who reminded him of his mother. He loved her, but she never tried to protect him against his violent and twisted father. Eventually, he killed both his parents and took off, leaving a path of death in his wake. He was captured after four additional murders. It got some attention from the media, but it never got the kind of press Williams or Bundy got."

"Why is that?"

"It took eight years for him to murder his victims. I think the slow pace wasn't what the press wanted. Like I said, a few mentions, but that was it."

"But what is it about this guy that reminds you of the poem?"

"Kennedy dumped his victims in Lake Michigan. Every one of them except his second victim."

"But why do you think our killer will pattern himself off this model?"

Kaely exhaled. "Because it's the only thing that makes sense to me at this point. Am I sure this is the case he'll use? No. But we should look into it. I'd rather do something than nothing."

She began sorting through the file, pulling out pictures. "These are the four women he killed and dumped in the lake. Each woman had blond hair like his mother. They were bound, hands and feet. Hog-tied. He did that because he wanted to dominate them."

Noah gazed quickly at the pictures, his stomach turning over. Bodies that spent time in water were disturbing — and these pictures certainly qualified. He watched Kaely as she spread the photos out in front of them. Her expression never changed. How could she not react to these images? Maybe she had more in common with her father than he wanted to believe.

Even as the thought popped into his mind, he rejected it. There was substance to Kaely Quinn. Something special. Something rare. He wanted to understand her — yet he didn't know how close he could allow himself to get. He knew instinctively that he had to keep his defenses up. There was danger in those dark, bottomless eyes.

"So what does this tell us?" he said, pushing one of the pictures back toward her.

Kaely flipped through several of the reports in the file. Then she pointed at something. "Here," she said. "This is what I was trying to remember. We narrowed the body dump area to Silver Lake in Silver Lake

State Park. The lake consists of four miles of Lake Michigan shoreline. Once we narrowed the area and completed our profile, it wasn't long before we found Kennedy. He actually worked at the park. Made it easier for him. The profile was so spot-on, park administrators told us it sounded just like Barton."

"You said he dumped all the bodies in Lake Michigan except the second one. What happened with that body?"

"He had the body in the back of his car, but a police car was patrolling the area that night. It spooked him so much he took the body out of the state. He drove to . . ." Kaely stopped suddenly and her eyes grew large. "He's going out of state." She frowned, dropped the file, and pulled her laptop in front of her. Noah watched as she typed *Silver Lake* into the search engine. When the choices came up, she shook her head. Then she added *Illinois* into the search. This time, when the different selections came up, Kaely gasped. "This is it," she said, clicking on something and turning the screen toward Noah. "Silver Lake Park. Highland, Illinois. It's only forty minutes from here. I think this is where the next body will be found."

Noah wanted to believe she was right, but

was Kaely grasping at straws? "Why do you think we're going to find the next body in Illinois?"

"Because this is his second killing and he's copying Barton Kennedy. Kennedy needed another Silver Lake Park. The nearest he could find was a Silver Lake golf course near Chicago. That's where he dumped the body." As if she could read his mind, which in retrospect, she probably could, she said, "I know you think it's a long shot, Noah, but I believe this guy is stuck on patterns. On details. Call it a hunch, but I think he's compelled to copy Barton's second killing. That means the body will be in another state. Illinois is just over the river. He could still stay close to his comfort zone."

"But if he follows his pattern exactly, he'll kill someone here and transport the body. . . ."

Kaely stared at him. "Still means we'll find the body in Illinois." She shook her head as she chewed her lip. "It feels right. We've got to follow it up."

Noah had just opened his mouth to respond when the door to the conference room swung open and Grace walked into the room. "You two need to report to Solomon. We have a problem." The look on her face made Noah's stomach lurch. He looked over at Kaely. He saw the apprehension in her expression.

Had they been outplayed again?

He watched them work the crime scene. He realized he shouldn't have taken a chance they'd notice him. Wasn't it something profilers looked for? Killers who couldn't stay away from their work?

He'd left the body in the water near a dock, not because he wanted to, but because he needed her to be found right away. He couldn't afford to let her sink and only show up after it was too late to read the message he'd left behind. He walked slowly back to his car, trying not to garner attention. He laughed softly to himself. This was really much easier than he'd thought it would be. Kaely Quinn could be defeated. She wasn't the genius so many believed her to be.

He wondered what she was thinking. Did she understand he'd issued a challenge? Did she feel the darkness creeping closer? Could she sense that her judgment day was approaching?

He smiled. Now for the next one.

Solomon sighed as Kaely and Noah left his office, headed for Silver Lake Park in Illinois. A body had been found there. When it was pulled out of the water, the police found a note under the woman's jacket. Encased in a plastic bag and pinned to her blouse, it was a drawing of an elephant with a number 2 written inside.

Even though Kaely had been quiet when he told them about the discovery, Solomon knew her well enough to see that she blamed herself. Felt that if she'd figured things out faster, the woman might still be alive. Solomon doubted it. He was pretty sure no one else could have narrowed it down to the right location. This UNSUB was smart. And he was purposely staying in front of them.

Solomon didn't want Reinhardt to find out what had happened, but he knew he'd hear about it. Especially since CIRG was coming in to help their investigation. All he could do was pray Reinhardt wouldn't work against them.

He had a couple of calls to make. He'd wanted to send ERT to the crime scene, but he had to get permission from their local field office. Since the crime was so close to St. Louis and they were already handling the case, he was pretty sure the local office would agree. First he needed to call Jackie Cross. He had no idea when this killing would hit the papers, but he needed to warn her. Once again, they'd appeal for time to collect evidence and study the murder. Try to get the elephant component kept quiet. Not that the *Journal* would listen, but Jackie would try to get them whatever space she could. She'd also need to talk to someone from the Public Affairs Office at FBI headquarters since this could become a high-profile, national interest case.

Solomon hoped he wouldn't have to make too many more of these calls. They needed to put a stop to this piece of human garbage. Each murder brought him closer and closer to Kaely. And at this point, Solomon was afraid the UNSUB was winning.

TWENTY

It was almost eleven by the time Noah and Kaely got to the park. They drove to the area filled with police cars. Kaely was quiet on the way to the crime scene, second-guessing herself. Why hadn't she connected the second verse of the poem to Kennedy right away? It was clear she needed to focus on the poem. As she'd suspected, the writer was leaving clues. Still, she strongly felt she couldn't completely trust them. What if he planted false clues to lead them in the wrong direction? Trusting the poem too much could be a mistake. She sighed loudly. Study the poem . . . but don't trust it? Really? This UNSUB wasn't driven by a need to be understood like so many other killers. He simply wanted to outsmart her. Outthink her.

They parked as close as they could to the scene and walked toward the area where the police were working. After flashing their credentials at the cop who approached them, they were directed to the officer in charge, Captain Terri Weldon. She frowned as they approached. Kaely wondered if the captain would be as easy to work with as the police chief in St. Louis.

Noah held out his creds first. "Special Agent Noah Hunter, Captain. And this is Special Agent Kaely Quinn."

The captain's eyes widened. "Did you say Kaely Quinn?"

Kaely nodded. "I'm sorry. Do I know you?"

Captain Weldon smiled. "We've never met, but I've heard of you. Glad to have you here."

"Thanks," Kaely said. "Can you tell us what you've got?"

The captain waved them over to where the body lay on the ground, covered with a special tarp that protected trace evidence without transferring fibers to the body. She pulled it back. A woman with blond hair was bound at her hands and feet. Almost like a steer in the rodeo.

"Yellow twine," Kaely said. "It's a reef knot."

"That's right," the captain said, frowning.

"Any cameras around here?" Kaely asked.

Weldon shook her head. "Not in this section of the park."

Noah knelt down closer to the body. "There are scratch marks around her neck," he said. "She clawed at the rope."

Kaely nodded. The woman hadn't been in the water long. She almost looked as if she were sleeping. Pretty. Probably in her twenties. She wore a flowery dress, something that looked vintage.

"Any identification?" Kaely asked the captain as Noah stood.

"No. Nothing on her. We're searching for a purse, but we haven't found anything yet."

"I don't think you will." Kaely sucked in a deep breath. "Anything unusual on the body?"

The chief turned and called out someone's name. A crime-scene tech came over.

"Show them what we found pinned to her," the captain said.

The tech nodded and jogged back to his van. He grabbed something and came back, handing a plastic bag to the captain. It was the drawing of an elephant with the number 2 in the middle of its body. Even though they weren't surprised since Solomon had told them about it, Noah swore under his breath. Seeing it made an impact. Something the killer counted on.

"I take it this is tied to the murder in Forest Park?" the captain asked.

Kaely nodded. "Yes, it is. Will you send us what you have after you process it?"

"Of course. We'll get it to you as soon as we can." The captain hesitated a moment before saying, "Don't call me crazy, but this killing reminds me of something."

"Barton Kennedy." Kaely said it matter-of-factly.

Weldon gasped. "You see the same thing?"

"Our killer is mimicking other serial killers." She nodded at the captain. "That's not for public knowledge. We'd appreciate it if you could keep the picture quiet." Kaely sighed and forced herself to meet Captain Weldon's gaze. "We almost had it. Figured it out moments before the call came in."

The captain's no-nonsense visage slipped, and Kaely could see the compassion in her eyes. "Don't do that," she said quietly. "It will eat you up until there's nothing left. You're too valuable to second-guess yourself."

Kaely had to swallow back the feelings that welled up inside her because of the captain's kindness. "Thanks. You're right. But we've got to get this guy."

Captain Weldon put her hand on Kaely's shoulder. "I'll give you whatever I have. We're going to process the scene, but you're welcome to send your own people in to go over everything."

"We're checking with the local field office," Noah said, "asking them to let us send our Evidence Response Team in. I'm sure they'll be okay with it. We appreciate your willingness to help."

"We should be working together," Captain Weldon said. "This isn't the time for competition." She gazed deeply into Kaely's eyes. "We'll get him, Agent Quinn. I promise you."

Kaely desperately wanted to believe her.

Twenty-One

When they got back to the office, Kaely and Noah headed straight for the conference room. They passed a smaller room on the way where several agents were gathered for some kind of meeting. Noah noticed a couple of dirty looks cast their way. He imagined some of the agents weren't happy about being kicked out of the larger conference room. The new command center would be ready by Monday, but for now, they needed the huge table for all the files and notes they had. Grace had moved in a large dry-erase board for them, and Kaely immediately went to it and began to make notes. She wrote out the details of the first two murders, including who they were patterned after. Then she turned toward Noah.

"Read the third verse of the poem," she said. He tried not to be offended by the way she asked. More of a command than a request.

He sifted through the papers on the table until he found the poem. *"Five little elephants playing on the swings,"* he read. *"One grabbed a rope and ended up choked. Four little elephants called it a day. They packed up their trunks and they all ran away."* As he read, his stomach churned, and he felt a little light-headed.

Kaely frowned. "Swings? Oh, wow."

"We should have noticed this right away," Noah said softly. "I didn't realize."

"You're thinking this is Oliver Burgess."

Noah frowned. "Wait a minute. That wasn't a murder though. It was a suicide, wasn't it?"

"Actually, a lot of people believed he was murdered," Kaely said. "The FBI investigated, but there simply wasn't any evidence to support the claim. The ME was certain it was suicide. There weren't any defensive wounds. Nothing to indicate a struggle."

"Does this mean he really was killed? And that our guy knows something about it?"

Kaely sat down and opened her laptop. "That happened in . . . was it Georgia? Three years ago, right?" She shook her head. "I don't think so. Our UNSUB just recently went off the rails. His killings are a way to get at me. I don't think he's killed before. I could be wrong, but it just doesn't fit his profile."

Noah sat down next to her. "So are we missing something?"

Kaely scrolled through an old story about Oliver Burgess, then she accessed FBI files for the case. Noah moved closer so he could read along with her. The investigation was pretty straightforward. As Kaely had said, there wasn't any evidence whatsoever that Oliver had been killed. The FBI had no choice when it came to its conclusion. Oliver's parents weren't happy about the outcome. They were convinced their son was murdered, but evidence was evidence.

The family went to the media, and the FBI was accused of bungling the case. It was a black eye for the Bureau even though the murder aspect was never proved.

"How are you connected to this case?" Noah asked.

Kaely shook her head. "I'm not. I had nothing to do with it."

"I don't see how this fits, then."

"Wait a minute," Kaely said. "Our poem mentions a rope. Burgess used the metal chain holding up the swing to strangle himself." She paused. "Maybe that doesn't matter, but why did our UNSUB use the word *rope*?"

Noah pushed his chair back. Being so

close to Kaely was starting to bother him, and right now he needed to focus on stopping a killer. "Maybe we have the wrong case."

"Maybe."

Kaely typed in something and waited. When the new page came up, she leaned forward. "Yeah, here's something." She gasped softly. "Surely not."

"What is it?"

Kaely leaned back and turned the laptop so Noah could see the screen. As soon as he began to peruse the information online, he remembered the situation. Four years ago, an FBI agent in Iowa committed suicide on his daughter's swing set after she was kidnapped and killed by a man who blamed the agent for his own child's death during a shootout in a drug house.

"I remember reading about this," Kaely said. "The agent, Phillip Reagan, shot Andrew Barker during a drug raid. Reagan did the right thing and took the guy down, but later he found out Barker was only sixteen years old. The gun he'd pulled was a toy."

"Reagan had no way to know that," Noah said.

"Of course not, but he was overcome with guilt. Then his daughter was kidnapped, and they found her body three days later in a field. Barker's father was behind it. A revenge killing."

"So Reagan took his own life," Noah said. "He blamed himself for what happened. It's terrible, but what does this have to do with serial killers?"

"Who said our UNSUB was only using serial killers?" Kaely asked.

"I . . . I don't know. I just assumed . . ."

"We can't assume anything with this guy." She paused a moment. "So which case is it? Oliver Burgess or Phillip Reagan?"

"Both cases connect to the FBI," Noah mused. He stood up and walked over to the dry-erase board. He picked up the marker and wrote *Oliver Burgess* and then *Phillip Reagan.* "You think it's one of these?"

Kaely nodded. "They're the only two cases I can find with direct ties to the FBI. I guess this time I'm not directly connected, but the Bureau is." She crossed her arms over her chest and stared at the names Noah had written on the board. "You should send this to CIRG. Have them search ViCAP using *swings* or *swing set* as a search parameter. They might find something we're missing. Oh, and add the word *rope.*"

"Good idea," Noah said.

"Let's look at the message he's sending. If

it's the Oliver Burgess case, then he's going to kill a teenager."

The uneasy feeling returned to Noah's stomach. Their UNSUB was thinking about killing a kid? Really?

"Or he wants me to hang myself," Kaely said softly. "I'm pretty sure I'm not going to do that."

"That can't be it. Look at the last stanza of the poem. *One last elephant facing final judgment. She was found guilty and given no pity. Jessica Oliphant called it a day. She picked up a gun and blew herself away.* Sounds like his exact plans are for you to shoot yourself, not end up on the end of a rope."

Was that truly the end game? Kaely Quinn's suicide? What kind of power did this killer think he had over her? Was it strong enough to actually make her blow her brains out?

Kaely frowned at him. "I would never do that," she said as if she knew what he was thinking. "Never. No one who knows me would think I was capable of it. I'm too . . ."

"Stubborn?"

Kaely snorted. "No."

She was silent for several seconds, and Noah felt he needed to be quiet. He could almost hear the gears turning in her head.

Finally, she took a deep breath. "After we found out who my father really was, I thought about ending my life. Everything changed. Family friends deserted us. Our neighbors avoided us. I couldn't go to school. Had to be home-schooled. It was awful." She turned her dark eyes toward him. "But in the end, it made me strong. Determined." A small smile played at the corners of her mouth. "Okay, stubborn. But nothing — and I mean nothing — could make me put a gun to my head. I have God in my life now, and I've learned that He can get me through anything, that I never have to give up. What I'm saying is that someone who knew me would know that. So our UN-SUB can't be close to me."

"You thought it might be someone in your life?"

"My friend Richard brought up my brother's name. Jason's very angry about what happened to our family. Supposedly, he blames me and my mother for not exposing my father."

"Why didn't you tell me about this sooner?"

"I was going to. Richard just told me about it this morning. It might be wise to track Jason down. Find out where he is. But my point is that Jason knows I would never commit suicide. Even after all this time surely he would be convinced of that. So it can't be him."

He noticed the look of relief on her face. "I agree that we need more information before we rule him out, but I understand what you're saying. So we're back to someone connected to a case but possibly not closely connected to you. What does that leave us?"

"The person who died," Kaely said softly.

Noah looked at her, confused by her comment. "What do you mean?"

"I mean, a child died. First Oliver Burgess, then Reagan's daughter. Isn't that the connection?"

"But you don't have a child."

"No, I don't." Kaely stood and walked over to the dry-erase board. "It's here. I'm just not seeing it. And we've got to figure it out. Quickly."

Someone knocked on the door to the conference room, and Noah jumped. He hadn't realized he was so tense. Grace came in, carrying some papers.

"They ID'd the young woman found at the park in Illinois," she said. "Thought you'd want to see this."

"Thanks," Noah said.

Kaely didn't turn around to acknowledge

Grace. She continued to stare at the board.

"Sorry," Noah said in a low voice. "We're trying to figure out where this guy will strike next."

"I understand," Grace said. "Not a problem." She smiled at Noah. "I ordered pizza. It should be here soon." She left the room, quietly closing the door behind her.

Noah looked through the reports from the police in Illinois. The woman found in the water was Eleanor Duncan, a waitress who worked in Highland. The police located her original clothes in the trees, not far from where she was dumped. The dress she wore was similar to what Barton Kennedy's second victim was wearing when her body was discovered. The killer was doing everything he could to copy the original murders. Once again, the victim seemed to be picked because the UNSUB could get to her easily and she matched the description of Barton Kennedy's victims. There didn't appear to be any other connection to Kaely.

He looked up when he heard Kaely gasp. She turned around, her eyebrows knit together in a deep frown. "It's not the Burgess case. It's Reagan."

"So it's a threat toward you?"

"I don't think so, Noah. I think he's trying to tell me he's going after someone close to me. That's the connection this time." She bit her lip and stared at him without saying anything for several seconds. "I think you're his next target."

Twenty-Two

At first Noah wasn't certain he'd heard her clearly.

"He's going after someone I care about," she repeated. "That has to be it."

"But that wouldn't be me," he said. "We're not that close. Wouldn't it make more sense for him to target your friends? Your mother? Your brother?"

"My mother is in Nebraska, and I don't know where my brother is. Besides, I don't believe he'll strike that far away. He'll stay near his comfort zone. He wants me to see what he does."

"So who are you close to here?"

Kaely shook her head. "I think the FBI connection is important to him. That means you. He could have easily seen me with you at a crime scene."

"What about Solomon?"

Kaely was quiet for a moment. Finally she said, "No. I don't see him outside of work. I still think you're the most likely target."

Noah swiveled around in his chair and stared at the dry-erase board. "What if we're wrong? Maybe the Burgess murder is the right one."

She shook her head again. "No. It's the Reagan case. It matches down to the rope." Her dark eyes bore into his. "I'm not trying to overreact here, Noah, but you need to be especially careful. If he's watching me, he would see that you're the closest person to me in proximity. He may assume we're close friends."

"Well, I hope we're friends."

Kaely walked over, sat down in front of her laptop, and appeared to focus intently on the screen. "I . . . I think we are. But that just proves that you could be a target. Think about it. The person found hanging was an FBI agent. Promise me you'll be very careful."

For some reason the absurdity of the situation made Noah laugh. Kaely turned her face toward him, one eyebrow raised.

"Sorry for laughing, but what does that mean? I have to keep an eye on you and now you have to keep an eye on me? This is going to get really confusing."

"Not really funny."

"It kind of is."

Kaely nodded. "Okay. It kind of is."

"So what do we do now?"

"I don't know," Kaely said. "I need to think a bit." She waved her hand toward him. "Distract me. Ask me your third question."

Noah was confused by her request. Shouldn't they focus on the next line of the poem? Try to find the UNSUB before he struck again?

"You're thinking we need to focus on the next murder. I agree, but I need to step back from this for a few minutes. Looking at it too closely locks my brain up. I want to concentrate on something else for a bit."

Noah swallowed hard and seriously thought about changing his next question. He knew what he wanted to ask, but he didn't want to lose his partnership with Kaely. Working with her was turning out to be the most exciting thing he'd done since joining the Bureau.

"Don't talk yourself out of it," she said, looking closely at him. "Just ask."

"Actually, it's not my third question. It's the rest of the second one." He stared down at the table, his heart pounding.

"You want to know *why* I believe?"

Unable to find his voice, Noah simply nodded.

For a few seconds, Kaely just stared at him without saying anything. Finally, she said, "You see me as a very rational thinker. Someone who doesn't accept anything she can't prove."

She laughed lightly, and Noah was struck by how lovely and lyrical her laugh was. He wished he could hear it more often, but that just wasn't Kaely.

"So you want to understand how someone who talks to people who aren't there can rationally believe in God?"

The absurdity struck him, and he chuckled. "If you really believed serial killers were sitting down for a meal with you, I'd be worried. But you know better. I realize it's just a way for you to visualize them. I don't have any problem with it."

She nodded. "Good. Thanks for that."

Kaely rubbed her hands together and looked away for a moment. Then she focused her gaze on him. "We went to church when I was a kid. As you know, my father was an usher. The church we attended was . . . well, let's just say that it was built around following rules. Pointing out sin. Judging others. It certainly didn't spark a desire for God in my heart.

"But there was a Sunday school teacher who was . . . different. She was so positive.

So full of love. I wanted to know why she was that way. I actually stayed after class one Sunday and asked her to tell me about God. She didn't seem surprised, really. She sat me down and told me about a God who loved me. Who never judged me or thought bad things about me. Who sent His son to die for my sins so I could be free from guilt and condemnation.

"This was just two months before my father was arrested. We left the church after that. My mother took my brother and me to Nebraska. I never talked to that teacher again, but I never forgot what she said."

"And that was what led you to believe?" Noah asked. Frankly, he was disappointed in her response. He'd heard the same things from his wife, but that had never convinced him that God was a good God. Or that He deserved Noah's loyalty.

"No, that wasn't all of it," Kaely said. "After my father's conviction, I felt so . . . empty. Alone. My teacher's words did come back to me, but that wasn't enough to make me a believer. I needed cold, hard truth. According to many people, you have to believe God is real based on faith alone. It's like me talking to serial killers who aren't there. My own mind causes them to respond. They're not actually talking. I had no plans to pretend God was real too. Pretend He was responding to me. I needed to *know* He existed.

"I checked out several different religions, but they were worse than Christianity. Statues that had no life in them. Religion based on good works or hatred for others who believe differently. I realized they all had one thing in common. They demanded that I work hard to get their gods to respond to me. The god my teacher told me about seemed to be the only one who actually reached out to me first. He didn't ask me to be perfect before He'd pay attention to me.

"So I started reading about Christianity. The Bible, historical accounts. I found a book about the apostles. How they died." Kaely shook her head. "They actually wanted to be martyred. Wouldn't have been my choice, but it was theirs. They died horrible deaths, but they wouldn't disavow their faith. I realized that any rational person would have denied Christ's resurrection if they hadn't actually seen Him raised from the dead. The only answer was that Jesus was exactly who He said He was."

Noah chuckled. "So you profiled the apostles?"

Kaely actually grinned. "Yeah, I guess I did. Once I came to that conclusion, I started thinking about the world. The universe. To believe it just accidentally happened is . . . well, it's ludicrous. If it had been some kind of accidental explosion of particles, then where did the particles come from? And why weren't there mistakes? How could animals and man have been designed so beautifully? The human body is a miracle. It was clear someone, a master designer, was behind creation. I concluded God had to be real.

"Then I found a scripture that confirmed my conclusion. It was Romans 1:20 — 'For ever since the creation of the world His invisible attributes, His eternal power and divine nature, have been clearly seen, being understood through His workmanship, all His creation, the wonderful things that He has made, so that they who fail to believe and trust in Him are without excuse and without defense.' That's the Amplified version. I think it expresses the thought perfectly."

"So that was it?" Noah asked.

"Not completely. I decided that if God was real, if He was the God of the Bible, the creator of the universe, if I called out to Him, He would have to answer. So I asked God to reveal Himself to me. And He did." She stared at Noah for a moment. "I won't tell you how He did that because it's very personal. I would just encourage you to do the same thing . . . if you want to know Him.

"Since then? Well, as time goes by, I've gotten to understand Him more and more. And to understand myself. Yes, of course He speaks to me. He speaks to everyone who will listen. He's teaching me what a Father *should* be. It may take some time, but I'm convinced He'll never give up on me." She leaned forward in her chair and touched Noah's arm with her small, delicate fingers. He was surprised to see tears in her eyes. "Faith came after I knew He was real, Noah. I have a lot of issues leftover from my past. God has never condemned me for them. He just keeps leading me slowly but surely out of the dark, at the pace I need. I have a long way to go, but I believe I'll make it because of His love and faithfulness."

Noah considered what she'd said. Her reasons for believing were compelling, and as he figured, based on facts, not some pie-in-the sky belief you had to accept for no reason whatsoever. It seemed to work for some people, and that was fine. But it didn't work for him. He'd think about what Kaely said. He still wanted to know why Tracy died. Why hadn't God answered those prayers?

"I don't know why your wife died, Noah," Kaely said softly.

"I wish you wouldn't do that," he snapped.

"I wasn't reading you. If I were you, it's the question I'd have. I believe it's God's will for us to live out our lives. The Bible says His plan is to give us long life. So why do some people die early? I have no idea. All I can tell you is this. I know God. But I also know evil. I've looked into its eyes. The devil is real. We're in a war. No matter how hard soldiers try to stay safe, sometimes they get shot. It's really important to remember that the enemy may win a battle, but the truth is, he's already lost the war."

"What does that mean? Tracy's gone. That war was lost. She's not coming back."

"But your wife is with God, Noah. She's alive. She may not be here — but she's somewhere, living, being loved, seeing things we can't even imagine. And I know she wants to spend eternity with you. I really hope you'll find the courage to ask God to reveal Himself to you. Give Him a chance to respond."

"And if He doesn't?"

"He will."

How could she be so sure? For some reason, something rose up inside him that he hadn't felt in years. Hope. A reason to believe. Could he really see Tracy again? Look into her beautiful blue eyes? He wanted that more than anything. He'd held her hand as she slipped away. He'd never told anyone that she made him promise to reach out to God. And she'd promised to be there to greet him when he got to heaven. He would have said anything she wanted at that point, but maybe he could keep that vow after all. Maybe . . .

"It's definitely the Reagan murder," Kaely said suddenly, pulling Noah back to the present. It was like having cold water thrown in his face.

Kaely jumped up from her chair and went to the board. She picked up the pen and crossed out the notes about Oliver Burgess and circled the name Reagan. She turned to look at him. "I don't think our UNSUB will hesitate very long before he makes his next move."

Twenty-Three

He sat outside the FBI building in St. Louis, watching the entrance. He would wait until Kaely came out — no matter how long it took. Wherever she went, he would be there. Ernie kept him up to date on her comings and goings. Noah Hunter was next on his list. Their worlds were getting ready to collide.

"Read it again," Kaely said.

Noah sighed. *"Five little elephants playing on the swings. One grabbed a rope and ended up choked. Four little elephants called it a day. They packed up their trunks and they all ran away."*

She knew he was getting tired of repeating the stanza, but she was trying to see if there was something she'd missed. Finally, part of the verse got her attention. " 'One grabbed a rope and ended up choked,' " she said. "That doesn't sound like murder, does it? I mean, if the victim grabbed the rope and *ended up* choked . . ."

"It sounds like an accident," Noah said, frowning. "Or maybe the poem just sounded better written that way. How can we be sure?"

"We can't. Read the rest of the poem again." Kaely had memorized the entire thing, but having Noah read it out loud helped her zero in on the words.

Noah sighed once more, but he kept reading. *"Four little elephants playing with matches. One built a pyre and set himself on fire. Three little elephants called it a day. They packed up their trunks and they all ran away. Three little elephants sat down for a meal. One took a bite and then said good night. Two little elephants called it a day. They packed up their trunks and they all ran away. Two little elephants playing all alone. One knew the truth and told it to the sleuth. One little elephant called it a day. She packed up her trunk and ran far away. One last elephant facing final judgment. She was found guilty and given no pity. Jessica Oliphant called it a day. She picked up a gun and blew herself away."*

His voice got so soft by the end of the verse she barely heard the last part. "Something wrong with your voice?" she asked.

"No, Kaely. Maybe I don't like reading

things like this over and over. Some insane person wrote it. It's evil. I'm starting to hear this in my mind at night when I try to sleep. It seems nothing gets to you, but it's beginning to drive me nuts."

She was surprised by his reaction. "I . . . I didn't realize. I mean, it's just a clue, Noah. Something we have to crack. It's not personal."

His eyebrows shot up and his mouth dropped open. "It's not personal? Are you crazy? The guy is threatening you. It's incredibly personal. I mean, I know you. It's not like he's targeting someone I've never met."

As soon as the last word left his mouth, Kaely felt something akin to an electric shock go through her. "Someone I've never met . . ." she echoed.

Noah frowned. "What are you talking about?"

"The first victim. Albert Lawson." She got up and hurried out of the room. She could barely breathe as she ran to her office, pulled her filing cabinet open, and searched for a particular file. When she found it, she put it down on her desk, stood there a moment trying to calm her adrenaline-charged body, and then opened the file. Sure enough, there it was. She picked up the file and headed back to the conference room. Noah sat in the same place, looking puzzled.

"How about a heads-up before you run out of the room and leave me here wondering what's going on? It's disconcerting."

"Sorry. I . . . I'm a little impulsive sometimes."

"You think?"

She sat down, opened the file, and pushed it over toward him, pointing at one of the papers. "Remember the guy we found who was planning to bomb City Hall six months ago?"

Noah nodded. "Yeah. The one who wanted to join ISIS?"

"Yeah. Look at the list of attorneys assigned to the case. One of them was . . ."

"Albert Lawson," Noah said, his eyes widening. "Could be a coincidence."

"Maybe, but I don't think so." She got up and walked to the dry-erase board. "Eleanor Duncan. A waitress in Illinois. How could I possibly know her?"

"You have a great memory. Are you sure the name doesn't ring a bell?"

"Yeah." She ran the name *Eleanor* over and over in her mind. What was the nickname for Eleanor? Ellie? She didn't know an Ellie either.

"What about the last name?" Noah asked.

"Duncan."

"No, I . . ." As she stared at Noah, she felt as if she was going to be sick. It must have shown on her face.

"What?" Noah asked. "What are you thinking?"

"Hold on a minute." Kaely's fingers trembled as she fished her cell phone from her purse. She punched in a number and waited. When the phone was answered, she took a deep breath. "Hi, Marlene," she said. "I . . . I need to ask you a question. . . . What was the name of the woman who lived in my condo before I moved in?"

Although she knew what the condominium association manager was going to say, she prayed she was wrong. She wasn't. When Marlene responded, Kaely thanked her and disconnected. She stared at the phone, unable to meet Noah's eyes for some reason.

"Let me guess. Eleanor Duncan?" he asked softly.

She nodded.

"But you never met this Eleanor Duncan, did you? What about Albert Lawson?"

She shook her head. "No. I had nothing to do with the court case. I never met him either."

"So why is our UNSUB picking these

people?"

Finally, Kaely found the guts to look at her partner. "He's researched my life, and he wants me to know that. He's not just picking cases I've worked, he's choosing people connected to me in some way. He's breaching my personal boundaries. Taking away the distance between us."

"But who could do this, Kaely?"

"Anyone could find out who the trial attorneys were for the bomber case. And it's not difficult to get the name of the person who lived in my condo. This doesn't put us any closer to an ID."

"Didn't you mention some guy named Richard? Doesn't he know a lot about you?"

"You mean the man who's given up everything to support me? Who has taken the place of my father?"

"I don't care about that. We need to check him out."

"You can do that, Noah, but he was out of town during the first murder. He couldn't have had anything to do with it."

"He *says* he was out of town. I'm going to follow up. We have to be sure, Kaely."

She tried to dismiss her growing irritation. Noah was only doing his job. He'd rule Richard out, and Richard would never know they'd looked at him. It was best to just go along with Noah at this point, and keep her personal feelings out of it. She prided herself on being analytical and unemotional when it came to her job, but she'd never been a potential victim in a case before. She didn't like the way it made her feel.

"And we need to find out where your brother is."

"I understand, but I'm sure he's not involved." Even as she defended Jason, she had to admit there was a little niggling doubt somewhere in her brain. The truth was, she needed it not to be him. She loved her brother. Even though he'd walked away from her, she believed someday they'd be reunited. She hated thinking that Jason had followed in her father's footsteps. It couldn't happen twice in one family. . . . Could it?

"You don't have to talk to Jason," Noah said, "but we need to locate him. If he needs to be questioned, I'll do it."

Kaely faltered. She wanted to see her brother, but she was afraid she'd find out something she didn't want to know. If he was innocent but found out she suspected him of murder, it could destroy any slight chance they had of reconciliation.

"And then there's the elephant in the room," Noah said. "Pun intended."

"What do you mean?"

"Jerry Acosta. It's obvious, isn't it? I mean, the guy stalks you. Has tried to hurt you. And he wants to interview you for his book. . . ."

"He won't get much from me if I'm dead."

"That's not funny."

"It kind of is."

"Touché. But seriously, we need to check this guy out. Couldn't a newspaper reporter be considered a sleuth?"

"Maybe, but I don't think he fits the profile," Kaely said. "He certainly has given up a lot to follow me from Virginia to St. Louis though, hasn't he?"

"Yes, he has."

"Look, he wants that interview with me so he can write his book. But like I said, I really can't help him if I'm dead. I don't think he'd try to kill me."

"I'm not so sure of that. I don't want to gamble with your life just to prove a point."

Kaely nodded. "Okay. He stays on the list for now."

Kaely and Noah both sat down at the table. Noah picked up their copy of the poem. "Who could be called a sleuth besides Acosta?"

Kaely held her hands up in mock surrender. "As I pointed out before, I'm surrounded by *sleuths*, aren't I? Not sure that narrows it down much." She put her hands down and clasped them together. "The reference about fire bothers me. I told you about my friend Louis and his son."

"The guy who owns the restaurant?"

"Yeah."

"You think it refers to him?"

"I hope not, but it concerns me. I think we need to consider it. I don't want anything to happen to Louis."

"You know everyone here was pretty impressed when you nailed that arsonist."

"Yeah? Well, it sure didn't seem to make me any friends."

Noah was quiet for a moment. "Kaely, I'm sorry people haven't treated you kindly. Maybe if you tried again . . ."

Resentment spilled out before she could stop it. "If *I* tried. You talk as if it was my fault. When I got to St. Louis, I got the cold shoulder, save for Solomon and Grace. Besides, I had *friends* at Quantico. Thanks. Been there, done that. Don't want to do it again."

"Sometimes life is about taking chances. Without doing that we just exist."

Kaely ignored his comment and steered the conversation back to the case. She didn't need friends, yet somewhere deep inside, she wanted them. She was angry with Noah for stirring up feelings she had no time to deal with. Getting distracted now could cost lives, and she was determined to save everyone she could.

"I've been told the command post will definitely be ready by Monday morning," Noah said. "Solomon wants us to take the weekend off and start in again on Monday. I think we've done everything we can for now. I know we'll both be reviewing the case over the weekend, but maybe some time apart to think on our own is what we need."

Kaely frowned at him. She'd figured they'd at least work on Saturday. "Are you sure . . ."

"No sense in arguing about it. We're stalled. If you come up with anything, call me. Otherwise, I'll meet you here first thing Monday. We'll move our stuff to the CP and start working from there."

"You need to be careful, Noah. Really careful. Promise me."

"I promise," he said softly. "Don't worry. I'll be fine. You stay safe too, okay?"

She didn't say anything, just nodded. As she stood up and prepared to leave, she wondered if their UNSUB was taking the weekend off.

She seriously doubted it.

Twenty-Four

He ducked down when Kaely drove by. She wouldn't recognize his car, so he was safe. He watched carefully as she pulled up to the guard shack. After talking to Ernie, she entered the complex. He waited a few minutes and then started his car. When Ernie saw him, the smile he'd given to Kaely vanished. He knew Ernie was uncomfortable with their arrangement, but he was determined to get Kaely alone.

"I don't know about this," Ernie said when he pulled up.

"I'm sorry you're bothered by it, but you're too far in to pull out now."

Ernie's expression went slack. It was evident he had no choice. He sighed and pushed a button, causing the gate to slide open.

"Don't call her. Don't warn her. I mean it," he said before he drove past the guard shack. As he rounded the corner, he realized she was still sitting in her car. He quickly pulled into an empty parking space. Hopefully, the owner wouldn't show up before Kaely went inside. Finally, she got out of her car and headed for her apartment.

He smiled in the dark. He was nothing if not patient. He'd waited for the right moment. And it was now.

When Kaely pulled into her parking spot, she was so tired she sat there for a moment and tried to gather her thoughts. She and Noah had taken the poem apart several times and tried to make sense of it. She was still worried about the reference to fire. It was too close to Louis. She had to find a way to protect him.

She looked forward to moving to the CP, and she was grateful for the help that would be provided by CIRG and the police departments in St. Louis and Illinois. She was pretty sure Reinhardt would be there, but he was smart and perceptive. Even if he didn't like her, she welcomed his input.

She finally opened her car door and got out. She was hungry and glad she still had some chicken left. She unlocked her front door, went inside, then carefully locked the door behind her. She put her purse and briefcase down on the kitchen table and went to the fridge. She pulled out the roasted chicken, got a plate, pulled more meat off the bones, and stuck it in the microwave. While it heated, she grabbed a bottle of water from the refrigerator, along with the rest of the macaroni salad.

When the microwave dinged, she took the plate out, dumped the macaroni salad on it, and grabbed a fork. After carrying her food into the living room, she plopped down on the couch and switched on the TV. She selected the only news channel she trusted and watched for a while. Kaely could do without TV — especially the news — but she felt she should at least attempt to stay current with what was going on in the world, especially when it came to the Bureau. After she finished eating, she turned off the TV and headed to her war room, where she perused the notes and pictures she had on her boards. She opened her briefcase and took out new information. Copies of reports, notes she made while talking to Noah. After staring at the boards for several minutes, she sat down at the table in the corner. She didn't feel quite ready for this, but she was at a standstill. She needed to see the UNSUB a little more clearly.

She scooted a little closer. She had two

empty plates and glasses on the table. She didn't really need them, but it gave a sense of reality to what she was doing. She laughed to herself. Not that many people thought she had a close relationship with reality anyway. Over the past year, she'd felt herself moving away from her profiling technique more and more. Alex used to tell her she didn't need it, that it had become a crutch. Maybe he was right. But on this case she could use all the help she could get. She sat for a while, staring at the empty chair. She felt unsettled. Maybe it was a sign she really wasn't ready to proceed. But she had to try.

She stared up at the board and began. "You're a white male. Can't quite nail your age, but I feel as if you're in your thirties or forties. Maybe older. You don't feel young to me."

"You're in your thirties. Does that mean you're not young?" she heard in a whisper.

The more she used this method, the more control she seemed to lose. In the past, the UNSUB never spoke unless she allowed it. But lately, comments kept slipping past her. Even though she didn't like it, she realized it was just her subconscious and she probably needed to give it the freedom to speak. It helped her to understand her own thought processes better.

"I'm young enough to catch you," she responded with a smile.

"You won't win this one." The voice was low and menacing.

Kaely laughed and leaned back in her chair, ignoring a cold wiggle of shock that danced up her spine. "I always win. Always."

"You didn't win with your father."

She frowned and stared at the chair. Why was this coming up now? "That wasn't my fault. I was a child."

"You know better than that."

"That's enough," she said firmly. "You're not here to badger me. Shut up."

"What about that scar?" he hissed.

"I told you to be quiet. Now do it."

Her last rebuke seemed to finally quiet him. She fought the urge to reach up and touch the scar that ran along the side of her face, near her hairline. Her mother had told her she'd fallen off her tricycle when she was two and cut herself. She had no memory of it. Kaely's attention went back to her incident board, but ignoring the question about her scar was harder than it should have been. Why had he brought it up? Finally, she said, "This is personal. I've affected your life in some way. You're angry. You want more than to kill me. You want to humiliate me. Frustrate me. Show me you're smarter than I am."

"I am smart—"

"Quit talking!" Kaely said loudly. She was uncomfortable with the degree of anger and bravado coming from the UNSUB. Was she really this intimidated by him? She prayed silently for help from God. When she prayed, she felt something odd emanating from the other side of the table. What was it? Why did this feel so different from the many other times she'd used this procedure to profile an adversary? She cleared her throat. "You're taking the time to find victims who are connected to me in some way. But I'm not close to them. Why would you do that?"

There was no response. Nothing but silence. Time to move on.

Kaely sighed deeply. What else did she know? "You're educated. Successful. Not the usual loser who kills people to get his kicks. Something happened to set you off, but what? Did you get fired?" Even though job loss could prime a killer, it didn't feel right. "Someone rejected you? Or did someone die?" The death would have been recent. "Is this connected to the Reagan case?"

Still no response.

She paused for a moment. "Jason?" she

said finally, giving voice to a possibility she really didn't want to let into her mind. "Is that you?"

As soon as she gave voice to the fear that her brother might be involved, the lights outside her window shifted. Kaely jumped up from her chair and hurried to the stairs. She gazed down at her front windows. Something moved by them and stopped. Something or someone. As she watched, the lights from the parking lot made it easy to see the figure that stood outside her door, although he was only in shadow. Kaely hurried down the stairs and into the living room, where she grabbed her gun from its holster. She held her weapon in front of her and was headed toward the front door when the knob rattled. Someone was trying to open the door. Ernie was supposed to call if anyone else entered the property. Who could it be?

She took a stance and waited. The door slowly opened and a figure stood there.

"Hey, put your gun away," he said. "I would have called, but I was afraid you might tell me to go away."

Kaely took a quick, ragged breath and lowered her gun. "I could have killed you," she said, her voice higher than it should have been.

Alex smiled. "Yeah, I know. Thanks for not doing that."

Twenty-Five

Kaely carried her gun over to its holster and slid it back inside. Then she faced Alex, who had closed the door behind him but still leaned against it.

"Don't be angry," he said. "I had to see you. I've been here since yesterday evening. Randy Parker called me about the letter."

Randy had been Alex's close friend and worked in ERT. "He could get in a lot of trouble for contacting you."

"I know, but you won't turn him in."

She frowned at him. "How did you talk Ernie into letting you enter the complex?"

He grinned at her, and her heart thudded in her chest. That grin. She'd missed it so much. His sandy hair and blue eyes were like a balm to her soul. She was thrilled he was here — and angry that he'd gone behind her back.

"I've been talking to Ernie since Monday. He kept me up to date on your comings and goings. Tonight he let me in. Don't be upset with him. I convinced him it was the only way to keep you safe."

"By letting unauthorized people into a gated community?" she said angrily. "That's not really the way to keep anyone safe."

"No," Alex said, pushing himself off her door and walking toward her. "But letting in a trained FBI agent who wants to protect you is a pretty good way to look after someone. Ernie knows me, Kaely. It's not like he let a stranger into the complex. Leave him alone. Please. He'll never do it again. I'll make sure of it."

"You'd better." Alex stood about two feet from her, and she could smell his aftershave. She wanted to breathe deeply, take it in, but she couldn't. She couldn't allow herself to show him how grateful she was that he'd come. How much she'd missed him. How much she needed him. It would just start the whole thing all over again.

"So, just what is it you plan to do?" Kaely asked. She walked over to the couch and sat down. Her legs felt as if they couldn't hold her up.

Alex took off his coat and dropped it on the back of her chair. That ugly dark green wool coat. It had belonged to Alex's father, and Alex wouldn't give it up, even though it had seen better days.

He plopped down on the other end of the couch. "I'm not sure, but I intend to make sure this idiot doesn't get close to you."

"I'm surprised Detroit let you come here. You haven't been there that long."

"I took a leave of absence. I have some things to sort out. Besides, I was worried about you."

She started to question him further, but he held up his hand. "Not now. I'll talk to you about it when I can. You need to trust me."

"You know you can't help with this case, right?"

He nodded. "I know. I'm just here to offer moral support to a friend." He sighed deeply and rubbed his eyes. Kaely noticed for the first time how tired he looked. "Look, Kaely, I know you're not ready for a romantic relationship. I shouldn't have pushed. I made a mistake. Right now, all I care about is making sure you're safe. I promise I won't say or do anything else to make you uncomfortable. We were always great friends. Can we just go back to that?"

Kaely realized her fists were clenched so hard her nails were making deep impressions in her palms. She shook her hands open. She wanted Alex to stay. More than anything. But she wasn't sure he could live up to his promises. She knew he was deeply in love with her, and she knew people were driven more by their emotions than they liked to admit. Was it possible someday she could return his love? Maybe. But not now. Not for a long time.

"Of course we're friends," she said. "Stay for a while. Frankly, I'd like to bring you up to speed on what's been going on. I could use your insight." She peered deeply into his eyes. "But if I need you to leave . . ."

"As long as you're safe, I'll go."

Kaely jumped to her feet. "Then you need to go now. Either we do this my way . . . or we don't do it at all."

Alex looked away from her, his jaw working furiously. When he turned his head back around and their eyes met, he said, "That's the way it always is, right, Kaely? Your way or the highway?"

The anger she saw in his expression frightened her. Alex wasn't an angry person. Had she done this to him?

"Let me ask you this," he said. "If I were in danger, what would you do? If I asked you to leave?"

She couldn't tear her eyes away from his. He knew the answer. It wouldn't do any good to lie. "I'd stay until I knew you were safe."

The tautness in his face softened a little. "Okay. So let's leave it there. I'll do my very best to leave when you tell me to, but I honestly can't promise you anything."

Although she didn't want to accept his terms, she realized she didn't have a choice if she wanted him to stay. Finally, she said, "Okay."

"So, let's go to your war room. Show me what you've got so far."

"Fine. But first . . ." She held out her hand.

He sighed and reached into his pocket, pulling out the key she'd given him a long time ago. He handed it to her, not saying anything.

She put the key in her pocket and headed upstairs, Alex on her heels.

Noah recognized Alex almost immediately. He'd followed Kaely home and then watched Alex's red sports car pull up to the guard's gate. He was surprised to see the guard let him through. He was supposed to call Kaely to notify her when someone was there to see her, but he never picked up the phone. Obviously he was working with Alex. Noah waited almost an hour, but Alex didn't come out. The longer he waited, the more enraged he got. Was all this talk about not wanting a romantic relationship a lie? Was Alex going to be there all night? As he sat there, Noah only grew more upset. Why was this bothering him so much? He had no intention of falling into the trap Alex had. He kept telling himself that Kaely was the sister he'd never had, yet somewhere in his mind, he knew it wasn't completely true. He wasn't prepared to deal with those feelings, so once again he shoved them away, telling himself that whatever Kaely did or didn't do with Alex was her business. Not his. After a few more minutes, he started his car and drove away.

Alex followed Kaely into her special room. She sat down at the table in the corner while he perused everything she'd posted on the corkboard and had written on her dry-erase board. She didn't say anything, so as not to distract him. Finally, he turned around.

"Nothing from the poem? Can you use linguistic analysis to point toward the writer?"

Kaely shook her head. "That's really difficult with a poem. The writer chooses words that rhyme, and sometimes they're not exactly what they really want to say.

Although I believe our UNSUB has chosen his words carefully, he probably faced the same challenge. I couldn't find anything that stood out. We might have BAU give it a try though. I could have missed something."

"I doubt that," Alex said. "So you believe he wrote this himself?"

"Yeah. One of the first things I did was search for the poem online. It's never been published. I'm sure it's original."

He nodded and turned back to the wall. "So the next murder will be a hanging? On swings? I hope he's not talking about a child."

"I don't think so," Kaely said. "He seems focused on adults. Adults who have come into contact with me in some way. And so far both other murders were copycats of cases I worked."

Alex turned around quickly and stared at her. "What do you mean the victims were connected to you?"

She explained to him her relationship to the first two targets.

"Wow. But that's really . . . distant. There's no way to predict who he'll hit next."

"I know. It's incredibly frustrating."

"What happened after the poem appeared in the paper?"

"Just what you'd think," Kaely said. "Lots of calls from crazy people who are certain they know who wrote the poem. We're sending all calls to the police, who set up a special line with BAU to review everything. So far, they haven't gotten anything that seems promising. Of course, we also have the usual psychics who want to help."

"You mean the people who've never given us a single thing we can use?"

"Yeah, the same."

Alex came over and sat down across from her at the table. "You know, that's what some people think you are. Psychic."

She laughed lightly. "And some think I'm just psycho."

He smiled. "Yeah, I suppose some do."

She wanted to reach out and take his hand. Tell him how happy she was that he was here, but she didn't dare. It would just make things harder when he left. Yet, at that moment, she felt safer than she had since the poem arrived at the FBI. She liked Noah, but she still didn't trust him completely. She trusted Alex. If anyone could help her stop this guy, it was him.

"How about some coffee?" she asked. "I'd like to talk more about the case. We're taking the weekend off while the command post is set up. Monday morning we hit the ground running. We have two days to review everything we have so far. Are you in?"

His slow smile tugged at her heart. "There's nothing I'd like more."

Twenty-Six

On Monday morning, Noah gulped down a cup of coffee and was headed for the door when his phone rang. Who could be calling now? He was supposed to meet Kaely at the office, get their files, and then go to the new CP.

He took his phone from his pocket and looked at it. When he saw the name, he almost dropped the phone. He turned back and leaned against the kitchen cabinet. Before he answered, he took a steadying breath.

"Hello?" he said.

"Hey, Noah. Alex Cartwright."

"What can I do for you, Alex?"

A slow chuckle came over the phone. "You don't sound surprised to hear from me."

"I'm not."

Alex didn't say anything for several seconds, and Noah let the silence continue. He had no intention of telling Alex he was aware he'd been with Kaely.

"Look, I'd like to talk to you for a few minutes. It's important. Could you meet me at that coffee shop by the office? You know the one?"

"Yeah, I know it." Noah sighed. "I'm supposed to meet Kaely in thirty minutes."

"I know, but she's running late. I only want fifteen minutes. Please, Noah. If I didn't think it was vital, I wouldn't bother you."

Noah wanted to say no, but he found himself agreeing to meet Alex. When he hung up, he wondered why he'd said yes. Truthfully, Noah was curious. He wanted to know why Alex was here. And it *was* only fifteen minutes.

Twenty minutes later, Noah walked into Sips Café. He looked around the small shop, hoping no other agents were here. It was a favorite place to grab coffee, donuts, fruit, or even a protein shake on the way to work. Sips had something for everyone. Thankfully, he didn't recognize anyone except Alex, who sat at a corner table and waved him over.

Before sitting down, Noah went to the counter and ordered a cup of black coffee. The barista quickly filled a cup and handed it to him. After paying her, Noah headed to the table where Alex waited. Noah was determined to keep his cool, but just seeing Alex made his blood boil.

Alex was everything Noah wasn't. Blond with blue eyes. He had an easy smile that people seemed to respond to. Even though Alex left just a few months after Noah arrived in St. Louis, Noah remembered how much everyone liked him. How popular he was. Although Noah had friends, he wasn't all that comfortable around people. Sometimes he felt like the odd man out. He was pretty sure Alex had never felt that way in his entire life.

He sat down at Alex's table. "I don't have much time," he said. "What are you doing in town?"

Alex smiled at him. "Good to see you too."

Noah felt his throat constrict. "Sorry," he forced out. "I just can't be late today. We're moving to our command post."

"I know. Kaely told me about it."

Noah took a sip of his coffee. It was so hot, it stung his tongue, but he didn't let Alex know it had made him uncomfortable. "You've seen Kaely?" he asked when he put his cup down.

Alex laughed. "You know I did, Noah. I saw you parked outside her place Friday night."

Great. "Does she know?"

"I don't think so. I certainly didn't tell her, nor do I intend to. I suspect we're both concerned about her. Worried that this nut is going to hurt her."

"I'll protect her. You don't need to be concerned."

"But I am." Alex cleared his throat, clasped his hands together on the top of the table, and leaned closer to Noah. "Look. You've only worked with her a short time, but I need you to know that she takes chances. Dumb chances." He leaned back and shook his head. "She's liable to do something stupid. Put herself in danger if she gets too curious, or if she thinks she can draw the UNSUB out. Please don't let her do it."

"Surely she wouldn't do anything to purposely put herself in his cross hairs." Even though he didn't want Alex's help, Noah was surprised by his suggestion. Was Kaely really that reckless?

"I'm telling you, she will. We worked a case once where a drug dealer kidnapped a girl. Held her for ransom because her father planned to testify against him. Kaely figured out where he was holding the girl and went there alone. Didn't tell me what she'd planned."

Noah's mouth dropped open. "I don't understand. . . ."

"I know. And that's what worries me. You've got to watch her. Don't let her out of your sight." He ran a hand through his thick hair. "The job is everything to her, Noah. She'll do whatever it takes to close a case — even putting her life on the line. She seems especially obsessed with this killer, and he's gunning for her. I'm really afraid he'll kill her."

A shiver of apprehension ran through Noah. "I've never seen her act rashly."

"She's an incredible agent. You'll never work with anyone better. But she's still . . . damaged. It can make her careless. Just keep a close eye on her," Alex said. "Even if you don't trust me, don't take a chance with her life."

"I've got her back. Nothing will happen." Noah picked up his coffee cup and took another sip. The coffee stung his burned tongue. "Is that it?" he asked when he put the cup down.

"Yeah, pretty much."

Before he left, Noah wanted to ask Alex a question. He decided to take a chance. "Why does everyone call you her partner? We have partners for specific investigations, but we don't get assigned permanent partners."

Alex nodded. "Solomon was looking out for her. She hadn't been in St. Louis long when he first paired us. Obviously, I wasn't her actual *partner,* but we worked well together. And to be honest, a lot of the other agents didn't want to work with her." He glanced down. "Then I left. It's not like we were together for years or anything."

Noah nodded. "I guess that makes sense. I just don't want to be . . ."

"Her permanent babysitter?"

Noah didn't acknowledge Alex's conclusion, but he'd hit the nail on the head.

"I wouldn't worry about it. If Solomon continues to pair you with her, talk to him. Tell him how you feel. He's fair. But Solomon doesn't trust many people with Kaely. If you two work well together, Solomon might decide to pair you up frequently."

"Okay." Even though he really didn't want to be tied to Kaely forever, thinking about someone else working with her made him feel a little nauseated. Not a good sign. "I've got to get going," Noah said. "How long will you be in town?"

"I don't know. An old CI of mine texted me. Says he might know something about the case. I'm going to meet him. See what he has to say."

"You can't work this case," Noah said. "You could get in a lot of trouble."

"I know that. I'm not working it. Just talking to one old source. He probably just wants money. If he has anything you can use, I'll turn it over to you. You have my word."

"Are you sure this is safe? Maybe I should go with you."

Alex laughed. "You just reminded me that I can't officially be on this case. If you go with me, you'll just be putting your own career on the line."

"Then at least tell me where you're going."

"An old abandoned school in North St. Louis. Where my CI used to go before it was closed down." He grinned at Noah. "Obviously, the school wasn't great at turning out successful students. My CI has been in and out of jail more than a dozen times."

"He doesn't sound very trustworthy."

"Petty crime. Drugs. He's like lots of other confidential informants. Lost, sad, desperate. Throw him twenty bucks, and he'll find out whatever you need to know."

"Name of the school?"

"Parkview Elementary."

"Okay. Thanks."

Alex drained his coffee cup and put it down. "Don't get too excited. It's probably a wild-goose chase. But since I'm in town, I'll check in with him. Make sure he's okay. Drop some cash." He shrugged. "I just want to help."

Noah stood up. Alex rose from his seat and extended his hand. Noah took it.

"I'll keep in touch," Alex said. "And if anything happens on your side . . ."

"I'll be sure not to tell you."

Alex smiled. "I would expect no less." His eyes searched Noah's face. "Please don't tell Kaely we met. She wouldn't like it. I'm only trying to help her, but she won't see it that way. She'd probably be angry with both of us."

"I don't think I can do that. Lying isn't the way to get her to trust me."

"Just meeting with me will cause a problem," Alex said. "She'll feel we're trying to take care of her. She doesn't like that."

"Tell me about it. Solomon does enough of that for the both of us."

Alex nodded. "Yeah. He's always been that way with her. She tolerates it from him. But not from us."

"Look, I can't promise you anything. I'm sorry."

"Fair enough," Alex said. "Thanks for

meeting with me. You could have said no."

"You're welcome."

Alex turned and started to walk away. But then he stopped and walked back to the table. "For what it's worth," he said, "I didn't stay the weekend at Kaely's. I have a hotel room." Without another word, he left.

As the door to the coffee shop closed behind him, Noah wondered why Alex had felt the need to tell him that. It wasn't any of his business. Yet somewhere inside, he felt a sense of relief. As he headed to his car, he wondered if meeting with Alex had been a mistake. When he told Kaely, which he intended to do, how would she react? Would it damage their partnership?

He got to his car, unlocked it, and slid in behind the steering wheel. As much as he wanted to be honest with Kaely, he wanted even more to be near her.

Twenty-Seven

It took Noah another ten minutes to get to the office. When he entered the conference room, he expected to see Kaely already there, asking where he'd been. But the lights were off, and their files were still scattered on the table where they'd left them.

Noah waited until after nine o'clock to call her. Originally, they were supposed to meet at eight. When she answered the phone, she sounded surprised.

"Oh, Noah. I'm sorry. I got distracted. I'll be there right away."

She hung up before he could say anything. He'd already packed up everything they needed and had half a mind to go without her. Kaely Quinn was never late, and she never forgot an appointment. Obviously, being around Alex Cartwright made her turn into someone else. Someone far less reliable.

He went to get another cup of coffee, and

then sat in the conference room, waiting and stewing. As he went over what he would say to her when she finally arrived, he realized that chewing her out would be a huge mistake. She would immediately wonder why he was so upset. Being late wasn't worth the kind of tirade he'd created in his mind. Would she find out he'd followed her home Friday night? That he knew she'd been with Alex? Would she assume his reaction was out of jealousy? He gulped down his irritation and realized he was on the verge of doing something he'd never be able to take back. If Kaely felt he was crossing the same line Alex had, it would end their relationship. He sighed. How had he gone from wanting nothing to do with Kaely Quinn to being afraid of losing the chance to get to know her better?

When she walked into the conference room fifteen minutes later, he was relaxed and calm. When he saw her, he almost lost it again. For some reason she looked incredible this morning. Her face glowed, and her eyes sparkled. Her auburn hair was pulled up into its usual bun, but loose hair gently outlined her face in a way that made his breath catch in his throat.

"Noah, I'm so sorry. I've been going over the case and lost track of time. To be honest, I didn't get much sleep."

"Find anything new?" he asked, choking back the emotions that surged through him.

She frowned. "No, not really. I'll be interested to see what CIRG comes up with. Maybe their behavioral analysts will see something I've missed." She noticed the boxes on the conference table. "You've already boxed everything up. I'm so sorry. I should have helped you with that."

It took every ounce of self-control he possessed to smile at her and say, "Not a problem. I didn't have anything else to do anyway. Should we load this stuff up and get to the command post?"

She nodded. "I'll get us a cart to put everything on."

She hurried out of the room, leaving him to wonder if she would tell him about Alex. What if she didn't? Did she feel safer with Alex than she did with him? He tried to ignore the sting of insecurity that tried to writhe into his mind. Why did it matter who she preferred? Why did he care?

A few minutes later, Kaely came back with a large metal cart. They loaded the boxes and headed out of the building. Once his car was packed, Noah drove to the CP. He knew the area of town where the closed print shop was located. St. Louis had at least a thousand abandoned buildings, but the city's budget only allowed them to tear down about two hundred per year. That left many neighborhoods looking like they'd been bombed. The vandalism and graffiti certainly didn't help. Thankfully, the closed print shop was in a decent area. Even though the small strip mall where it was located was empty, it hadn't yet been struck by teens who thought destroying property was a form of entertainment.

The front windows were covered with paper so no one could see inside. Most of the cars were parked in back in an attempt to avoid unwanted attention. Although it was obvious something was going on, anyone who was curious would never suspect the building was being used by the FBI.

Noah pulled around to the back so they could unload. After Noah and Kaely showed their credentials to the agent at the door, a couple of guys came out and grabbed their boxes. Noah left Kaely at the door while he parked the car. When he jogged back to the entrance, he found her waiting for him, and they went in together.

His first look at the command post impressed him. Desks and computers had already been set up. There was a large table at the back of the room with chairs around it, obviously for meetings. Noah felt a little twinge of regret at the realization that he and Kaely wouldn't be sharing the case alone anymore, but calling in CIRG was the right move. Their expertise and resources would give them every advantage they could hope for. This was now a group effort.

Noah nodded at Ron Wilson, the assistant special agent in charge from their office. Ron would help oversee the operation. Solomon might stop by from time to time, but he needed to be available for other cases. Ron looked more like a college professor than an FBI agent. Tall and skinny with large black glasses, he was actually a lot tougher than he looked. Ron was here to approve any major decisions Noah made in regard to the investigation. He could also request additional agents from other squads if they were needed. But one of his main roles would be to handle any conflicts between agencies.

Donald Reinhardt was talking to someone Noah didn't know. He assumed it was one of the detectives assigned to the task force by either St. Louis or Illinois. He hoped Reinhardt wasn't planning to fight him for control of the team. Noah was the agent in charge, and Reinhardt would simply have to accept that.

Robbie Mantooth, a local prosecutor, was setting himself up at a desk. He'd be sworn in by a local judge as a Special U.S. Attorney so he could prepare federal subpoenas, affidavits for search warrants, or anything else they might need when they were ready to make a move. Robbie would be replaced by someone else before it was all said and done. They could end up with several attorneys throughout the process, but they needed at least one on site at all times.

Noah wasn't sure who the other people were, but there had to be at least one logistics unit member on all shifts to make sure equipment was working and to help everyone access the ORION case management system. Among the other agents in the room there would also be a ViCAP analyst and a couple of information specialists.

Standing against the wall, watching the team set up, were two BAU agents from Quantico. Noah recognized them. Lela White and Beau Lagoski. He waved at them. They raised their hands and smiled in response. He and Beau had been friends. He didn't know Lela well, but she had a reputation as an outstanding agent. He wanted to talk to them, but first he and

Kaely needed to get set up.

Noah was scouting out desk space when he noticed Reinhardt headed their way, a phony smile pasted on his face.

"Here we go," Noah said softly to Kaely.

"You're the case agent, Noah. You need to establish your authority from the start. Reinhardt is a master of manipulation. Watch yourself."

Noah stuck his hand out as Reinhardt approached. "Good to see you again, sir," he said.

Reinhardt shook his hand and then turned his attention to Kaely. "Special Agent Quinn. SAC Slattery has nothing but good things to say about you. Seems you're doing some outstanding work."

"I'm pleased to hear my SAC is satisfied with my work, sir," Kaely said.

Noah was amazed at how genuine her reaction seemed, especially after everything Reinhardt had done to her.

Reinhardt tossed Kaely a brief nod and then turned his attention back to Noah. "I understand you're the agent in charge, Noah. Although we're still setting things up, I think we're prepared to have you bring us up to date on the case. Are you ready to meet with us?"

Kaely's words about establishing his

authority drifted into his mind. "Actually, I'm not," he said quickly. "Kaely and I will find a place to work, and when we're settled in I'll let everyone know."

Reinhardt didn't seem offended. "Sure. Sounds good. We'll be waiting for you." With that, he turned on his heel and walked over to a younger agent who was working diligently on his computer.

"That's his way of telling you everyone is prepared — except you," Kaely whispered. "Don't pay any attention. Let's find some desks and get set up."

"Okay." He stared down at Kaely. "I want you to speak up in the meeting, okay? I need your expertise and your opinions. We all have to put down our egos for a while so we can catch our UNSUB." He waited for a reply, but she didn't say anything. "You won't let me down, will you?"

"No."

Noah could tell she was distracted. Was it because of Reinhardt?

"Kaely, is something wrong?" he asked.

She looked away. "I know Lela and Beau. It's just . . ."

Noah sighed. "Why didn't I realize? I'm sorry."

She tossed her head back as if she wasn't

bothered by their presence, but he knew she was.

"Lela and Beau weren't involved directly in what happened at Quantico. It's not fair of me to hold anything against them."

"But they didn't speak up for you, did they?"

"No, but I understand why. They were intimidated by Reinhardt — and by the Bureau." She raised her eyes to meet his. "I'll be fine. I promise. And I'll give my input. Just be prepared that Reinhardt won't like it."

"Tough," Noah said gently. "Like you said, he's not in charge here."

Kaely flashed a quick smile. "Good for you. I hope you can keep up that stance. It might not be that easy."

"I know, but I don't like the idea of someone pushing us around when we're dealing with such a dangerous threat. Reinhardt needs to drop his attitude. This isn't about him."

"I agree," Kaely said. "But I don't see that happening anytime soon."

Noah grabbed the handle of the cart and pulled it close to him. "Let's unload and jump into this thing."

As they proceeded through the room, looking for a couple of desks together, Noah reminded himself that he would have to draw on all the experience, confidence, and strength within him as he led this task force. Lives depended on him.

He hated drug dealers. Sniveling little rats, looking to make money from the desperation and hopelessness of their fellow human beings. But from time to time you had to dance with a small devil before you could confront a major demon.

He pulled the vial out of his pocket and smiled. Buying LSD had been easier than he thought. He had it all planned. Kaely Quinn would be forced to confront her nightmares before he finally put an end to her.

It was time to send another message. This time, he'd hit her where it would really hurt.

Twenty-Eight

Most of the people working at the CP were gathered around the table. One of CIRG's analysts was still glued to his computer, doing research work that was vital to the team's success.

Noah and Kaely spent almost forty-five minutes bringing everyone up to date and giving them their opinions as to the next place their UNSUB might strike.

When Noah felt he'd shared everything he could, he asked for questions.

One of the investigators from the police department in Illinois raised his hand. "So you believe the next murder could be someone Agent Quinn knows?" he asked. "Have her friends, family, and acquaintances been afforded protection?"

"The two people already killed didn't know Special Agent Quinn. Their deaths are the result of a copycat killer who is familiar with Agent Quinn's previous caseload, but the victims themselves had never actually met her. At this point we don't feel there's anyone close to Agent Quinn who's in danger." He didn't mention himself, but he had no intention of putting himself in the UNSUB's cross hairs. He planned to stay close to Kaely — and his team.

Kaely nervously cleared her throat. Noah knew this was hard for her, and it made him angry. Kaely Quinn should never feel uncomfortable around other LEOs. She was the most talented agent he'd ever met. The way she'd been treated by the Bureau made him furious. He took a deep breath and forcefully tamped down his emotions. This wasn't the time or place to give in to them.

"It's important to remember that our UNSUB has specific targets in mind. I doubt Kaely's friends fit his narrow parameters. He wants victims who fit previous scenarios. They will have similarities to victims of the crimes mentioned in the poem."

"It sounds like he's already selected them," Lela said.

"We believe that's true," Noah said.

"What about the threat of fire, Agent Quinn?" Beau asked. "You know someone in St. Louis who might be targeted for the fourth murder, isn't that right?"

"Yes, Louis Bertrand," Kaely said. "He's

being closely watched, and he's been questioned thoroughly. We're looking for anyone suspicious who may have contacted him recently." She shrugged. "His is the only case I've been involved in that had to do with fire. But it was done on my personal time, so no one really knows about it. Maybe Louis is the target, but if that were true, our UNSUB would have to know me or Louis pretty well."

"Thanks. You also mentioned something about the Phillip Reagan case," Beau said. "Supposedly it was a suicide, not a murder. Could the UNSUB know something we don't? Could he have been involved?"

"I don't think so," Kaely said. "Our guy just recently went off the rails. Phillip Reagan died several years ago. But as we said, we can't afford to rule it out at this point."

"Do you really think your brother could be involved?" Lela asked Kaely.

She stared at Lela for a moment before answering. "I just don't know. After . . . after my dad . . ."

She stopped and took a deep breath. Noah could see she was trying to gather her courage.

"After my father was apprehended," she continued, "my mother took Jason and me out of the state to start a new life. Jason was just nine years old, but it affected him greatly. He shut down. Became uncommunicative. My mother got him counseling, but it didn't seem to help. When he turned eighteen, he took off. He basically told us he didn't want anything to do with us." She cleared her throat and looked away for a moment. "A friend of mine, a therapist, has been in touch with him occasionally. He says Jason is convinced my mother and I knew the truth about my father. That we kept it to ourselves. Of course, this isn't true, but since he won't talk to me, I can't convince him of that. A few years ago, if you'd asked me if my brother could do something like this" — she swept her hand toward the large incident board they'd set up — "I would have said absolutely not. Now? Well, I just don't know."

"Are you looking for him?" Beau asked.

"I've already done some preliminary work," Kaely said. "He moved to Colorado after he left home. Lived there a couple of years. Then he changed his name and moved again. I believe we can find him, but it will probably take some legwork."

"I'll assign someone to look into that," Ron said. "We'll need some information from you, Kaely, to get started."

"Not a problem," she said. "I'm not sure I

have much more information beyond what I just gave you, but I'm certainly willing to do what I can."

"Thanks, Ron," Noah said. "When we finish here, why don't you get with Kaely and let her give you whatever she has, then turn that over to an investigator? Let them see what they can find out."

"The only other suspects we have right now are friends or family of Michael Edmonds and Archie Mason?" Lela asked.

"As far as Edmonds and Mason," Noah said, "we don't feel either of them are strong possibilities. Archie's family doesn't seem like people who would murder innocent human beings to make a point. And Michael Edmonds's girlfriend, who was pretty insistent that he was innocent, has moved on." Noah pulled two files from the stack and tossed them in the middle of the table. "But we need to follow up anyway. Just in case.

"We're also looking at Jerry Acosta," Noah said, "the reporter who wrote about Kaely in Virginia. As you know, he's here now and was the one who brought us the poem."

"But he's not a prime suspect," Kaely added. "He doesn't fit the profile. I think we need to move him off our list for now."

"Then I take it you've come up with a profile," Lela said.

"A rough one. Nothing official. I'm happy to hear what you've got."

"We've looked over the case materials and have some ideas."

"Kaely, why don't you share your insights first?" Noah said.

Kaely glanced at Lela and Beau before nodding at Noah. "It's tough to profile this guy," she said softly.

"Why do you say the UNSUB is male?" The person asking the question was someone Noah didn't know.

"Most serial killers are white males," Kaely said. "The forcefulness of his language makes me believe he's male. Also, he was able to overpower two victims so far. I would assume he's male because of his physical strength."

"Can you speak up?" the detective from Illinois, Peter Bridges, said. "Go back to your profile."

"Sorry," Kaely said. "I said he's very hard to profile. His MO is copied from previous crimes, and it changes from victim to victim. We're focusing on his motive. What's driving him. His determination to challenge me . . . and then kill me. I can tell you that he's very organized and he's been planning this for a long time. As Lela mentioned, his victims were chosen some time ago. I believe something happened recently . . . a stressor that set him off. Whatever happened brought it to the forefront." She took a deep breath before continuing. "I believe he's somewhere between thirty and fifty-five. I'm a little confused by his age. He seems mature. Either he's younger and very developed emotionally, or he's older. We know that certain experiences increase emotional maturity faster than chronological age."

"What do you mean by being developed emotionally?" Ron asked.

"Because of the patience and planning behind this," Kaely said. "An older person would be more capable of this kind of behavior, yet most serial killers are in their twenties or thirties. There are always exceptions. Like Dennis Rader, who went back to killing when he was in his fifties.

"I believe he has a good job. Is respected. He probably dresses well. Presents himself well. He's smart. Personable. Relates to people. He seems able to move around in public without much trouble. Something about him puts people at ease. He appears to have a lot of time on his hands to plan his crimes. He could be on a sabbatical, or perhaps he's on family leave." She frowned and looked down at the table. "Tox screens on our victims haven't shown any drugs in their systems so, as I said, he's strong enough to physically subdue them." She walked over and pointed at the large cork-board on the wall. "Here's a map that shows the two killings. I've marked the areas I believe are in his comfort zone, but it wouldn't hurt to have a geographic profiler take a look at this." She turned and gazed at the group gathered around the table. "He's connected to me in some way. Obviously I've done something that has really angered him."

"Does this profile point to your brother?" the detective from St. Louis, Jeff Armstrong, asked.

"I don't think so. Can I rule him out completely? No, but my gut says it isn't him."

"But if you haven't seen him in years, how can you be sure?"

"I can't. I'm going on instinct."

"So our UNSUB's signature is his hatred of you?" Beau asked. "Can you elaborate on that a little?"

"Yes. He wants to humiliate me. Eventually, he wants to kill me. But first he has to prove he's smarter than I am. This fulfills his emotional need."

Reinhardt scoffed. Noah scowled at him. "If you have another point of view, we'll be glad to hear it after Kaely's finished."

To his credit, Reinhardt flushed.

Noah looked at Kaely. "Sorry. Go ahead."

Although Kaely didn't flinch at Reinhardt's rude reaction, Noah noticed the knuckles on her right hand turn white as she gripped her pen.

"He's very creative. Used to getting his way. His hatred for me is everything to him. He is completely dedicated to punishing me for whatever crime he believes I've committed. He's a psychopath and has no feeling for his victims." Her eyes swept around the table. "And he won't stop. He'll play this out until the end. To him, the game is everything. And it is a game. A deadly game. He is playing me, and he intends to win."

"Is that it?" Lela asked.

Kaely hesitated a moment before saying, "Yes, for now." She came back to the table and sat down.

Noah nodded at Reinhardt. "Anything you'd like to share?"

Reinhardt stood. "Yes, I would." He grabbed a briefcase next to his chair and put it on the table. Then he opened it and pulled out some papers. After putting his briefcase back on the floor, he cleared his throat and started reading. "I believe the UNSUB is between twenty-five and thirty-five. A loner. Someone who obsesses on people he thinks have wronged him in some way. I see him as someone who either lives alone or is still at home with one or both parents. If he has a job, it's probably part time. Minimum wage. He has a lot of time on his hands to come up with this elaborate plot. Probably reads books about serial killers. That's how he knows about these particular cases. Old car. Probably full of trash." He glanced at Kaely. "I agree with Special Agent Quinn about one thing. He's smart. Probably not book smart, but he has natural intelligence. He's just not living up to his potential. In fact, teachers and people who know him say this very thing about him — frequently."

Noah realized his mouth was hanging open by the time Reinhardt finished. He quickly closed it and then looked at Ron, who seemed just as shocked as he was. This profile didn't make sense to him. Sure, it did seem the UNSUB had put a lot of effort into his plans — and he was intelligent. But the rest of Reinhardt's profile seemed unlikely.

"Agent White and Agent Lagoski, do you agree with this profile?" Noah asked.

Lela and Beau looked at each other.

"We're not sure," Beau said slowly. "We

really haven't had much time to work on a profile."

"We knew Kaely was working this case, so we didn't feel it was our job to profile this UNSUB," Lela said.

Reinhardt's expression turned stormy, and Lela noticed. "But we certainly have confidence in Donald's experience and expertise," she added quickly.

Noah noticed she threw another quick glance at Beau. Noah looked at Kaely. It was obvious she'd seen it too. What was going on?

"I'm really disappointed in the differences in these profiles," Noah said. "We need to be together on this."

"I'm sorry to disagree with Special Agent Quinn," Reinhardt said, "but this is my opinion. It will be up to you to decide who's right. I would think my proficiency in the area of behavioral analysis would speak for itself."

"Let's table these profiles for now," Ron said forcefully. It was obvious he was upset. "We have other things to work on." He turned his head and stared at Noah. "Where do you want to start?"

Noah pointed at Detective Armstrong. "Jeff, you look for the brother. See what you can come up with." He stared down at a list of the people working the case. Then he nodded toward the detective from Illinois. "Detective Bridges, will you and your team look into Edmonds and Mason? Check out friends and family members. We need to be certain there's no one connected to them who might be our UNSUB. As for Jerry Acosta, let's move him to the end of the list for now, but if anyone finds a reason to move him back up, let me know."

Noah stood. "Let's get busy. Everyone has a copy of the poem. Our next victim has already been selected. Kaely, Lela, Beau, and Donald. You're with me. Let's pull this poem apart and see what we can come up with. I think it's our strongest lead right now." His gaze swept around the table. "That's it for now. Let's catch this piece of trash."

As everyone moved toward their stations, Ron walked up next to Noah. "I'd like to talk to you for a moment," he said.

"Get started," Noah told Kaely and the others. "I'll be with you in a minute."

As Kaely, Beau, Lela, and Reinhardt walked away, Noah turned to Ron. "Before you say anything . . ."

"What was that?" Ron said in a loud whisper. "That was completely unprofessional and never should have happened in front of the rest of the group. If you or Solomon had any idea this kind of disagreement might occur . . ."

"Look," Noah interrupted. "I knew there was tension, but I never anticipated that Reinhardt would undermine Kaely like this. I thought he was more professional."

"Well, you were wrong." Ron pointed at him, his face flushed red. "You get this straightened out, Noah. We need to present a united front to the task force. That's not what happened here."

"I agree," Noah said. "I'll take care of it."

"You'd better." Ron turned and walked away.

Noah watched him, wondering just how he was going to handle the situation without one profiler feeling he was choosing the other. Suddenly being the agent in charge didn't seem like such an honor.

TWENTY-NINE

Jerry had just finished his third cup of coffee and was thinking about lunch when the guy from the mail room dropped off the day's stack of mail. Ever since the story came out about Kaely Quinn and St. Louis's newest serial killer, he'd been inundated with letters. Most of them were from nuts who were sure they knew the identity of The Elephant, the public's nickname for the killer. Jerry sent all of them to the police. They'd set up a hotline for tips and were going through all the mail received by the *Journal.*

Not that they needed more help. They were getting deluged by crazies too. Supposed psychics who had important details that the police desperately needed. Unfortunately, they had to investigate every tip that came in, just in case. Of course, he was pretty sure the old woman who was convinced her cat was psychically linked to the killer didn't warrant a visit from the cops. Maybe someone from the psychiatric wing of the local hospital.

He leaned back in his comfortable new desk chair. Banner had moved him from the dark corner where his previous beat-up desk had been situated. Now he was sitting behind a brand new desk near the editor's office. Life had gotten better, and he was enjoying it. He glanced back at John, who sat several rows behind him. John just happened to be looking his way, so Jerry gave him a big smile. John's reaction was less than magnanimous and involved the middle finger of his right hand.

Jerry laughed to himself and removed the rubber band that held the mail together. As it spilled onto his desk, one envelope caught his eye. The block lettering used by the sender was familiar. Jerry felt his chest constrict. He coughed, trying to calm his breathing. Could it be from The Elephant? He got up and tried to look nonchalant as he strolled over to the area of hooks near the door to the newsroom where everyone hung their coats. He found his and reached inside his pocket to get his gloves. With his back turned to the rest of the room, he quickly stuck them into the pocket of his jeans. Then he walked back to his desk, hoping no one had noticed him. He gazed around the room, but everyone was busy working. He sat down and hunched over the envelope, trying to keep it from prying eyes.

He was aware that there would be lots of fingerprints on it already, but he pulled his gloves on anyway, then he grabbed a letter opener from his desk and slid it under the edge of the envelope. Once it was open he carefully removed the folded piece of paper inside, slowly opening it. Sure enough, the familiar print, written in thick black ink, confirmed his suspicions. Another letter from the killer.

Jerry took a deep breath and read the message:

> Jessica Oliphant swinging in a park
> Went so high she began to cry.
> This little elephant called it a day.
> He said good-bye and drifted away.
> Dedicating this one to you, Jessica. How does it feel?

Jerry felt the hairs on the back of his neck stand up. He grabbed his cell phone and found Jacqueline Cross's number at the FBI. When she answered, he quickly told her about the letter.

"Please don't touch it," Jacqueline said. "I'm sending someone from our Evidence Response Team over right away to pick it up."

"Okay," Jerry said. Of course, he planned to keep a copy, but he didn't tell her that.

"Can you hold on a minute?" she asked.

"Sure."

She put him on hold, probably arranging to have an agent retrieve the letter. After a couple of minutes, she was back.

"Now, can you read the message back to me, Jerry? I want to pass it along right away."

Jerry slowly read each word until she had it down.

"Is there anything else?"

Jerry suddenly remembered that the letter containing the poem had a message for him on the back of the paper. He carefully turned it over but the back side was blank. "No, that's it. Nothing else," he said.

"Okay, thanks. Jerry, can you please hold this just a bit? It sounds like a very specific threat. Someone is probably in very real danger. Please. Let our agent in charge check out this message before you publish it. You could be saving a life."

"I've got to notify my editor," he said, "but I'll wait until after you pick this up."

"I'm asking for a day or two, Jerry. We need some time."

Jerry sighed. He had too much at stake. Holding back the note wouldn't work with his overall plan. He'd waited too long for this. "I'll do the best I can," he said, trying to sound as if he meant it. Which, of course, he didn't.

"Thanks, Jerry."

From the tone of her voice, he could tell she knew he had no intention of holding the story. But this was how the game was played. It wasn't his fault.

He said good-bye and hung up. Then he switched to the camera on his phone and snapped several pictures of the letter. After he had several clear shots, he got a plastic bag from the bottom drawer of his desk, thankful he'd bought a box of gallon-sized storage bags just in case he heard from the killer again. He realized that a box of surgical gloves would be a good idea too and decided to buy some when he got off work. After resealing the original letter and envelope, he picked up the bag and hurried to Bannon's office.

Kaely grabbed some of the pizza Ron ordered for lunch and joined Detective Jeff Armstrong at his desk. As they munched on pizza, Kaely gave him all the information she could in hopes it would help him find Jason. Jeff had tracked Jason from Colorado Springs to Fort Collins, where he'd changed his name. He couldn't find anything about him after that. Jeff called the police in Fort Collins and asked for their help. They agreed to go to the last address they had for Jason and interview neighbors to see if anyone knew where he'd gone. In the meantime, Jeff planned to search various databases, trying to find something that would help him locate Kaely's brother. His job was made harder because Jason had stopped using his Social Security number.

"Probably got a number from someone who died," Jeff said. "Employers often don't check the National Death Index when they hire someone. They just accept the number and go on. We're not going to find him that way."

Kaely saw the rest of her team assembling at a small table in the front room. How was she going to work with Reinhardt? Beau and Lela were going to support him no matter what. She dreaded working with them.

Kaely was about to join them when Noah suddenly showed up at Jeff's desk. "Meeting now," he said gruffly.

"What's going on?" Kaely asked.

He shook his head. "Not until everyone's together." Then he walked away.

Kaely's body tensed. Something was wrong. Please, not another killing.

She got up and headed toward the big table with Jeff following behind her. It took only a couple of minutes for the team to gather. The silence in the room was evidence that everyone was worried the news would be bad. Every person who died before they could find and stop their UNSUB was a defeat for them. A person they'd let down. That never got easier.

"There's been another message from the killer," Noah said. "We've got someone from ERT on their way to the *Journal* to get the original note, but this is what it said."

As he read the odd message, Kaely tried to figure out what it meant. A park? Again? She hadn't seen that coming.

"He's going back to Forest Park," Reinhardt said with authority. "We need to get people there . . . now."

"Kaely, what do you think?" Noah asked.

"I would be surprised if he went back to Forest Park. He doesn't seem to be the kind of person who likes to repeat himself."

"Nonsense," Reinhardt said. He pointed at Noah. "We need to send some people out there right now."

Noah scowled at Reinhardt, his lips thin and his eyes narrowed. Kaely was certain Reinhardt was wrong, but she didn't want to argue with him in front of everyone. There was already too much tension.

Finally, Noah said, "Ron, let's send some people to the park to check it out. But not everyone."

Ron nodded his agreement.

"I can dispatch some additional people from our office," Jeff said.

"Do that," Noah said. "You know where the playgrounds are located?"

Jeff nodded. "Take my kids there all the time."

Kaely stayed in her chair, surprised that Noah had so quickly agreed with Reinhardt.

"Ron, why don't you give the detectives some instruction? Tell them what to look for. Donald, go with him. Offer any insight you think is important." As Ron, Reinhardt, and Detective Armstrong got up and walked away, a few other people started to stand.

"Sit down," Noah said in a low voice. "I haven't dismissed anyone else."

He waited until all three men were out of earshot. Then he turned to Kaely. "Okay, now tell me what you see in this note." He handed her the piece of paper with the message.

Kaely felt her face grow hot as everyone at the table stared at her. It was pretty obvious Noah just wanted Reinhardt out of the way. She read the passage out loud. Slowly. *"Jessica Oliphant swinging in a park. Went so high she began to cry. This little elephant called it a day. He said good-bye and drifted away. Dedicating this one to you, Jessica. How does it feel?"*

She let the words run through her head several times, turning them over, looking for the meaning behind them. Finally, she said, "This isn't about Forest Park. It's personal. *I'm* swinging on the swings." She looked at Noah. "I haven't been on a swing since I was a kid in grade school." Realization ran through her, making her tremble. "Park. I attended Parkview School in Des Moines."

Noah made a strange noise, and Kaely turned to stare at him. He'd turned as white as a sheet. "Alex," he choked out.

"Did you say Alex?" Kaely asked. Her heart leapt in her chest.

He nodded. "I spoke with him this morning. He told me he was going to meet a CI at Parkview School in North St. Louis."

"What?" Kaely jumped to her feet. She felt sick. "We've got to get there right away."

"Okay," Noah said. "You're with me." He

yelled out Ron's name. He came running over.

"What's wrong?" he asked.

"We have an agent in danger. Call SLMPD and ask them to send officers to the Parkview School in North St. Louis. Now. We also need backup from the office."

Ron nodded. "Of course. Go."

Kaely and Noah grabbed their coats and ran toward the back door. They jumped into their car just as Reinhardt and Armstrong pulled out. Noah ignored them and turned the car north. Kaely just prayed they would get there in time.

THIRTY

Kaely and Noah actually made it to the school before anyone else. They could hear sirens behind them, so the police weren't far away. Kaely wanted to ask Noah why he'd met with Alex, but she was so afraid for Alex, she couldn't concentrate on anything except getting to the school.

Noah drove around the building, looking for the playground. The place was in bad shape. Broken windows, trash piled up outside, graffiti everywhere. They found the playground behind the school. As soon as they pulled up, they could see someone on one of the swings. It looked as if he was just sitting there, enjoying the day, but the man's posture was wrong. Limp and at an odd angle.

Noah and Kaely jumped out of the car and began to run toward the swings. Suddenly, Noah grabbed Kaely's arm and pulled her back.

"What are you doing?" she asked. When she saw the look on Noah's face, her chest tightened and her heart felt as if it were in her throat.

"Stay here," Noah ordered. "I mean it, Kaely. Don't move."

She looked over toward the swings and felt her knees go weak. She could taste the sour bile that forced its way into her throat as she recognized that dark green coat. Before she knew what was happening, she sank down to the ground. "No. No, please, no."

Noah squeezed her shoulder. Two police cars pulled up and parked next to them. The officers got out and ran toward them. Noah yelled at them to hurry.

"Call an ambulance," he said. "And stay with her. Don't let her near the crime scene for any reason, do you understand?"

The cop closest to them nodded while the other one called for an ambulance.

Kaely watched as Noah jogged over to the swings. He leaned over the body on the swing and put his fingers on Alex's throat. Two more police cars pulled up, with additional officers running toward them. Noah straightened up and gestured wildly at them.

"I need some help!" he yelled. "He's still alive!"

The officers who'd just arrived ran over to Noah, who was removing the chain wrapped around Alex's neck. Then the three of them gently lowered him to the ground. Kaely felt as if the whole world had just stopped in its tracks. She struggled to get to her feet. The young officer who'd stayed with her helped her up, but when she tried to walk away, he pulled her back.

"You need to stay here," he said gently. "Let everyone do their jobs. Interfering won't help."

Rage filled her with a strange kind of strength. She glared at the officer. "Take your hands off me. Now. Or you'll be sorry, I swear it."

She couldn't tell if it was fear or just surprise that made him step back, but when he did, Kaely began to run toward Alex and Noah. She was surprised she was still upright since her legs felt numb. Noah saw her coming and waved her away. She ignored him.

"Don't tell me what to do," she said as she reached them. She dropped down on her knees next to Alex. His face was pale, and there was blood running down his cheek. He looked dead.

"He's got a pulse," Noah said. "I think we made it in time." He gestured toward the swing. "It was set up to strangle him slowly. The more he resisted, the tighter it got." He pointed to the blood. "Someone hit him on the head. That's how he got him into the swing." He looked into Kaely's eyes. "You may have saved him, Kaely. If we'd been even a few minutes later . . ."

Kaely leaned down and put her hand on Alex's cheek, tears running down her face. "It going to be okay," she said. "Hang in there, Alex."

She heard another siren and looked toward the street. She whispered a prayer of thanks when she saw it was the ambulance. The EMTs jumped out, grabbed their equipment, and began running toward them. When they reached Alex, Noah grabbed her and pulled her out of the way. She didn't resist. She wasn't sure she could have moved on her own.

The EMTs began checking Alex over. They gave him oxygen and inserted an IV.

"We need to transport him," one of them said.

"Can I come with you?" Kaely asked.

"Kaely, I really need you," Noah said. "Let them do their job. I need your eyes and your insight. You can go to the hospital as soon as we're done here, I promise."

Kaely felt torn. She wanted to go with

Alex, but she also wanted to catch the person who did this to him.

"Please, Kaely. We might be able to stop him if we can understand what happened here."

"You need to decide, miss," the EMT said. "We've got to get him to the hospital. Now."

"I . . . I'll stay." As soon as the words left her mouth, she wondered if she'd made the wrong decision. She watched as the EMTs carried Alex away on a stretcher.

Noah reached over and took her arm, pulling her toward the swings. "He'll be all right," he said gently. "Now, let's bring him some justice."

Kaely struggled to look away from the EMTs. "What was he doing here?" she asked. "I saw him last night. He didn't say anything about coming here. It doesn't make sense." She exhaled. "I'm sorry I didn't tell you he was in town. I was going to . . ."

"I planned to tell you that I met with Alex this morning. I was just waiting for the right time."

"You said he was contacted by an old CI?"

Noah nodded. "He said he'd put out some feelers, told me he got a text from his confidential informant. I told him he couldn't work this case. He insisted he wasn't, that this CI probably didn't know anything. But Alex still wanted to check up on him. Make sure he was okay. If I'd had any idea he was walking into something dangerous, I would have stopped him."

"I know that, Noah."

Kaely walked closer to the swing set and looked closely at the swing Alex had been tied to. There wasn't anything unusual about it. Just a rusted old swing, but there was a long chain attached to it. The chain that had been wrapped around Alex's throat. It was obvious it had been attached in a way that would have forced Alex to sit up as straight as possible to keep him from being choked to death. No one could sit that way for long. When his back began to hurt, and he slumped, even a little, it would become harder for him to breathe. As he became weaker and weaker, due to a lack of oxygen, it would eventually be impossible for him to remain rigid.

She noticed plastic ties lying on the ground, under the swing. "Were his hands tied?" she asked Noah.

"Yeah. And his feet. I cut the ties off."

"We need to check everything for DNA and fingerprints," Kaely mumbled. "I'm afraid we're not going to get footprints. Too many people running around."

"There was something else," Noah said. He reached into his jacket and pulled out a plastic bag with the crudely drawn picture of an elephant they were used to seeing. Inside the elephant's body was a number 3.

"He wanted Alex to suffer. To take a long time to die. We just happened to get here before it was too late." Kaely shook her head and stared down at the ground. "We almost didn't make it." Her voice broke with emotion.

Noah walked over and put his arm around her. Kaely almost pushed him away, but it felt good to have someone to lean against. She gulped several times, trying to get rid of the fear that seemed to have taken over her entire body. She needed to get her act together and work the case.

"But we *did* make it, Kaely," Noah said, "because you figured out the newest poem."

She looked up into Noah's face. The compassion in his bluish-gray eyes almost made her lose it again. She gently pulled herself out of his grasp just as ERT arrived to go over the scene. Noah went over to tell them what had been disturbed in an effort to assist Alex. She watched as he handed them the elephant picture. As they prepared for the transfer of evidence, she began to think about the UNSUB's latest attack.

He'd tried to re-create the death of Phillip Reagan. But that wasn't the work of a serial killer. It was a suicide. Maybe it wasn't significant, but it was a change from his previous pattern. So what did that mean?

Although she wanted to keep the case foremost in her mind, right now all she could think about was going to the hospital and checking on Alex. Maybe he'd seen the UNSUB and could give them a description. But more than anything, she wanted to sit next to Alex's bed, hold his hand, and tell him everything was going to be all right. Noah was leaning against the car as she approached.

"I'll drive you to the hospital," he said.

"Thanks, but don't you need to get back to the CP? Just take me to my car. That way, you won't have to wait or come back and pick me up. I'm okay. I'll be fine." She suddenly stopped where she was and stared at him, her mind racing.

"What is it, Kaely?" Noah asked.

"He wants to distract me," she said quietly.

"What do you mean?"

"This has nothing to do with a serial killer. He picked a case that was linked to the FBI. But it occurred years ago. Something happened to our UNSUB fairly recently. No longer than six months. I doubt whatever made him snap had anything to do with Phillip Reagan." She paused a moment before saying, "We all agree that he's planned all of this out meticulously, right?"

"Right."

"How could he know Alex would come to town?"

Noah stared at her without responding.

"He couldn't," Kaely said.

"You're right. He chose Alex because he was here. Changed his plans. Changed his victim."

"Because he knew killing Alex would distract me. Give him an advantage." Kaely shook her head. "I'll go to the hospital, but after that I need to get back to the CP. Our killer has strayed from his strategy. That means he might have made a mistake, and we have to find it. As quickly as possible." She grabbed Noah's arm. "We're gonna get him, Noah. I'm sure of it."

Thirty-One

On the way to pick up Kaely's car, Noah listened as she called Ron at the CP and asked him to double check on Louis Bertrand. Noah knew she was worried about him.

"So you definitely think the poem refers to Louis?" he asked after she disconnected the call.

"It's the only arson case I worked, and Louis is someone connected to me. It seems to fit." She was silent for a moment and looked out the window. Suddenly she turned back to look at him. "Wait a minute. There *was* another case. In California. I'd almost forgotten."

"What are you talking about?" Noah asked.

"I hadn't been at Quantico long. There was a series of forest fires set in California, a few miles apart from each other. It began to look like they were being set on purpose.

The FBI was contacted for help. A profile was developed about the arsonist. It was so accurate, they caught the guy a couple of weeks after the profile was given to authorities. I didn't help with it, but I saw it happen."

"I remember that," Noah said. "Donald Reinhardt was responsible for that profile, right?"

Kaely nodded. "Yes, he was. His work was instrumental in catching the arsonist." She was quiet for a moment. "Doesn't fit our UNSUB though. It's too broad. He can't ensure fatalities. Besides, any forests around here are probably out of his comfort zone."

"You're sure?"

"Yeah, I didn't work it, and the help the Bureau gave wasn't widely known. Doesn't fit our UNSUB's MO." She shook her head. "Never mind. I'm grasping at straws."

"How do you feel about Donald's profile for this case?" Noah asked. "Being so different from yours, I mean?"

"I don't know," she said with a heavy sigh. "I'm fairly confident about my profile. How could he think someone with such organization could be . . . disorganized? I don't understand. He knows better."

"I'm not sure he said the UNSUB was disorganized. Just that he was a loser. A loner. Someone who had time to come up with this plan. He thinks he's smart, just like you do. I guess it's just the lifestyle that varies."

"Yeah, I'd say it varies." She appeared to study him, making Noah feel a little nervous. "Do you agree with him?" she asked finally.

"No. Not really." He met her gaze. "I can see it both ways, frankly. But I have to go with you. I've seen you work, and I have confidence in your abilities. Reinhardt has had some wins, but not like you." He smiled at her. "His visit to Forest Park won't help his cause much."

"I'm glad he went to Forest Park," she said quickly. "As I've said before, I'm not always right. Covering both places was the smart move."

"Very magnanimous of you."

"No, just being practical."

Noah stifled a smile. Kaely's relentless logic was as soothing as it could be frustrating. She seemed to be recovering from the shock of finding Alex at the school, but Noah felt confused. Was she actually in love with him? There was certainly something between them. Something strong. Maybe her rejection wasn't based on how she felt toward him. Maybe it was just as she'd said

— she didn't want any romantic entanglements right now. He found himself fighting a twinge of jealousy, but it didn't make any sense.

He wasn't in love with Kaely Quinn. He had to admit that he had feelings for her, but it wasn't real love. Not like he'd felt for Tracy. That love was so big, so strong, he didn't have room for anyone else. He couldn't see himself with another woman — ever. Surely what he and Tracy had only happened once in a lifetime.

He realized his attention had wandered, and he shifted back to the case. "So now we need to take a close look at the next attacks," he said. "What about that next verse? After fire? Sounds like poison to me."

"To me too," Kaely said. *"Four little elephants sat down for a meal. One took a bite and then said good night."*

"Have any ideas about this one?"

"I've gone over and over it," she said. "I never worked a case with poison. I know it happens, but usually it's not a serial case. Just a husband or wife trying to get rid of a spouse so they can collect insurance money."

"The only serial poisoning I can think of was the Tylenol scare in the eighties. You probably weren't even born then."

"No, I wasn't," she said. "John Davis came to Quantico and talked about it. Fascinating. He also talked about how he and another guy started the Behavioral Analysis Unit back in the day. They used to call it the Behavioral Science Unit. The Unabomber was one of the first major cases they profiled."

"I heard him too. He and his team coined the term *serial killer.* At first they called them 'sequence killers.' "

Kaely suddenly grabbed Noah's arm, causing the car to swerve.

"Hey," he hollered. "What are you doing?"

"Noah, is that it? I mean, I didn't work the Tylenol case, but I listened to John Davis. So I'm connected in a way. I wasn't involved directly in the case, but the FBI was."

Noah glanced at Kaely. Her face was white, her eyes wide with terror. "Is he planning to randomly poison people? That would make it almost impossible for us to anticipate his next move."

"Surely not."

"But it's possible." She turned away for a moment. "While I check on Alex, you let everyone at the CP know our concerns, okay?"

"All right, if that's what you want. But

shouldn't we concentrate on the next threat instead of jumping ahead?"

"If he decides to copy the Tylenol poisonings, we need to get ahead of it. Now. We've done everything we can about the threat of fire. Louis is secure."

Kaely was quiet during the rest of the ride. Noah was worried about her. Whoever the UNSUB was, he wasn't just waging war on innocent victims. He was doing everything he could to destroy Kaely. Noah was determined to make certain he didn't succeed. He had no intention of letting some psychopath kill Kaely Quinn.

After Noah let her out at the CP, Kaely got her car and drove to the hospital. After parking, she went inside, found the front desk, and asked for Alex's room number. The woman she spoke to informed her that he had just left the ER and was being transferred to a private room. She told her to have a seat and she'd notify her when she could visit him. About thirty minutes later, Kaely had a room number. She rode the elevator upstairs, praying he was okay. The last time she'd seen him, he'd looked terrible. She couldn't get the image of his pale face out of her mind. If Noah hadn't told her he'd found a pulse, she would have assumed they were too late.

When she got out of the elevator, she went to the nurses' station. One of the nurses came up to see what she wanted.

"I'm here to see Alex Cartwright," she said, showing the nurse her credentials. "But I also wanted to talk to his doctor."

"The doctor is with him now," she said. "If you'll wait just a minute . . ."

A dark-haired woman in a white coat walked up to the station. The nurse, whose name tag read *Cindy,* nodded at her.

"Dr. Silver, this woman is here about Mr. Cartwright. She wants to find out his status."

The doctor turned toward Kaely. "I'm sorry, but I can't release any information about Mr. Cartwright unless you're family."

Kaely reached into her pocket and pulled out her creds again. "Not blood, doctor," she said. "But family nevertheless. He's my partner."

The doctor smiled. "Why don't you come over here with me?" She gestured toward a waiting room just off the corridor. Kaely followed her into the small room. When the doctor sat down, Kaely took the chair next to her.

"Agent Cartwright will be fine. He sustained a blow to the head, but it's not serious. His neck has bruising and a few cuts, but there wasn't any permanent damage to the throat. If he hadn't been rescued when he was, we'd be having a very different discussion. As it is, I'm keeping him the rest of today and overnight. I want to make sure there aren't any lasting effects from a lack of oxygen."

"Thank you, Doctor," Kaely said. Relief flowed through her like a flood. "Can I see him?"

"Sure, but don't stay too long, please. He needs rest. And no stress. If he gets excited . . ."

"I won't upset him, I promise."

"One of your people is with him now. He's collecting his clothes, taking DNA samples and hair samples."

"An agent from our Evidence Response Team. Standard procedure."

"Yes, I believe that's who he said he was. He should be through any minute now." She frowned at Kaely. "If you're the person who will pick him up in the morning, just call first and we'll let you know what time he'll be released. He needs to take it easy at home for a couple of days, but I get the feeling from Mr. Cartwright that he has no intention of taking that advice. Maybe you could convince him?"

Kaely wanted to assure the doctor, but she knew Alex well enough to know the last thing he'd want to do was lie around. There wasn't anything anyone could do about it when he made up his mind.

"I take it from your silence you have little hope he'll follow my instructions?"

"I can't say that for certain, Doctor, but Alex doesn't do well with inactivity. I'll do my best to make sure he's careful. You have my word."

The doctor smiled again. "This isn't the first time I've worked with law enforcement. Beyond a doubt, you're my most stubborn patients. I guess I'll have to accept your rather feeble assurance since that's probably the best I'm going to get."

The doctor held out her hand, and Kaely shook it. After the doctor got up and walked away, Kaely headed for Alex's room. She fully intended to keep her promise and do everything she could to keep Alex calm, but as the doctor suspected, she wasn't certain it was possible. Right now, she was just grateful he was alive. The killer had made a big mistake. Alex was a trained FBI agent. He could have noticed something that would help them catch this killer. Maybe the UNSUB's trail of death would come to an end today.

Thirty-Two

When Noah got back to the command post, everyone seemed busy. Reinhardt was talking to Detectives Armstrong and Bridges. Noah was headed their way when Ron intercepted him.

"Armstrong and Bridges have some information about Michael Edmonds, the nurse in prison for killing four patients."

"Oh yeah? What's up?"

"Seems Mr. Edmonds was adopted. About three months ago, his biological father popped up. Contacted Edmonds. Even visited him in prison."

Noah frowned. "What are you saying?"

"This guy, his name is" — Ron looked down at a piece of paper in his hand — "Marvin Chambers. Seems Chambers has a long rap sheet, and he's angry. Says his son is innocent. A guard at the prison overheard Chambers telling Edmonds he would 'get the people who put you here.' "

"Really?" Did they finally have a lead? "Where is he now?"

"We're looking. He seems to have dropped off the map."

"We need everyone on this," Noah said. "We have to find this guy right away. Put out a BOLO on him. Name, description, any known vehicles registered to him. You know the drill."

"I'll take care of it," Ron said. "Do you want me to call a meeting?"

"Yeah, we need to brief everyone and talk about the poem. Kaely and I have some concerns."

Noah could tell Ron wanted to ask more questions, but instead he gave one of the agents working at a nearby desk instructions about issuing the order to be on the lookout for Chambers. Then he began to inform the team to meet at the conference table.

Noah stood where he was, trying to figure out what he was going to say to them. Should they go after Chambers — or should they concentrate on the killer's next move? Noah had been honored to be named lead agent on this case, but he needed to make the right decision here. With authority came great responsibility. And that responsibility weighed heavily on his heart and mind.

■ ■ ■ ■

When Kaely got to Alex's room, an agent from ERT was just leaving. After showing her credentials to another agent guarding Alex's room, she pushed open the door. He was sitting up in the hospital bed. When he saw her, he gave her a rather strained smile. He looked tired. Not himself.

"How are you?" she asked.

"I feel like I've been bashed on the head and strangled. How are you?"

In spite of her concern for him, Kaely laughed lightly. "I'm fine. Just worried about you."

Alex reached up and grabbed her hand. "Seriously, I'm gonna be okay. The doctor says there's no permanent damage. I'll recover completely."

"I know. I just talked to her. But she also said you need to take it easy, Alex. Don't push it. I want you to come and stay at my condo while you're recuperating. It's a perfect place to recover, and you'll be safe there."

"Thanks, Kaely, but I don't think I'll need to do that. I still have that room at the hotel, and I have no intention of lying around for two days anyway."

"You're going to need protection when you leave. I'm not sure the hotel is the safest place for you."

"I can take care of myself."

"Yeah, I saw how you took care of yourself. Besides, it's policy. We have to make sure our UNSUB doesn't come back and try to finish the job. You know how it works."

Alex's expression tightened. Kaely knew that look. "Please work with us, Alex. We just want you to stay safe." She reached over and brushed a lock of hair off his forehead. "And you've got to listen to the doctor. If you don't . . ."

"If I don't, what? I don't have a concussion. My head's fine. No damage to my throat or vocal cords. Lying around isn't going to change anything." He let go of her hand and shook his finger at her. "And as far as brain damage, you know me. I'm not any more damaged mentally than I was before that creep wrapped a chain around my neck."

"And here I was hoping somehow you'd actually improve."

"Funny. Knock the injured guy."

She closed her eyes for a moment and sucked in a deep breath. "Look, don't fight us. Take the doctor's advice like an adult. I know it's hard for you to sit back, but if anything happened to you because of me . . ."

"Because of you?" Alex shook his head. "Of course I'm worried about you, Kaely. But people are being murdered and my job — and yours — is to keep them safe if we can. It's what we're trained for." His eyes locked on hers. "You wouldn't step back before you got your guy — and neither will I. But I will be as careful as I can. You have my word."

"Your SAC may have something to say about it, you know. Solomon's going to tell him what happened. You'll probably be ordered back. Not only for your own safety, but also because you're not supposed to be working cases right now."

"Guess I'll face that if it happens."

Kaely didn't need an ability to read people to see that Alex had already made up his mind. When he got like this, there was no way to reason with him.

"Okay," she said with a sigh. "I guess that's the best I'm going to get." Kaely leaned closer to him. "I need to know what happened, Alex. Everything. I'm hoping you can recall something that will help us."

He blew out a quick breath. "After he hit me, I can't remember . . ."

"Start at the beginning. Why were you there?"

He frowned at her. "I got a text from Fish. One of my old CIs. Do you remember him?"

"Sure. You talked about him a lot. Wasn't he pretty unreliable?"

Alex nodded. "Yeah. But I'd sent out some feelers looking for information. I thought there was a slight chance he'd come through."

"And if he couldn't, you planned to make sure he was eating and taking care of himself?"

Alex shrugged.

"You're a good man, Alex Cartwright," Kaely said gently. "But it almost got you killed."

Alex tried to sit a little straighter in the bed, and Kaely saw him wince. He was obviously still in pain. "I know now it wasn't Fish, but at the time I had no reason to think otherwise. Except . . ."

"Except what?"

"The message was spelled correctly. Fish's spelling is atrocious. I should have caught it, but it just didn't occur to me until later."

"ERT has your phone?"

Alex nodded.

"Do you remember what the message said?"

Alex squinted with an effort to remember. "It was something like *I heard you're looking for information about The Elephant. Meet me at the playground at Parkview School in North St. Louis. I may have information.*" Alex shook his head. "That's as close as I can get it."

"No specific time?"

"No, but that was normal for Fish. I was always supposed to go immediately to meet him when he texted me. As soon as I could, I headed over there."

"Alex, how many people know about Fish?"

"Almost everyone I worked with. Since I never used his real name in public, I didn't see the need to keep my relationship with him private."

"And you went without questioning who this really was?" Kaely asked. She was angry at him for being so naïve. "You should always take backup in a situation like this, just in case. You know better."

"I really didn't think he had any pertinent information, Kaely," Alex said again. "And at the time I really thought it was Fish." He rubbed his face with his free hand. His other arm was hooked up to an IV. "It was stupid. I realize that now."

"Were you going to tell me you met with Noah?"

"I don't know. Maybe. I was just trying to protect you."

"I don't want you to *protect* me, Alex." She sighed in frustration. "Between Solomon, you, and Noah, it's a miracle I'm allowed to get out of bed in the morning. Seems all my FBI training was for nothing. I don't need it with you guys watching over me."

He didn't respond to her comment, just began to finger an unopened container of green gelatin sitting on the tray in front of him.

"Okay, let's go back," Kaely said, trying to keep the frustration out of her voice. "Tell me what happened after you got there."

"I got out of the car and walked around the building, trying to find the playground. I turned a corner and spotted the swings. But suddenly someone came up from behind me and hit me on the head. Hard. I passed out. When I came to, I was on the swing with the chain around my neck." He lowered his voice. "I was really scared, Kaely. To keep the chain loose I had to sit perfectly straight. And I was woozy from the hit on the head. Every time I started to slump, the chain tightened. Toward the end,

I'd almost decided to give up. Just relax and let nature take its course."

This little elephant called it a day. He said good-bye and drifted away. Kaely shivered even though the room was warm. "Can you remember anything about him, Alex? Even the smallest detail could help."

He shook his head. "I'm sorry, I can't. He never spoke, and I didn't see him. The doctor said from the way he hit me he was probably of medium height. Strong. Right-handed."

"That's not much help."

"I know. Sorry I can't tell you more."

"Okay. Maybe ERT will come up with something," Kaely said, choking back her disappointment. She'd expected him to have more information, but she knew he was doing his best and didn't want to push him.

"Is there anything I can do for you before I leave?" she asked.

"No, but thanks. You need to get back to the CP and work the case. I'll be fine. Really. With my watchdog outside, no one can get to me."

"You call me tomorrow morning when you're ready to go, and I'll pick you up."

"Thanks. Now get going and catch this guy." Alex reached up to pat his thick blond hair. "He messed up my hair, you know, and

I can't abide that. You know how much I like my hair."

Kaely grinned at him. "Yeah, I know. You hated it when we worked cases in bad weather. Especially when it was windy."

He returned her grin. "I have my priorities."

"I'm relieved to see you haven't changed." She bent over and kissed him on the cheek. "I'll call later to check on you, okay?"

"Sure, but make it after dinner. I'll probably be taking a nap." He laughed abruptly. "I can't believe I just said that. I haven't had a nap since kindergarten, but I feel one coming on today."

"That's because your body is telling you what it wants. It's pretty good that way. Learn to listen."

"Yes, ma'am." Alex saluted her.

"That's more like it." She patted his shoulder. "I'm so glad you're okay, you big goof."

He smiled at her, but Kaely noticed he wouldn't meet her eyes for more than a few seconds and his right hand tapped lightly on the bed. Signs of deception. She tried to chalk his actions up to her imagination, but her concerns weren't so easily vanquished. Was there something Alex wasn't telling her?

Thirty-Three

Once the team was gathered around the table, Noah asked Detectives Armstrong and Bridges to fill them in on Marvin Chambers. Armstrong took the lead and laid out the information they'd gathered.

"We're looking for Chambers," he said. "We feel he could be our UNSUB. The timeline is right. He finds his son about three months ago — then discovers he's in prison. Starts insisting he's innocent. This could be the trigger that started his campaign against Agent Quinn."

"Why would he seek out Quinn?" Reinhardt asked. "Why not the judge . . . or his son's attorney?"

"Jerry Acosta wrote an article that insisted Kaely single-handedly brought Edmonds down," Lela said. "Targeting her makes sense to me."

Noah frowned at her. "I don't know. He just found his son. Why would he be so emotionally invested? Shouldn't it take a while for them to form a bond strong enough to warrant this kind of commitment?"

He wished Kaely were here. She could see this much more clearly than he did. Maybe Marvin Chambers was their UNSUB, but for some reason it just didn't feel right — and this guy certainly didn't fit her profile.

"Do you have any leads as to where Chambers is?" he asked Armstrong.

"No, not yet. He seems to be hiding. Moved out of his apartment a couple of weeks ago. Just disappeared. We're checking his phone, his bank, the DMV, the Department of Labor in case he's got a job, and the post office, in case he's filed a change of address. We'll also check fingerprints. Maybe he's been in prison. We also need to issue subpoenas for visitation records at his son's prison. Get surveillance videos of Chambers and copies of any mail coming from or going to Chambers from the prison."

"Good. Make sure you get all the proper warrants." He gestured toward Robbie Mantooth. "Keep everything legal, Robbie."

"I will," he said, giving Noah a big smile full of overly bleached teeth. Robbie was a small guy. Short and thin. But underestimating him was a mistake. He was a bulldog when it came to his job. Noah wasn't worried they'd get in legal trouble with Robbie around.

"I want to talk about Agent Cartwright," Noah said to the group, "but first I want to see if we've come up with any other leads."

"I think we've got a lead on Agent Quinn's brother," Jeff said. "Police in Fort Collins talked to his next-door neighbor, a nice elderly lady who likes to keep tabs on the neighborhood."

"A busybody?" Noah said, grinning. "Great." Nosy neighbors had helped the FBI in more cases than the Bureau could count. "What did she say?"

"She used to take care of Jason's . . ." Beau paused a moment and quickly perused a report he held in his hand. "Excuse me, *Darrin McDonald's* dog. A chocolate lab named Fancy. Seems Fancy has diabetes and needs regular injections. We're looking at veterinarians in Colorado. Hopefully, we can locate Fancy — and Jason."

"Great work," Noah said. "Anything else before we talk about what happened to Agent Cartwright?"

"We're ruling out anyone connected to Archie Mason," Lela interjected. "His family still believes he's innocent, but there's absolutely nothing that indicates a propensity for something as twisted as our UNSUB is doing. They're a nice family that has a hard time believing their son and brother is capable of rape. None of them have been out of the state lately. There's just nothing there."

"Super," Noah said. "Anything that narrows our list helps."

Peter Bridges raised his hand, and Noah nodded at him. "I know you said we should put Jerry Acosta at the end of our list, but this guy concerns me," he said. "He's followed Agent Quinn from one town to another. He will do anything to promote himself, and he's obsessed with writing a book about her father. What better way to inject himself into her life than to become a serial killer, forcing her to confront him?" He looked around the table. "Right now, I'm checking with his friends and coworkers, trying to see if they feel he's capable of doing something like this." He pulled some papers out of a file. "Agent Quinn told me that during the first murder, Acosta may have actually been at the Bureau, but after talking to the ME, I think Acosta could have done it and then gone to the Bureau. The ME set time of death about five to six hours before the body was found." He studied Noah for a moment. "If you want me to back off of him, I will. I just felt compelled to take another quick look."

Noah frowned at him. "I'm not convinced he's our guy, but if your gut tells you something else, stay with it — for now, anyway. You're right about one thing. No one seems to benefit more than he does from the emergence of this UNSUB."

Peter nodded.

After checking to see if anyone else had new information, Noah said, "As you know by now, we found Agent Alex Cartwright at an abandoned school in North St. Louis. Thankfully, he's alive and recovering. If we hadn't arrived in time, we would have lost him."

"Can you describe the scene to us?" Lela asked.

"Sure. ERT is there now, so we'll have more details when they complete their investigation." Noah told the group everything he could remember. He ended with, "The chain was around his neck, and his hands and feet were bound. As long as he sat up as straight as he could, he could breathe. But if he slumped even a little, the chain would tighten."

"I don't understand something," Beau said. "Was Agent Cartwright conscious when the UNSUB tied him up? I mean, if he wasn't, wouldn't he have been asphyxiated almost immediately?"

"I . . . I don't know the answer to that question. Maybe the UNSUB waited to apply the chain after Agent Cartwright had somewhat regained consciousness."

Silence around the table made it clear others also had a problem with the scenario. Noah had to admit it didn't make sense. Before anyone could make another comment, the back door opened and Kaely walked in. Noah waved her over.

"We're talking about the situation at the school," he told her as she approached them. She took an empty chair next to Noah.

"I just left Alex at the hospital," she said. "Unfortunately, he doesn't remember anything about the UNSUB. He was unconscious after sustaining a blow to the head. When he came to, he was trussed up on the swing."

No one said anything for a moment, but several people exchanged looks. Kaely noticed.

"Is something wrong?" she asked.

Reinhardt, who'd been unusually quiet since the meeting started, cleared his throat. "Has it occurred to you, Agent Quinn, that if he'd actually been unconscious, he would be dead? From what Noah tells us, the chain was set up to strangle him if he didn't keep himself upright. Hard for an unconscious person to do."

Kaely frowned. "I'm sure there's an explanation. Maybe the UNSUB waited until he started to come to and then put the chain around his neck. He wanted Alex to suffer. To panic. Difficult for an unconscious person to do." The last sentence was said with a hint of scorn.

"Maybe," Beau said, "but it's a good point. One that needs to be examined."

"Tell us why Agent Cartwright was at the school," Reinhardt said to Kaely.

"He got a text from one of his old CIs — or at least he thought it was from him. He was told this person had information about our UNSUB."

"And he didn't tell anyone else?" Lela said. "That's not protocol."

"He told me," Noah said, "but he didn't think this CI really had anything we could use. He wasn't concerned."

"He was way out of line," Reinhardt said abruptly. "He had no business interfering in this case."

Noah nodded but didn't say anything. Reinhardt was right. Unless his SAC had given him permission to join their case, he wasn't supposed to be involved. Alex could get in big trouble for his actions.

Noah looked over at Kaely. He knew she wanted help, but he wasn't sure what he could do. "Let's get back to looking for our UNSUB," he said. "We're not here to criticize one of our own. Thankfully, Kaely was able to figure out where our UNSUB would strike next. That's the reason Agent Cartwright survived."

He hoped Reinhardt would take that as a warning that if he continued, Noah could point out Reinhardt's erroneous assumption that the UNSUB's latest murder would be carried out in Forest Park.

"I suggest we direct any further questions about what happened to Alex himself," Kaely said. "Can we move on? I think we need to concentrate on the next verses in our poem. I'm really concerned about the fifth verse."

"Before we look at that," Noah said, "what's going on with Louis Bertrand, Ron?"

"I visited with him," Ron said. "Finally got him to shut down the restaurant for a while. He won't leave town, but we've got him under surveillance. He's secure."

"We can assign some officers to watch him too," Jeff said.

"Thanks, Jeff. I'll talk to you privately after the meeting. I'd appreciate the help."

"Thank you both. That's a huge relief to know he's safe," Kaely said. "Now I'm really concerned about the next verse in our poem, as I haven't worked any poison cases. The only connection I have is sitting in on a lecture by John Davis back at Quantico. He talked about —"

"The Tylenol poisonings in the eighties," Reinhardt finished. "Surely not. I mean, that could be . . ."

"Disastrous," Noah said.

"Do we need to issue a public warning?" Beau asked. "I mean, I realize it would probably cause a panic."

"Yes, it would, and since this is only a guess at this point, we need to know a lot more before we do anything." Noah nodded at Reinhardt. "You've done a lot of research on the Tylenol case, Donald, and you're friends with John Davis. Maybe you could share some insights. Give us some suggestions."

"Sure. I'd be glad to, but can I have some time to write something up? I want to be thorough. TYMURS happened a long time ago."

"Sure. All of you need to press hard on whatever you're working on. I'll send out for supper."

As everyone got up and hurried back to their desks, Noah felt unsettled. He had no reason to suspect Alex's story wasn't true, yet it didn't seem plausible. But why would he lie? Maybe he should talk to Alex himself. Could he have something to hide?

Thirty-Four

After an update from Ron about the attack at the school, Solomon asked Grace to put him in touch with the SAC in Detroit. He wanted to let him know what happened to Alex and that he was recovering.

A few minutes later, his phone rang and he picked it up. "I have Special Agent in Charge Paul Gladstone for you."

"Thanks, Grace," he said. "Put him through."

Solomon heard a click. "Paul?" he said.

"Yes. What can I do for you, Solomon?"

"I'm calling about Alex Cartwright. As I'm sure you know, he used to work with us. Not sure if he told you he was coming here during his leave of absence. You've probably heard we're trying to take down a serial here?"

All Solomon heard was silence. "Did you hear me, Paul?" Had he lost the connection?

"Yes, I can hear you," Gladstone said finally. "Of course we know about the case you're working. Everyone does. I'm just a little concerned about Alex. Great agent, but the past month or so he seemed to lose concentration. It's like he was somewhere else. Then he requested leave but wouldn't tell me why. Said it was personal. We tried to get him to stay, but he had made up his mind. Something happened, Solomon. Whatever it was took him back to St. Louis. Can you tell me why you felt the need to call me?"

Solomon explained what had happened at the playground — the *Reader's Digest* version. "He's recuperating nicely. The doctors say he'll be fine."

"I'm happy to hear that, but I think you need to keep a close watch on him, Solomon."

"What do you mean? Do you think we need to be worried about him?"

A deep sigh came over the phone. "I don't know. Frankly, I wish you'd talk to him. Maybe you'll get more out of him than I could. You had a good relationship with him, right?"

"Yeah, we did. I'll see what I can do."

"I really hate to see him throw away a stellar career." Gladstone cleared his throat.

"He shouldn't be getting into your case without my permission, you know."

"I know that. I don't think he meant to. I'm thinking this experience will force him to sit back and take it easy for a while."

"Well, let's hope so. He's walking a dangerously thin line. I'd appreciate it if you could keep me updated."

Solomon promised to keep in touch, then thanked him and hung up. Was there something going on with Alex? Should they be worried? He was determined to uncover the truth. He picked up the phone and called Grace.

"I'm going to the hospital," he told her. "I'll be gone for an hour or two."

"Sure, boss," she said.

Solomon grabbed his coat and car keys and headed out of the office. He and Alex had been close, and Solomon was convinced he could find out what was really going on.

Noah was doing his own research about the Tylenol case when Detective Bridges walked up to his desk. He looked up. "Yes, Peter?"

"You asked me to follow up on a Dr. Richard Barton?"

Noah had forgotten about Kaely's friend. He didn't suspect him of anything, but he wanted to be thorough. Make sure there wasn't anything there to be concerned about.

"Yeah, I remember now. What did you find?"

"As Agent Quinn said, he was in Des Moines during the first murder. I asked someone from the PD there to check with his neighbors. . . ."

"Neighbors? I don't understand. I believe he lives here."

"Yes, he does, but he has a house there too. His next-door neighbor said he plans to move back to Des Moines someday."

"Probably when he feels Kaely doesn't need him anymore," Noah said, more to himself than to Bridges.

"Well, anyway, he was there. The neighbor talked to him. She said his car was in and out of the driveway until the day he flew back to St. Louis. I think you can cross him off your list."

"I didn't really suspect him," Noah said. "I just felt it was smart to check out anyone Kaely is close to."

Bridges handed him the report. "I also found Marvin Chambers. He's not our UNSUB. He's been in the hospital for a week now. Cancer."

"So there goes another possibility," Noah said. "At least we don't have to spend any more time on him."

"What do you want me on now?"

"Why don't you see if Jeff needs help finding Jason Oliphant? I'd really like to know if we can rule him out as well."

"Or know if he's our UNSUB?"

"Yeah. I hope for Kaely's sake it's not him. That would be hard to take. A serial killer for a father . . ."

"And a brother who follows in his father's footsteps?"

"Exactly."

"Okay. I'll get back to you."

"Thanks, Peter."

Noah sat back in his chair and gazed around the busy room filled with the *click click click* of fingers on computer keyboards or voices talking on the phone. What did they have? Was the UNSUB really planning to carry out mass poisonings? It would be harder to pull off now, but not impossible. Noah remembered hearing about a case where someone threatened to put cyanide in the beer at a pub where FBI agents regularly hung out. Since they were all eating at the CP and he picked different restaurants every time, he doubted this was the plan. There was no way for the UNSUB to guess what place he'd order from next.

His mind drifted back to the Tylenol case.

The killer actually removed containers of Tylenol from the stores, took them home, added poison, and then took them back and put them on the shelf. The first victim was a twelve-year-old girl. She was home from school, sick, and her mother gave her Tylenol, just like any concerned parent might do.

Noah ran his hand through his hair. Twelve years old. How could someone do something so heinous? Of course, he'd seen the evil humans do to each other, but it still shocked him. Maybe the day things like this didn't bother him anymore would be the day he would need to get a different job.

"Noah?"

He jumped when someone called his name. He turned around to find Reinhardt standing next to his desk.

"The write-up is ready. Just wanted to look up a few things, make sure I had it right."

"Thanks, Don." He shook his head. "Boy, I hope we're wrong about this."

"I don't see how we could stop it, Noah, with all the different stores and different kinds of groceries or medicines."

"I know." Noah sighed and stood up. "At this point all we can do is our best."

"Sometimes our best isn't good enough."

"We need to pray that this time it is."

Reinhardt didn't say anything, but his expression mirrored the uncertainty in Noah's mind. It seemed this case was going to get much, much worse before it got better.

When the guy from the mail room dropped off the late mail on Jerry's desk, he immediately noticed the box with the same block-style letters. Jerry grabbed it and turned around in his chair to see if Banner was still in his office. He was just sitting at his desk. Didn't look too busy. Jerry thought about opening the box himself, but at the last second he decided to let Banner do it. Give his editor a thrill. It should only make him value Jerry more.

First he took a picture of the writing on the box with his phone. Then he pulled a pair of the latex gloves he'd just bought from his desk drawer, picked up the box, and walked over to Banner's office door. When he knocked, Banner looked up and motioned for him to come in.

"We've got another one, boss."

Banner's sour expression disappeared. He almost looked happy. Almost. "What is it?" he asked.

"I thought you might like to open it." He

held out the pair of gloves to his boss.

"Thanks, Jerry."

Banner took the gloves and slid them on. Ever since the *Journal* started writing about The Elephant and posting the missives he sent them, their subscriptions had tripled. Life was good for Jerry and Banner.

"Is there a way I should do this?" Banner asked. "I don't want to destroy evidence."

Jerry could have told him that the best thing would be for them to call the FBI and let them open it, but they might not tell them what was inside. And they couldn't risk that.

"Just don't destroy any writing," Jerry said as if he were an expert on the subject.

Banner smiled and nodded. He picked up a letter opener and cut through the mailing tape that held the box shut. Then he carefully pulled it off and slowly opened the lid.

The blast blew out the windows in Banner's office and knocked staff out of their chairs in the outer room.

Banner and Jerry would end up being the *Journal*'s next headline.

But they'd never know it.

Thirty-Five

Reinhardt and Noah told everyone to meet at the table, but Peter held up a finger asking for some additional time. Noah nodded at him, and then headed to the back of the room.

"Don's going to tell us what he can about the Tylenol case," Noah said as everyone took their seats. He looked around the table. "If anyone has any other idea as to what case our UNSUB is referring to, please share. This was the only one we could tie to Kaely, but it doesn't seem to fit our guy's MO."

"I've gone over every case I've ever worked," Kaely said, "and there aren't any poisonings. It seems like a stretch, thinking it's the Tylenol case just because I heard John Davis talk about it at Quantico."

"Most poisonings are one-on-one," Noah said. "One family member trying to get rid of another. Usually there's money involved.

This doesn't sound like something our UNSUB would be interested in." He nodded at Don. "Go ahead. Tell us anything you think might help us."

"I'm not exactly sure what it is about this case that will assist us in finding our UNSUB since he has a different motive and a different signature," Reinhardt said, "but here's a quick overview of that situation." He looked down at a piece of paper in front of him. "The case was referred to as TYMURS by the Bureau, a portmanteau of *Tylenol* and *murders.* It happened in 1982, and there were seven deaths. The first was a twelve-year-old girl who stayed home from school because of a cold. Her mother gave her extra-strength Tylenol. The girl collapsed and died in her bathroom.

"Next to succumb was a twenty-seven-year-old postal employee. After his death, the man's brother was so upset he gave himself a headache. Both he and his wife took Tylenol and died. Thanks to the work of two sharp firefighters who realized the deaths were related, the Tylenol bottles were confiscated and were found to contain potassium cyanide."

Reinhardt's eyes swept over everyone at the table. "Cyanide inhibits the blood from taking oxygen from the lungs and transporting it through the body. The victim becomes starved for oxygen. Blood pressure crashes and the heart stops." He paused and pursed his lips before saying, "God help us if our UNSUB is going to copy TYMURS."

"But because of this case, product packaging was changed, right?" Ron asked. "Wouldn't it be difficult for someone to duplicate these poisonings?"

Reinhardt shook his head. "Maybe more difficult, but not impossible. Although the person behind the Chicago deaths used a powdered form of cyanide, it's soluble. It could be injected into something. Fruit. Vegetables. And we can't rule out other packaging. How many of you have opened something like a jar of mayo or salad dressing and wondered if you heard that seal break?"

Some uneasy looks were shared by those around the table. Noah had to admit it had happened to him, but he'd convinced himself the product was probably alright. He'd never do that again.

"See? It could be done." Reinhardt cleared his throat and went back to his notes.

He was getting ready to continue when Ron's phone rang. He looked down at it and frowned. "Just keep going," he said. "I have to take this." He got up from the table and walked away. Noah could hear him talking on his phone, but he couldn't make out what he was saying.

"Chicago police, Illinois police, and the FBI all worked the case," Reinhardt continued. "More than one hundred LEOs pored over every bit of information they had. The makers of Tylenol pulled the product off the shelves. No one was ever charged for the Tylenol deaths. Investigators' number-one suspect moved away. He's still considered to be the person behind the poisonings, but the evidence needed to indict him was never found." Reinhardt turned his notes over. "Here's a brief profile, although, as I said, I'm not sure what this has to do with our case. The UNSUB was profiled as a loner. Someone who had probably failed in many areas of his life: jobs, romance, social situations. A white male in his late twenties or early thirties. As with all of these cases, something happened. A precipitating stressor — a *trigger.* Could be the loss of his job, girlfriend, or wife. The death of someone close to him."

One of the analysts raised his hand. Noah couldn't remember his name. "Is there always a trigger in these cases?"

Reinhardt nodded. "In my experience there is. I must say that I've seen a few cases where someone had a life-changing experience years earlier but buried it until something brought it to the forefront. Something that made them feel as if the abuse . . . or whatever . . . just happened. That makes it harder to uncover the original trigger."

The analyst nodded and thanked him.

"Anyway, the Tylenol guy feels life has given him a raw deal, and he wants someone to pay — but he doesn't want to get his hands dirty. He's a coward. So he found a way to kill from a distance. Davis's profile pointed out that he might have a disability. Could be in therapy for psychological problems. Was probably the kind of person to write letters to those in authority, complaining about what he considered to be the injustice in the world. As it affected him, of course."

"I believe there was at least one other poisoning case linked to product tampering," Noah interjected.

"Yeah," Reinhardt said. "A woman gave her husband extra-strength Excedrin laced with cyanide. Then she put tampered bottles of medicine in one particular store. She killed an innocent woman before she was caught."

Noah sat back in his chair. "So what do we do if our UNSUB starts murdering random consumers? Is there anything that could help us stop him before he starts?"

"If there is, I can't find it," Reinhardt said matter-of-factly. "We should probably alert grocery stores and pharmacies to be particularly careful and stay on the lookout for someone who might be tampering with products. But we can't count on every employee to be vigilant or even to know what to look for. I also think we need to ask hospitals to watch for any unexplained deaths, ask them to test for cyanide. Unfortunately, that only applies to people who are already impacted."

"The profile for the UNSUB sounds more like the one you presented," Lela said hesitantly. "But he's hiding behind other profiles, making it hard for us to see him."

Noah glanced at Kaely, who'd been noticeably quiet. He wondered what she was thinking. He was pretty sure she was still confident in her original profile.

"How far in advance could our guy have tampered with these products?" Beau asked.

"Good question," Reinhardt said. "Cyanide is pretty corrosive. He couldn't plant the items very far in advance. He'd have to do it when he was actually ready to kill."

"Should we give this story to the press?" Jeff asked.

"Not yet," Noah said quickly. "We'd start a panic. Besides, we're not sure this is what our UNSUB is planning. However, I agree with Don. We should start contacting stores and pharmacies — and the hospitals."

"What about shutting down sales of cyanide?" Robbie Mantooth asked. "Sorry. I know I'm just an attorney, not trained like you are, but I just wonder if we could cut this off at the source."

"It's a good idea," Reinhardt said, "but cyanide is incredibly easy to obtain. Cyanide and cyanide-containing compounds are used in pesticides, among other things, and dye. Drug companies also use them. It's even in the pits of some fruits. Once we have a suspect, we can certainly check to see if he purchased cyanide, but checking ahead of time? It would be tough. Where would we start looking? There are just too many ways to appropriate it."

Noah sighed audibly. "So is there anything here you think *will* help us, Don?"

Reinhardt was quiet for a moment. Finally he said, "Except for the suggestions already mentioned, I don't think so. I'm afraid it's the best we can do."

Noah bit his lip and stared down at the table. "Okay," he said after a long pause. "Let's get started. Detectives, please start with the places Don suggested. You'll need help from your departments."

"What do you want me to do?" Kaely asked.

"Stay here. I want to talk to you." He waved his hand at the rest of the people gathered around the table. "Move quickly. We may not have much time."

"Hold up."

Noah looked up to see Ron standing at the other end of the table. His face was white. It was as if he'd seen a ghost.

THIRTY-SIX

After Ron told everyone about the explosion at the *Journal*, all Kaely could think about was that she'd missed it. The UNSUB had copied the Unabomber. Even though Louis seemed like the right target, she should have at least entertained the possibility that it could be someone else. Gilbert Banner and Jerry Acosta were dead because she'd made a mistake.

Noah was talking to Ron, but he'd asked her to stay in her chair until he could speak to her. She wondered why. He seemed to think Reinhardt had a better feel for this UNSUB than she did. She was trying not to take it personally, but it was difficult. She'd tried to read him, but it was impossible to figure out what he was reacting to. The case? Reinhardt? Her? What just happened at the *Journal*? Frankly, she wasn't sure why she was still part of the task force. Maybe that's what Noah was going to tell her. Fine with her. She'd just go home and work the case on her own.

But as soon as she had the thought, she knew it wasn't what she really wanted. She liked being part of this team. She enjoyed the energy. Being part of something special. But it was frustrating when she felt others were going in the wrong direction. Looking in the wrong places.

Noah waited until almost everyone was gone before he said something to her. "You're too quiet. What are you thinking?"

"Well, for one thing, I missed it. I should have considered the Unabomber. Acosta and Banner are dead because I was so focused on Louis."

Noah sat down in the chair next to her. "That's ridiculous. Knock it off. None of us considered anyone except Louis. This isn't your fault. You're no good to me when you start getting down on yourself."

"I'm sorry." Kaely looked away. "I'll try not to blame myself if you tell me not to, but I intend to learn from this. Unfortunately, that won't help Acosta or Banner."

"No, it won't, but I'm glad you're not planning to punish yourself for something out of your control." Noah frowned. "Why Acosta? I mean, that guy made your life hell. Why would someone who wants to destroy you take out a man who caused you so much trouble?"

Kaely sighed. "I don't think it had anything to do with that." She shook her head. "It was the perfect setup. I should have seen it."

"What do you mean?"

"The UNSUB set Jerry up. Sent him letters. So when the package came . . ."

"He never thought to be suspicious."

Kaely nodded.

"Wow. Believe me, I don't respect our UNSUB, but that was pretty smart."

"Yeah, it was."

"Which points back to your profile."

Kaely didn't respond.

"Kaely, you were bothered about something even before we got the news about what happened at the *Journal.* What's on your mind?" Noah asked softly. "The truth."

She raised her head and met his gaze. She could see the sincerity in his face. "Look," she said, "I think Reinhardt's profile is wrong. I stand by mine. Someone who has planned all this out is very organized and smart. Not a loner. Not a loser. I think Reinhardt is confusing our UNSUB with the perpetrators connected to the cases he's imitating."

"And I completely agree. I'm going with

your profile." He frowned at her. "Is there something else bothering you?"

She was relieved to hear he supported her conclusions. She tapped her fingers on the surface of the table, asking herself the same question he'd just posed. Finally, she said, "I think we're headed in the wrong direction. Wrong for us. Not necessarily for him." She stared at the carefully constructed incident board full of crime photos and notes. "The Tylenol case? Really? Is this guy actually going to travel around the city poisoning food or over-the-counter medicine? Does that sound like one of his preplanned scenarios? It would be unlike anything else he's done."

"Well, I guess he could have prepared for this ahead of time."

Kaely shook her head. "He might have planned it, but he couldn't set up the poison. Remember what Reinhardt said? Potassium cyanide is caustic. It eventually degrades anything it comes in contact with."

"Yeah, you're right." Noah rested his chin on his knuckles, staring at the papers in front of him. He straightened in his chair. "And I see what you're saying. It doesn't fit with the rest of his actions. It's too random. He can't control it — and he can't pick his victims. Are we following the wrong case?"

He leaned back in his chair. "What did we miss?"

"I'm not sure we missed anything. But while we're running around, checking out grocery stores and pharmacies . . ."

"We're not looking in the right direction."

"That's what I think. I believe this clue is bogus. He's trying to distract us."

"So, what do we do now? We can't make a mistake here. If we're wrong again . . ."

Kaely didn't respond. She didn't need to.

Jeff, who'd stayed at his desk during the meeting, rushed up to the table. "Sorry to interrupt, but I've been on the phone with a detective in Fort Collins."

"About my brother?" Kaely asked. The look on the detective's face caused a frisson of fear to shoot through Kaely. It couldn't be Jason. It just couldn't.

"Another one of Jason's neighbors mentioned Durango, Colorado, so I contacted the Durango PD. One of their detectives began calling vets in the area. I think we found him."

Kaely swallowed hard. She wanted to ask Jeff for details, but she couldn't seem to find her voice. As if he realized she needed help, Noah spoke up.

"Are you sure it's him?"

"Yeah. A guy named Joe Tucker has a

chocolate lab with diabetes. The Durango PD went to his apartment manager with a picture of your brother from an old driver's license. She identified him as Joe Tucker."

"Did they talk to him?"

Jeff shook his head. Even though Kaely felt the need to prepare herself for what was coming, she was shocked by what she heard.

"His landlord said he left his dog with a friend and took off two weeks ago. Told her he was going to visit his sister."

Kaely gasped. "What?"

Noah reached over and grabbed her arm. "Listen to me. That doesn't mean he's here. And it certainly doesn't mean he's our UNSUB. He may have used that excuse just to get off work . . . or because he didn't think his landlord needed to know his business. Don't jump to conclusions."

"It's pretty hard not to," Kaely said, having to work hard to croak out the words. "How could he hate me so much?" She felt tears fill her eyes, and it made her angry. She was better than this. More professional. She had to look at Jason as just another possible suspect. Period. She frowned at Jeff. "Did you happen to find out where he works?"

He nodded. "An auto body shop. A rather specialized one dealing with vintage cars.

Pretty prestigious place, I guess."

"He always loved cars," Kaely said quietly. How odd that his interest in automobiles hadn't changed that much.

"We need to put a BOLO out on Jason," Noah said. "I'm sorry, Kaely, but we have to know where he is. Jeff, get a copy of his driver's license and his vehicle registration. Send it to me. Then contact law enforcement with that BOLO."

"Right away."

"I know you need to follow up on this," Kaely said to Noah. "I understand and I agree."

"I'll take care of it," Jeff said. "I'm really sorry, Kaely."

"This doesn't mean our UNSUB is Jason," she said, giving Jeff as much of a smile as she could muster.

He nodded and walked away.

"What do you really think?" Noah asked. "Is it possible?"

Kaely perched on the edge of her chair. The muscles in her back were so tight they hurt. She intertwined her fingers on the table in front of her, trying to ignore the pain. "I . . . I don't want to believe it's him," she said. "My profile stands, but I have no idea if it fits Jason. I haven't seen him for years. I don't know who he is now. But . . .

in my gut . . . it just doesn't feel right." She tried to change her position, but it didn't help. "Obviously I'm too conflicted to look at him honestly. Maybe I should remove myself from the team."

"No, Kaely. We need you. Take the rest of the night off. Relax. I think you should distance yourself a bit. Get some sleep. You'll see things more clearly in the morning."

Although she wanted to argue with him, Kaely felt the need to get away from the group, think about the case on her own. There was something she wasn't seeing. Something out of place. But what was it?

"Okay. I'll take you up on that." She locked her eyes on his. "But call me if you need me. And please keep me updated."

"I will. You can count on it. And if you hear from Jason . . ."

"Trust me. I'll let you know right away."

She stood. "I'll be back first thing in the morning." She glanced over at Reinhardt. He'd probably feel as if he'd won some kind of victory if she left, but she couldn't be bothered by that. The case was the important thing. Not Reinhardt's overblown ego.

She'd just started to head out when the back door was pushed open with so much force it shook the windows around it. Solomon Slattery walked in, his face creased in a deep scowl. He pointed toward her and Noah.

"Stay right there. We have a situation."

He strode quickly to where Noah and Kaely waited. Everyone on the team stopped to stare at him, and work came to a standstill. When he reached them, Kaely could only stare. Had there been another death?

"What's going on?" she managed to choke out.

"I just left the hospital," Solomon said. "Alex Cartwright is gone."

THIRTY-SEVEN

Kaely stared at her boss, trying to understand what he'd just said. She grabbed the edge of a nearby chair to steady herself. "What do you mean he's gone?" she asked, her voice shaking like an old woman's. "Is he . . . is he dead?"

Solomon's eyes widened. "No. No, Kaely. I'm sorry. Let me start again. Alex left the hospital."

"How is that possible?" Noah asked. "We had an agent stationed outside his door."

Solomon grunted. "Seems Alex talked the agent, a friend of his, into getting him a milkshake from the cafeteria. Our agent felt it would be okay since he wouldn't be gone long and the nurses' station was nearby. We think Alex slipped out right after he left. No one noticed him take off."

Noah blew out a quick breath of air. "So, what does this mean? Why would he do something like this?"

"I talked to the SAC in Detroit. He couldn't get Alex to explain the reason for his leave of absence. He's worried that Alex is in crisis."

Solomon pulled out a chair and sat down while Kaely slipped back into her own chair. What was going on? This wasn't Alex. He'd always been her rock, so steady and reliable.

Kaely noticed Jeff headed toward them, but Solomon glared at him and waved him away. It was clear he wasn't ready to bring this new situation to the team. Jeff stopped in his tracks, and then turned around and hurried back to his desk.

Noah cleared his throat. "I really hate to say this, but I have some concerns as well."

"What are you talking about?" Kaely demanded.

Noah closed the file in front of him and then swiveled his chair toward her. "Look, Kaely. The scenario with the swing. It really bothers me. If he was really unconscious, he would have choked to death."

"Explain what you mean," Solomon said.

"Whoever set up the swing carefully constructed it so that if the victim slumped even a little, the chain would cut off his air supply. So how could Alex have been unconscious when we arrived? Or how could he have been unconscious when he was attached to the swing? Shouldn't he have been dead?"

"Now wait a minute," Kaely interjected, unable to keep the anger from her voice. "He obviously passed out right before we got there. There's no other explanation. We saved his life. Why are you trying to make it sound like something else?"

"You're probably right, but there's another explanation. One you won't want to consider."

She could hear the suspicion in his tone, and indignation rushed through her. "You think Alex is our UNSUB? That's ridiculous." She turned toward Solomon. "Tell him. Tell him it couldn't possibly be Alex."

Solomon paused for a moment. Not long, but just long enough for Kaely to understand the implications.

"How could you possibly —"

"Now hold on a moment," Solomon said harshly. "Don't tell me what I'm thinking. I can do that for myself, thank you."

Kaely was ready with a sharp retort, but when she saw the look on Solomon's face, she clamped her lips together. Solomon rarely got angry with his agents, but when he did, it was time to shut up.

"You profiled this UNSUB as very organized," Solomon said. "You said he could get around easily in public. That he's smart."

"And you called him creative," Noah said, picking up Solomon's thought. "Successful. Had a good job. Something that people respected." He leaned toward her. "You said something happened to him lately. A stressor that set him off. That he could have a grudge against you. That what set him off could have been the loss of someone close to him. And that he may have recently taken off time from his job."

"You also said we'd be surprised when we caught him, Kaely," Solomon said more gently.

Kaely took a deep breath, trying to rein in the anger that threatened to break through. How could they think Alex had anything to do with killing innocent people? Didn't Solomon know him better than this? "I remember what I said," she said evenly. "I also profiled our UNSUB as a psychopath." She caught Solomon's eye. "Do you really believe Alex Cartwright is the kind of person who would kill innocent people just because I wouldn't date him?"

Solomon frowned at her. "Did you think your father was a serial killer?"

The impact of his statement was like a punch to the stomach. It took her breath away. She wanted to respond, wanted to yell at him, but she couldn't find her voice.

Noah picked up on her distress. "That's not really fair," he said to Solomon.

"Maybe not," he agreed. "But I want her to understand that no matter how smart we are, how well trained we are . . . even if we have incredible natural talent . . . we can be fooled. It's happened to me. It's happened to you." He stared at Kaely for a moment. "I'm not trying to be harsh. I'm really not. But I want you to be prepared."

"For what?" Kaely managed to croak out. She cleared her throat. "So, is my brother trying to kill me? Or one of my very best friends? Which should I hope for?"

"It might not be either one of them," Noah said gently. "We have other suspects."

"And one by one we're eliminating them." She took a deep breath and exhaled slowly. "I'm afraid to look at who's left."

"Right now we have to consider the possibility that our UNSUB plans to come after you. He certainly has confrontation as part of his end game."

"He can't touch me," Kaely said. "I'm around you guys all the time, and when I'm not with you I go home to a gated community. Our UNSUB can't get in. There's a guard at the gate." Even as she said the words, she wondered. Ernie had allowed Alex in. Of course, he knew Alex and he thought he was protecting her. Would he let someone else in without her permission? Should she worry?

"I'm going to send someone out to talk to the guard and to make sure you're safe," Solomon said.

His declaration didn't leave an option for discussion. Solomon said it as if he were quoting the law — and he was. The law of Solomon. Kaely kept her mouth shut.

Solomon stood. Kaely could see the conflict on his face. This was hard for him.

"I need you to be as professional as you can, Kaely," Solomon said. "Put your personal feelings aside. You've always been good at that." He shook his finger at her. "I need Special Agent Kaely Quinn to show up and do her job. I know I'm asking a lot, but I'm certain you can do this. I have absolute faith in you. Always have. After filling Ron in about what's happened, I'm going back to the office. If I hear anything else or if we find Alex, I'll let you know immediately."

With that, he turned and walked away, leaving Kaely feeling somewhat shell-shocked. Still, she understood exactly what Solomon meant. She prided herself on being analytical, not swayed by unhelpful emotions. This case had ignited something inside her she hadn't known existed. She had to get a grip. If she couldn't, she was useless. More people would die.

"Look, Kaely," Noah said. "Solomon wasn't trying to be unkind. . . ."

Kaely held up her hand to stop him. "I know, and he's right. About everything." She paused for a moment, thinking. Finally, she said, "I'm going home. I need some quiet time to regroup and think everything through. Right now my thoughts are jumbled up and confused. I have to sort them out. Make sense of this case. Of myself." She offered Noah a small smile. "I'm not any good to you right now, Noah."

"I think taking some time for yourself is a great idea," Noah said, "but I don't want you leaving until your security guard has been interviewed and your place has been cleared." He pointed at her. "You stay right here. Don't go anywhere. Drink some coffee. There's still some barbeque left from supper."

She nodded and leaned back in her chair. "Just chilling out, okay?"

"Okay." After staring at her for several seconds, Noah turned and walked into the main room where people were working hard, trying to bring this nightmare to an end.

Once she was certain Noah was busy, Kaely pulled some files close to her. She'd been over and over the information, but she still felt there was something she wasn't seeing. Going over these again wouldn't hurt.

She jumped when her phone rang. She dug it out of her pocket. Richard. She answered.

"Hey," he said. "How's it going?"

"Not well. I'm actually going home in a bit. I need a break."

"Well, this may be perfect timing," he said. "Remember how you said you wanted to have me over for supper?"

"Of course I do," she said. "I'm sorry. I've been so busy, there just hasn't been time."

"I know that," he said. "So why don't I bring supper to you? Tonight? I could be there by the time you get home with nice, hot Chinese food. My treat. And if you're too tired to visit, that's fine. I'll leave the food and take off."

She started to turn him down, but at the last second she realized his suggestion sounded wonderful. One of her best friends, her favorite food, and no strings. "You know what? That sounds awesome. You've got a deal."

"Good. When will you be home?"

"Believe it or not, my place is being secured. It shouldn't take more than an hour before they allow me to leave here."

"Secured?" Richard said. "Is everything okay?"

"Sure. Just protocol. Nothing to be concerned about." Richard was already worried about her. The last thing she wanted to do was make him any more paranoid.

"Okay, if you say so," he said skeptically. "I'll be there in an hour or so. See you then."

"See you," she said. "And Richard?"

"Yeah?"

"Thanks."

"You're welcome, Kaely. Happy I can do something to make you feel better."

She chuckled. "You have no idea how much this means to me."

"Good-bye, honey."

"Bye." She disconnected the phone call and smiled to herself. A few hours to rest her mind and enjoy Richard's company sounded fantastic. She not only liked being around him, she could talk to him about anything. Maybe he could give her a new perspective. She so desperately needed the kind of help he could give her.

About an hour later, Noah came back. "Your place has been checked out. You can go home now."

She stood up. "Thanks. I'll be back tomorrow. I know we don't have a lot of time." She reached over and put her hand on his arm. "If you hear anything about Alex . . ."

"I'll call you right away."

"Thank you. I still don't believe —"

"I know. You're probably right." He offered her a small smile. "Don't worry about it."

"As if that's possible." Kaely strode toward the back door, grabbing her coat on the way out. She ignored the eyes that followed her. She had to figure this out and fast. Not only for anyone else targeted for death, but also for Alex. She needed to clear him . . . or stop him. And right now she wasn't completely sure which scenario she'd have to face.

He watched her leave. Although he was too far away to see the expression on her face, he was certain she was confused. Good. That was exactly what he wanted. If he could get her to look in the wrong direction, she'd never see him coming. Kaely Quinn was too smart for her own good. He'd never be able to defeat her head-on. The only way to bring her down was to distract her — and then pounce when she wasn't looking.

The time had almost come. The end of Jessica Oliphant.

Although it wasn't his job, Reinhardt offered to go with some of the detectives who planned to look for recent large sales of potassium cyanide. Research had given them several local leads. Although, as Reinhardt had said, it was probably a waste of time, they had to do something. It was possible they might get lucky and find that proverbial needle in the haystack.

Several other detectives were working the phones, contacting hospitals, pharmacies, and grocery stores. The list of places was long and would take some time.

Noah wasn't ignoring what Kaely had said — that product tampering was a red herring, something that would distract them from what was important, but they had to act as if the threat were real. They had no choice. But if she was right, what was it the UNSUB didn't want them to see? Noah riffled through the files on the table, looking for something . . . anything . . . that would give him some clarity. He'd noticed Kaely doing the same thing. If there was something they'd missed, he wasn't seeing it. Who hated Kaely so much he'd go to this much trouble? The hate would have to be strong. Really strong.

"Excuse me."

Noah jumped at the sound of Ron's voice. He hadn't seen the ASAC approach the table. "Sorry," he said. "I've been going through these files again, hoping to find something that will send us in the right direction, but so far, it hasn't happened."

"We're all doing the best we can," Ron said, patting him on the shoulder. "We'll get him. I'm certain of it."

Noah leaned back in his chair. He'd been fighting a stress headache all day and had been popping over-the-counter pain meds, trying to win the battle in his head. Unfortunately, he seemed to be losing. "I hope you're right," he said.

"Kaely went home?"

Noah nodded. "She needed some time by herself to think through the case. She's our best weapon. If she can just figure this out, we really will catch this guy."

Ron sat down in the chair next to Noah. He noticed Ron's bloodshot eyes and the tension in his face. Obviously, the stress was getting to him too. Ron was a nice-looking man with an old-fashioned burr cut, lean and fit for forty-eight. But today he looked a lot older. Noah understood. He felt as if he'd aged a few years himself.

"I'm glad Reinhardt's out for a while," Ron said. "Between you and me, he's driving me nuts. He seems to think he should be in charge of this investigation."

"I know. I'm trying to handle him, but I really didn't appreciate his profile. I'm relying on Kaely's input. Not his."

Ron nodded. "Good. I agree. I think Lela and Beau are afraid to disagree with him. We'll get a break when he goes back to Quantico, but they have to face him every day."

"Yeah, you're right. That must be tough."

"I still find it strange that he arrived in town just three days before the letter arrived."

Noah felt his stomach clench. "What are you talking about?"

Ron frowned at him. "I said several things. What are you referring to?"

"I thought Reinhardt came to town after someone at the police department contacted him about the first murder."

"No. He called me on Monday. Told me he'd flown into town on Sunday. He just happened to be here when the first murder occurred."

Noah tried to digest what Ron had told him. "Did he say why he was here?"

Ron's eyes narrowed. "No. To be honest, I didn't think much about it. He has several friends here." He paused a moment. "Did he tell you he got here on Tuesday?"

Noah shook his head. "No. I got that from Solomon."

"He told Solomon he arrived on Tuesday?"

"I don't know," Noah said. "But we'd better find out how he anticipated murders that hadn't happened yet."

Ron's face went white for the second time that night, and he pulled his cell phone out of his pocket.

Thirty-Eight

It was almost seven-thirty when Kaely pulled into her parking spot. She'd talked to Ernie when she pulled up to his guard shack. He'd already been questioned, and the complex searched. Everything was secure. Ernie had apologized for letting Alex in without contacting her. Ernie was a simple man. Easy to read. It was obvious he went along with Alex because he thought he was helping. She was glad they'd spoken. She wasn't angry with him, but she made it clear he wasn't to ever let anyone else in without her knowledge. He promised her it wouldn't happen again and informed her Richard was already here.

"Do you still want me to let him in whenever he comes to visit?" he'd asked.

Richard had permission to come and go as he pleased. She came close to telling Ernie the same held true for Noah, but she wasn't quite ready to give him the same kind of access she'd given Alex and Richard.

Someone tapped on her window, causing her to jump. It was Richard.

"I'm sorry," he said, stepping out of the way so she could open her door. "Did I frighten you?"

Kaely smiled at him. "Not really. Lost in thought. Wasn't paying attention. Sorry."

He returned her smile. "I stopped by that Chinese place you like. We have more food than we could possibly eat in one sitting. Might take two or three. Sound good?"

Kaely sighed, grabbed her purse and her briefcase, then got out of the car. "You have no idea how great that sounds. Thank you, Richard. How do you always manage to show up when I need you?"

He chuckled. "I have no idea. I just had a feeling you might like some company."

She'd thought she wanted to spend the evening alone, but now that Richard was here, she was glad. Maybe talking things out with him would help. It usually did.

"I'll get the food and follow you up," he said. He hurried over to his car, grabbed several bags, and joined Kaely.

"Wow. You really did buy out the restaurant," she said. "This could feed me for a week."

"That was the idea. You forget to eat, you know."

"That's what Alex always said." Her voice caught in her throat.

Richard studied her for a moment. "Looks like we really do need to talk. Let's get you inside, full of Chinese food, then you can tell me what's going on."

"Okay." Kaely blinked away the tears that filled her eyes. "Thanks again, Richard. I'm so grateful you showed up tonight."

"Me too. Now, move it."

She laughed. "Yes, sir." Kaely hurried over to unlock the door. Once it was open, Richard carried in the bags and dumped them on the kitchen table. After Kaely poured a couple of glasses of iced tea, they sat down to eat. Kaely was hungrier than she'd realized, and after some crab rangoon, she finished off one helping of orange chicken and another of honey-walnut shrimp before she'd had enough. She decided tonight was not the time to worry about whether or not the food was fried. It was a night for comfort food, and this fit the bill perfectly.

"That was delicious," she said with a smile. "I owe you big-time. When this case is over, I'll cook something for you. I promise."

"Sounds good," Richard said. "You sit

there while I put the rest of this in the fridge." He gestured toward the coffeepot. "Do you want me to make some coffee?"

"That sounds great. I might actually have some pumpkin spice creamer that hasn't expired yet."

Richard's lips twitched. "For you, that's quite a feat."

"Hush."

After putting the food away, Richard checked inside the refrigerator door and pulled out the container of creamer. "Hey, you're right. In fact, you still have three days until this has to be thrown out. I'm impressed." He poured them both a cup of coffee and added the creamer.

Kaely giggled. Thanks to Richard, she already felt better. It had always been that way with him. Even before her father was arrested, Richard and Bella were people who'd encouraged her, who'd told her she was special. Her parents weren't the nurturing type. They did their duty, and they were there for her and Jason when it came to providing the physical necessities of life, but praise was rarely forthcoming.

A few minutes later, Richard carried two cups of hot coffee to the table. "Okay, so what's going on? Tell me what's bothering you."

His comment brought back the emotions she'd felt when she heard Alex had left the hospital. She told Richard that the UNSUB had targeted Alex, but that they'd reached him before it was too late. He'd met Alex several times and looked as shocked as she felt.

"Thank goodness you figured out what the second message from the killer meant," he said. "You obviously saved his life."

Kaely nodded. "But now someone on the task force thinks Alex is our UNSUB."

"He left the hospital. We don't know where he is. He probably had another reason. Kaely, Alex isn't a serial killer. Seriously. I mean, I realize he was upset when you told him you couldn't return his . . . affection. But to do this?"

She clasped her hands together and rested her chin on her fingers. "I don't know what to think. I mean, it all adds up, Richard. I supplied the trigger, he's taken leave. Is unaccounted for . . . But how could someone who said he loved me want me dead now?" Before Richard could respond, she waved his comment away. "I know. I know. It's happened. But these were people who were already unstable, had serious issues with self-esteem. I never saw that in Alex." She fixed her gaze on him. "Did you?"

Richard didn't hesitate. "No. I didn't. I absolutely can't believe it." He rubbed his forehead, something he did when he was thinking. "You mentioned he got a message from Fish telling him to go to the school? Why would he tell you that it didn't sound like him?"

"You mean why bring up a detail like that if he's lying? People don't generally do that."

Richard nodded. "And how could he have put that chain around his own neck? Do you really think he could have set that up by himself?"

"I don't know. Our Evidence Response Team will take that setup apart. If it turns out Alex couldn't have done this alone, they'll tell us. But right now . . . well, I'm confused."

"If it makes any difference, I don't buy it," Richard said. "I believe what he said about Fish. I remember that he used to talk to him a lot. Makes sense that he wanted to make sure he was okay. He hadn't seen him for months."

Richard was a talented therapist. His reassurances meant a lot to her and helped to confirm that she wasn't just seeing what she wanted to see. "Some people on our task force don't seem to believe Alex should have survived. He was unconscious when we found him. They say he should have been dead."

For the first time, doubt flashed in Richard's eyes, and it made Kaely's stomach lurch.

"Obviously he'd just passed out," Richard said. "I mean, right before you arrived. It's the only answer."

"That's what I've been saying, but between you and me, it would take a miracle of timing." She hesitated before saying, "They think he did it himself and pretended to be unconscious."

Richard picked up his cup and took a long, slow sip of coffee. Kaely knew him well enough to realize he was weighing the facts. Trying to find the truth.

"Richard, be honest with me. Is there any chance he's our UNSUB? What about Jason? He's disappeared. Said he was coming to see his sister. Isn't he a better suspect?"

"Yes, he is. In fact, I tried to tell you I was concerned about him."

"Except he doesn't fit my profile. He's been working in an auto body shop. Not exactly the successful professional person I envisioned."

Richard shrugged. "I guess it's how you see it. To people in that profession, working at a vintage car shop may be considered successful. It's just a guessing game at this point." He sighed and took another sip of coffee. "Weren't you looking seriously at that reporter? He seems like someone who would do anything to get what he wants."

"You haven't heard?"

Richard frowned. "Heard what?"

Kaely reached up and took out the band holding her hair up. She shook it out. "Jerry Acosta received a package from our UNSUB. Took it to his editor's office . . ."

"Oh no." Richard's eyes were wide with shock.

Kaely nodded. "It exploded. Killed him and his editor."

"Was anyone else hurt?"

"The last I heard there were other injuries but none of them are life-threatening."

Richard exhaled sharply. "I guess that's something." He looked confused. "Why would your UNSUB want to kill Jerry Acosta? I mean, he wasn't really a positive influence in your life."

"I think he set him up from the beginning. He sent him letters, they're making him famous, he looks forward to them. Then when the package comes . . ."

"He doesn't stop to think about it."

"Right." Kaely couldn't stifle a yawn. "I'm sorry, Richard. It's been a long day. I'm exhausted."

"I'm not sure I helped you much. I'm sorry."

"Actually, you did. I obviously need to expand the search beyond Alex, no matter what anyone else thinks."

"I believe you're right. It's hard for me to imagine that anyone is looking seriously at Alex."

She nodded. "Unfortunately, they are. If he's behind this, I need to quit my job. It's clear I have no idea what I'm doing."

Richard reached across the table and took her hand. "That's self-pity. Don't you give in to it. You have a wonderful talent that the world needs. Don't turn this situation inward. It's a huge mistake, and it could keep you from catching a very bad man."

Kaely smiled and squeezed his hand. "Thanks. Again, I'm glad you came over."

"So my advice is better than Georgie's?"

Kaely chuckled. "Yeah, I would say so. This time anyway."

Richard laughed and downed the rest of his coffee. "Okay, I'm going. Call me tomorrow and let me know how you're doing, okay?"

She frowned. "Humor me. Call when you get home."

"I'll be fine, Kaely. Your bad guy isn't

coming after me."

"I don't think so either, but it would really make me feel better."

He put his mug in the sink and rinsed it out. "All right. I'll call as soon as I get in."

"Thanks." She started to stand up, but he put his hand on her shoulder and gently pushed her back down. "You don't need to walk me out. You take it easy." He leaned over and kissed the top of her head. "I love you, Kaely. I'm here whenever you need me."

"I know. Thanks, Richard."

He nodded and headed for the door. When it closed behind him, Kaely got up and locked it. She got another cup of coffee and headed toward her war room. She had an appointment with a serial killer, and she was determined to leave that room with a name — and a way to stop him.

Thirty-Nine

Kaely sat down at the small table with her cup of coffee. After a few sips, she set the cup down. As she ran different facts of the case through her mind, she prayed, asking God to give her clarity. Help her to shake the truth out of all of the confusion. Almost immediately, something she'd heard popped into her head. She sucked in her breath, trying to make sense of it. As awful as the truth was, there could be only one conclusion. She felt like she was going to be sick.

She stared at the chair across from her. "I was wrong when I said you don't know me. You do, and you hate me because of something you think I did to you. For some reason, you're focusing on my father. I think you're angry and you need to find a way to justify your hate." She peered at the empty place across from her, her eyes narrowed, her heart racing. "How could you connect me to him? I had no idea what he was up to."

A dark shape began to form in the other chair. "You knew," it whispered.

"No, I didn't. You're wrong," Kaely argued.

"I'm not wrong."

"There's something else. Something you're not telling me. I wish I knew what it was," she said.

"You will."

"Is that your plan?" Kaely asked angrily. "To prove I knew my father was a monster? Will that give you the strength you need to . . . kill me?"

Silence.

"The timing is strange. Why did it take you so long to come after me? Why now?"

"Don't you know?"

"Not exactly, but I'm sure you're going to tell me. That's what comes next, right? Hearing the truth?" She shook her head. "I have to admit, you've kept me in the dark for quite a while."

"You don't know who I am," the voice hissed.

Kaely looked away. "Yeah, I do. You made a mistake, you see. Now I know exactly who you are." She stared at the person sitting across from her at the table. He was fully formed now. She couldn't stop the tears that flowed unchecked. "You've broken my heart," she whispered. "You really have."

"Then we're even. You broke mine too."

Kaely stood to her feet, waving the image away. She went back into the kitchen and picked up her phone. She quickly placed a call.

"Thanks for picking up," she said.

"You knew I would, didn't you?"

"Yeah, I guess I did," she said. "I know who we're looking for. I need your help."

"Who is it?"

When she said the name, there was silence from the other end of the phone.

"What do you want me to do?" he said finally.

"I'm going to get a call soon, asking me to meet him. When it happens, follow me. Don't let me out of your sight. But be careful. Stay back and don't allow him to see you. Don't call for backup until the last possible moment. I have to be completely sure. If I'm wrong, I could ruin a life. Besides, we need a confession. Do you understand?"

"Yeah, I get it. I'm on my way."

Kaely hung up the phone. She went to her bedroom and changed out of her work clothes. She'd just pulled up her jeans and was choosing a sweater out of her closet when she heard something outside. She pulled up the window shade. Rain. Great. It would make it harder for her backup to keep her in sight. But she couldn't worry about that now. This had to end, and it had to end tonight.

Everything was ready. Tonight Jessica Oliphant, alias Kaely Quinn, would face final judgment. Once she admitted the truth, he would kill her. Then he would finally be free. He began preparations for the moment he'd been waiting for. A feeling of euphoria charged through him. His plan had worked perfectly. There was one incident he hadn't expected, but it actually helped him. Gave him a way to get her to come to him.

He smiled. Kaely Quinn had only hours to live.

Kaely waited in the dark. Even though she sat in her warm living room, watching the clock next to her television, she was almost certain she could feel cold, deadly fingers reaching in from the outside, trying to touch her. Trying to warn her. Of course, that was impossible, but nevertheless, the steady sound of rain drummed a frightening message into her brain. Someone might not survive the night, and it could be her. This could actually be her last night on earth.

She was okay with that. She knew God would simply take her home. She believed in heaven with all her heart, but if she had her choice, she'd want to live. She had things to do. Monsters to capture. Before she left this world, she needed to make an impact. A real difference. She wanted to know that people lived because she did.

She desperately wanted to talk to Georgie. Listen to her encouragement, but there wasn't time for that. When it was all over, if Kaely survived, they'd talk. Bouncing her thoughts off Georgie gave her balance. Made her calmer and more focused. She realized suddenly that she needed someone else even more than Georgie.

"Stand with me tonight, Lord," she prayed quietly. "You've always helped me. Always been by my side. Is there anything I should know? Something I need to do?"

She waited silently but didn't hear anything. When her phone went off, she jumped, even though she'd been expecting it. She picked it up and read the message. *I need to talk to you. Meet me in front of the abandoned warehouse at 17th and St. Louis Avenue. Come alone! Alex.*

She sighed and texted back: *On my way.*

Kaely slid the phone back into her jeans

pocket. Then she grabbed her coat and her gun. Before walking out the door, she picked up two additional magazines and put them in her purse. When her phone rang again, she took it out of her pocket. When she saw it was Richard, she answered.

"The bogeyman didn't get me. I made it home safely."

"Thanks for letting me know, Richard. I'll sleep better knowing you're safe."

"Get a good night's sleep, Jessie. I'll talk to you soon."

Kaely saw another message on her phone. Noah. She listened to it. He was warning her about Reinhardt. Kaely smiled and turned off her phone. She couldn't let anyone distract her now. She had to deal with this on her own. She put the phone back in her pocket. Now she was ready.

Noah cursed in frustration. Why wasn't Kaely answering her phone? He tried Reinhardt again, but his phone went straight to voicemail. He'd talked to one of the detectives who had gone with him. Reinhardt had suggested they split up, and the detective hadn't heard from him since. He'd tried to call him too, but just like with Kaely, all his calls had gone to voicemail.

Was Kaely in danger? He called for backup

and sent them to her condo. But would they reach her in time? And who were they looking for? Her brother? Alex Cartwright? Donald Reinhardt? Someone else? Noah had no idea. How could they protect Kaely if they didn't know where the danger was? Noah's stomach was tight with worry. This situation was out of control, and his gut told him Kaely Quinn was in trouble. Terrible trouble.

In her rearview mirror, Kaely saw flashing lights approach her complex. She breathed a sigh of relief. If she'd waited a little longer, they'd have stopped her. She pushed down on the accelerator, making certain she was out of their line of sight, yet being careful not to lose the car behind her.

It took her almost twenty minutes to reach the warehouse. She pulled up in front and looked around, but she didn't see anyone. She glanced into her mirror to make sure her backup couldn't be seen. She'd told him to be careful. If he was spotted, they could lose their UNSUB. Thankfully, she couldn't spot him, which likely meant no one else could either.

She almost screamed when someone knocked on her window. She hadn't noticed a man wearing a hoodie and a ski mask approach her car because she was so focused on the person she believed would keep her safe. She rolled down her window. "What happens now?" she asked.

He didn't answer. Instead, he reached in and covered her face with a cloth. She grabbed his arm and tried to wrestle it away, but the chloroform was too strong, and she felt herself drift away.

FORTY

When Kaely came to, she realized she was tied to a chair. She squirmed, trying to find a more comfortable position, but she couldn't. She looked around. She was in an old room, paint peeling from walls covered with faded clippings that seemed to be cut from newspapers. She realized most of them were articles about her father. Photos of his victims, newspaper columns devoted to Des Moines's Raggedy Man. A single light bulb hung from the ceiling, right over her head. Although the spot where she sat was illuminated, the rest of the room was black. It was so dark she couldn't tell how large the room was or if she was alone.

A musty odor permeated almost everything. It was overpowering. She twisted around as far as she could, but it didn't help. Her gun was gone. So was her phone. She had no way to call for help. No way to defend herself. There was only one person who could rescue her. Where was he? He'd promised to call for backup. Where was it?

Across the room, she heard a door open. It squeaked loudly, but she couldn't see who entered the room. Of course, she didn't need to. She knew who it was.

When he entered the circle of light, she almost didn't recognize him. His expression was so different. Filled with such anger and hate.

"Where are we?" she asked.

His expression went slack. "You don't look surprised to see me." The disappointment in his voice was obvious, and it made Kaely's stomach turn over. The man who stood in front of her wasn't the man she thought she knew. He was someone else. Someone who hated her.

"I'm not. I knew it was you."

"I don't believe you."

"Fine. Whatever you want to believe."

"If you knew it was me, you wouldn't have come alone."

"I didn't."

He laughed as if her comment was the funniest thing he'd ever heard. "Actually, you are. Even if someone saw the address I sent you, they wouldn't know where you are now. I moved you."

Fear grabbed Kaely by the throat and

shook her. She felt a spike of adrenaline — the instinctive fight-or-flight reflex. Was he telling the truth? Had she lost the only person who could help her? "You're lying."

"No, I'm not. And you know that." He gazed at her through hooded eyelids. "How could you possibly know it was me?"

"You made a mistake."

His face twisted with anger. "No, I didn't. I haven't made any mistakes. Not one."

"I told you that Alex was the killer's target, but I never mentioned the second letter sent to the newspaper. It hasn't been printed yet. There's no way you could have known unless you wrote it."

It was obvious Richard was running their conversation over in his mind. Suddenly, his eyes widened. "You're right. What have you done?"

"I called someone. Asked him to follow me. He should be here any moment."

Richard walked out of the light and back into the darkness. Kaely heard a scraping sound. He pulled another chair with him. He positioned it a couple of feet away and sat down. "I hate to disappoint you, but we weren't followed. We were only at the warehouse for a minute or two. When we left, there was no one behind us. They must have lost us in the rain. You're totally alone."

Kaely didn't want to believe him, but she could tell by his direct gaze and the way he leaned in that he was telling the truth. At least as he knew it. Of course, he'd been lying to her for a while and she hadn't caught it. Probably because she wasn't looking. She'd trusted him for so long, it hadn't occurred to her to look for signs of deceit. They were probably there. She'd been sloppy. Let down her guard. Now she was going to pay for it.

"I assume you have questions?"

She nodded. "Did you ever love me?" She hated the vulnerability she heard in her voice, but she couldn't help it. Richard and Alex were the only people she'd fully trusted. How could she have been so wrong?

For just a moment, Kaely thought she saw something flicker in Richard's eyes. Regret? Compassion? But as soon as it came, whatever it was disappeared.

"Yes, I cared for you. For you and Jason."

"So what happened?"

He snorted and rolled his eyes. "You mean what was the *trigger*?"

She nodded. "It's been twenty years. Why would you do this now?"

He reached inside his jacket and pulled out a couple of envelopes. "You remember what I told you about Bella's sister? About the letters her daughter gave me?"

"You're talking about Doreen? Yeah, I remember."

"I was going through the letters Bella sent to her. And I found . . . these." Richard's voice shook, and the rage in his features turned to grief. "Let me read you a section." He cleared his throat and took a deep breath. *"I don't know what to do, Doreen. Ed and I were together at his house and Jessie came home early from school. Ed made up some story about why we were in his bedroom, but I don't know if she believed us."* Richard glared at Kaely. "You knew Bella had an affair with your father?"

Kaely's mouth dropped open. "No! I . . . I don't believe it."

Richard leaned in and slapped Kaely across the face. She cried out in surprise and pain. Her reaction seemed to only fuel his anger. "You knew. You should have told someone. Told your mother. Put an end to it."

"I didn't know, I swear." Kaely tried to think back, to recall the incident Bella referred to. A long-forgotten memory sparked in her mind. "Wait a minute. I do remember something. I was sick at school. I called my mom, but she couldn't leave work. Then I phoned my dad, but he didn't answer. I finally called our neighbor, and she picked me up and drove me home. I came in the door and went to the kitchen to get something to drink. A couple of minutes later, my dad and Bella came down the hall. I had no idea where they'd been." She grimaced as she tried to pull up the rest of the buried memory. "I . . . I think my dad told me Bella came over to borrow something, but I can't remember what it was. I wasn't really paying attention. I had the flu. The thought that they were having an affair never entered my mind. Never."

"You're the smartest person I've ever known," Richard said, "and you want me to believe you didn't know about your father and Bella? You also had no clue your father was a serial killer? Either you're incredibly stupid or you're a liar. And you're not stupid."

"Richard, I was twelve the day I saw Bella and my dad together. And fourteen when he was arrested. I was a child. Children don't automatically assume people are cheating on their spouses . . . or that their father is a coldhearted, twisted murderer!" Kaely could hear the panic in her voice, but she recognized that Richard was detached from reality. He wouldn't hesitate to mete out some kind of delusional justice unless she could change his mind.

Richard's eyes were dark and emotionless. He put down the letter he'd just read and opened the other envelope. "Bella wrote this four days before she died." His fingers trembled as he held the letter. *"I can't take it, Doreen. How could I have cheated on Richard with someone like Ed Oliphant? He's evil. Vile. How could I have allowed him to touch me? I feel defiled. Dark inside. There's no place left for me in this world. I don't belong anymore. I will never be able to face Richard again. Or look at myself in the mirror. I have no idea why Ed didn't kill me too. He should have. Maybe he did."*

Kaely gasped. "You said Bella died of a heart attack."

"She had a bad heart, but she overdosed on Valium and alcohol. On purpose. Her heart couldn't take the reality of who your father really was. And what he did to her."

"Bella killed herself?" Even in the bizarre situation she found herself in, Kaely's eyes filled with tears. Bella had always been kind to her, and Kaely had loved her. Her show of emotion seemed to only stoke Richard's rage. For a moment, Kaely thought he was going to strike her again.

"Don't pretend you care," he growled.

"I do care, Richard. About Bella and

about you. You're hurt and angry. In shock. But I didn't cause any of this. I wish I'd been aware of what was going on. Maybe you're right. Maybe I could have stopped it. But I didn't do it on purpose."

"You're lying," he snarled, "and I'm going to prove it."

"How in the world can you prove something like that?" Kaely asked, frustration overtaking her. "You can't get into my head. You have to believe what I'm telling you."

"No, I don't. You see, I'm going to make you face the truth you've been running from for years."

"And how do you intend to do that?" Kaely's eyes kept darting toward the door. Where was Alex? She needed him now.

Richard reached into another pocket inside his jacket. This time he pulled out a small plastic box. Kaely watched as he opened it and removed a syringe.

"What's that?" Kaely asked, fear clutching at her chest.

"Lysergic acid diethylamide," he said, a slow smile spreading across his face.

"LSD?" The tension in Kaely's chest grew stronger until she wasn't sure she could catch her breath. "No," she whispered with effort. "Don't, Richard. Please."

"Don't, Richard. Please," he repeated in a

singsong voice. He leaned close to her, a few inches from her face. "We're going to visit your nightmare, Jessica. I'm going to prove you knew the truth all along. Maybe your mind is trying to hide it from you, but you knew. All you had to do was tell someone. People are dead because of you. Bella is dead because of you."

Richard held up the syringe. He tapped the needle, and a small squirt of clear liquid bubbled over. Then he turned it around and plunged it into Kaely's upper arm, completely ignoring her screams.

Forty-One

Noah raced up the street, pulling over when he saw Alex's vehicle in front of the empty warehouse on 17th. Alex stood in the rain, next to his car. When he saw Noah, he ran over and made a circle with his hand, encouraging Noah to lower his window.

"I don't know where they are," Alex said as soon as the glass separating them slid down. "I had them until a few blocks back, but a semi truck slid on the highway and blocked me for several minutes. When I got around him, I couldn't see her anymore. I drove here as fast as I could. I found her car, but she's gone. I'm really worried."

For the first time, Noah noticed Kaely's car pulled up next to the building. "You have no idea where she might be?" Noah asked.

"None. I looked for a while, but I didn't want to miss you, so I came back here."

Noah picked up the phone in his car and

selected a number. "I need you to find Kaely's phone," he said. "Quickly. I think her life is in danger." After a few seconds, Noah hung up. "Hopefully, she still has her cell phone and we can —"

A sound cut through the rain and the mist. Alex cursed loudly and jogged away from the car. He came back with a phone clutched in his hand. Kaely's. He opened Noah's passenger door and slid into his car.

"What are you doing?" Noah asked as Alex's fingers worked the phone.

"Checking her last text. She told me she was expecting one." He stopped. "Yeah, here it is." He sighed loudly. "That creep told her he was me. She figured that's what he'd do. He knew deep down inside she trusted me, that if I asked her to meet me, she would."

"You're sure our UNSUB is Richard Barton? He had an alibi for the first murder. We never looked at him that seriously, but we checked anyway, just to make sure we covered all our bases. Besides, I thought he was her longtime friend. She said he was one of the only people she completely trusted."

The look on Alex's face was grim. "I'm sure he made it look as if he had an alibi, but obviously it was a lie." He sighed. "I can't imagine what this will do to her."

"Before we worry about her emotional state of mind, we need to save her life." Noah frowned at him. "Why didn't you call me sooner?"

"Kaely made me promise. She didn't want to bring the Bureau in until she was sure she was right. She always planned for me to call you. She wasn't going to take on Richard alone."

"Yet she is. Great."

Alex looked over at him. "I warned you about this. I told you she could put herself in danger — ignore protocol. I was so grateful she called me I didn't think it through. Not that she gave me much time. But you're right. I should have told you everything from the beginning."

"Yeah, you should have."

Noah took out his own phone and dialed a number. When the person on the other end answered, he said, "I need you to hack into Kaely Quinn's phone. Find the source of the last text she received. Whoever sent it said he was Alex Cartwright, but he wasn't. We've got to find the location of his phone. Kaely's life depends on it." He waited to get a response before saying, "Hurry. Do it as fast as you can. Text me when you have something." He hung up but held the phone in his hand as if somehow that might make it ring sooner. "There's nothing we can do but wait. Backup should be here soon. I called for it as soon as you contacted me."

"I hope we have something to tell them." Alex was quiet for a moment. "Hey," he said suddenly, "we need to have someone check Richard's records. Look for property with his name on it."

"You're right." Noah dialed another number. "Ron, have some of our people check property records in the name of Dr. Richard Barton. Now. Highest priority."

"Who is Richard Barton?" Ron asked.

"Our UNSUB. He's got Kaely somewhere. I doubt she's at his main residence. Have it checked, but I'm more interested in a second property, someplace he's tried to keep private."

"Okay. On it. I'll get back to you as soon as we find something. You need to bring me up to speed when you can. I'll call Solomon and tell him what I know — but it's not much right now."

"Sorry. I'll get back to you with more information the first chance I get. Thanks."

Noah and Alex sat silently in the rain. Noah was certain they were both trying to come up with any idea that could help them find Kaely before it was too late.

"So, how did Richard commit the first murder if he was in Des Moines?" Noah asked. "That's what we turned up anyway."

"How did he get there?" Alex asked.

"If I remember, he flew. And flew back. Neighbors said he was home."

"How would they know he was home the entire time?"

Noah thought for a moment. "They said they saw a blue car in the driveway."

Alex grunted. "Richard has an old green Ford Explorer. If he flew, that had to be a rental car. He could easily drive back to St. Louis in the middle of the night, commit the first murder, and drive back before morning. The neighbors wouldn't have noticed."

"Yeah, you're right. I should have thought of that. Why didn't I look closer?"

Alex shook his head again. "Kaely was so convinced it couldn't be him, you reacted to her instead of investigating the way you should have. It's easy to accept everything she says because she's so smart. So intuitive."

"So broken."

Alex took a quick deep breath before saying, "Yes. Very broken."

"She believes God is healing her. Making her stronger."

Alex turned to look at him. "And you don't believe that?"
"No, not really." He met Alex's gaze. "Do you?"
"Yeah, I do."
Noah felt a rush of irritation. "Has it occurred to you that encouraging that kind of . . . *faith* could cause her even more hurt? More disappointment?"
"You mean because you think God failed you?"
Noah's irritation turned to anger. "You have no right to say that to me. You don't know me at all."
Alex sighed and stared out the window at the rain. "I was just like you when I first met Kaely. After knowing her a while, I changed. I believe a lot of things now that I never used to."
Noah shook his head and started to spit out an angry remark about not being as gullible as Alex. Instead, he said, "I find myself wanting to protect her, but I know I can't. She'd get angry. Push me away."
"I know. I felt the same way. As time went on, my feelings got deeper. Stronger. I made the mistake of telling her."
"Alex, why did you take a leave of absence? Was it because of Kaely? Your feelings for her?"

Alex chuckled. "No. It had nothing to do with that. But if you don't mind, I'll keep that to myself. For now anyway. I'll just say that I finally realized I was made to do something else."

"Okay," Noah said slowly. "So, why did you leave the hospital?"

"Because I knew Kaely might need me, and I had to be available. I couldn't legitimately work the case, but neither could I just stand by and watch her die."

"Do you know that some of us thought you were the UNSUB?"

"I wondered if that would occur to you, but I couldn't let that stop me."

Noah started to ask him to explain why he hadn't been strangled on the swing, but before he could get the words out, his phone rang. He answered and tilted the phone toward Alex so he could hear too.

"Sorry, Noah," Ron said. "We can't find anything under the name Richard Barton. There are some Bartons, but none of them are named Richard."

"What about a spouse? Someone named . . ." He tried to remember Richard's wife's name. Had Kaely mentioned it?

"Bella," Alex said. "Ask about Bella."

"Is there a Bella?" Noah asked.

"Yeah, there is," Ron said, an edge of

excitement in his voice. He rattled off an address. "Can you text that to me?" Noah asked.

"Sending it now."

A few seconds later, Noah's phone beeped, and he said, "We've got it. Thanks."

Noah glanced at his rearview mirror. He could see the blue flashing lights from a few blocks away. Then suddenly the lights stopped. Backup had arrived. They were running silently and without lights so as not to alert their UNSUB. As the unmarked police cars pulled in behind them, Noah got out and made his way to the main car. The window lowered, and he could see Jeff and Peter, along with several other officers.

"We brought SWAT," Jeff said. "Where are we going?"

Noah gave him the address. "Follow us. No lights or sirens. I don't want to spook him. I'd like to get Kaely out of there alive."

"It's your call," Jeff said, "but we'd better get there fast."

Noah nodded and ran back to his car. "You wanna come with me?" he asked Alex.

"Yeah, if it's okay."

"Well, let's see. You're completely unauthorized to even ride in a Bureau vehicle or take part in an official case. And I assume you're armed and don't have a Missouri concealed carry permit?" Noah took a deep breath. "Sure. Why not?"

"I actually do have a permit for my gun. But even if I didn't . . ."

"I know. You'd ignore anything I told you and go anyway."

Alex nodded. "I love her, Noah. I have no intention of sitting this out."

Noah held up a hand, signaling Alex to stop talking. "Don't say anything else. We're both already in too deep."

As Noah put his car in gear, his phone rang and he answered it. "Good," he said after a few seconds. "Where is it?" He nodded as he listened. "That confirms what we already know. Thanks." He hung up the phone. "They tracked Richard's phone to the same address we got from Ron. We're on the right track."

"Let's get Kaely and put an end to this monster," Noah said.

"Amen, brother."

Forty-Two

It didn't take long for the drug to take effect. Kaely tried to fight it off, but it was impossible. The air around her became alive, a moving thing full of vibrating colors. She stared at Richard, but his face had become twisted, frightening. He looked just like the theater mask of tragedy, but his features shifted and danced in a macabre ballet. Every few seconds, she could see him peering at her through the empty holes in the mask, but suddenly everything changed. She found herself staring into the eyes of her father.

She'd clamped her lips together, determined Richard wouldn't break her, but the sound of sobbing surrounded her. Was it coming from her? She couldn't tell.

The tragedy mask came nearer, within a few inches of her face. "Now we're going back, Jessie. You're in the dream again. You're running down a dark hallway. Something is coming after you."

"It's in the walls," a child's voice said. "There's a monster in the wall."

Kaely wanted to reach up and pinch her lips together. No matter how hard she tried to keep them closed, the voice seeped out. She couldn't control it.

"We have to find out what's behind the wall," the man behind the mask said.

"Why?" Kaely asked. "Don't let the monster out. Please, please."

"Jessie!"

Someone shouted her name as if she'd done something wrong. It was her father's voice. He'd yelled at her when she . . . when she what? She tried to pull up the memory, but she couldn't. Then she heard someone whisper. She looked away from the mask and peered into the shadows. Someone else was calling her. Not as Jessie. Her new name. Who was it?

"Who are you?" she asked. "Can you help me?"

I will never leave you. Never forsake you.

Kaely felt something slowly seeping through her, as if someone had poured warm honey on the top of her head. But this warmth had something else in it. Peace. Extreme peace. She let it wash over her entire body.

"Jessie, what's in the wall?" Richard's voice hissed.

She couldn't see him anymore. Where Richard had been sitting, there was a void. A dark void, but no person. Just a feeling of evil. A voice in the darkness. She turned back toward the shadows from which the peaceful voice had come.

It's okay. I want you to see. Don't be afraid.

Kaely took a deep breath and put herself back in the hallway. She realized for the first time she was inside her childhood house. She walked to the end of the hallway and stopped. There was nothing there. What was she supposed to see? Suddenly, a light began to shine from the wall. It highlighted the edges of the green wainscoting on the bottom half of the wall. Kaely reached for it and found a loose spot near the top. She pulled at it, and a hidden door swung open.

"It's a secret place," she whispered. Her voice echoed and bounced around the room. The colors and patterns intensified. Everything wiggled and shifted with the colors. They made an odd sound. Like a buzzing but not really unpleasant. She could hear words. Lyrics. The colors made music, but not any kind of music she'd ever heard before.

"Go inside. Everything will be okay." The

voice came from somewhere. It sounded far away.

Kaely pulled the door open and scooted past it. The space on the other side wasn't very large. Just big enough for Kaely and all the things stuffed inside. She started to look at them, but bile rose in her throat, and she felt like she was going to be sick. Panic raced up from her stomach and seized her around the throat. "Help me," she choked out. Dust flew around her, but it wasn't regular dust. It sparkled and pulsed. In some other context it might have been pretty, but it was clear this wasn't a pretty place. This was a bad place. An evil place. There were pictures. Bad pictures. Knives. Scarves covered with something dark. Was it blood? The entire space began to fill with blood, and Kaely was afraid she was going to drown. She started to scream. Then something grabbed her from behind and yanked her violently. Her head scraped against the side of the wall and a nail pierced the skin on her face. She could feel warm blood running down her chin and her neck, onto her clothes.

She found herself lying in the hallway. She looked up to see her father standing over her, his face distorted by something she couldn't comprehend.

"You will forget what you just saw, do you understand?" he said. "You'll never bring it up. Never." His face moved just inches from hers. "Do you hear me, Jessie Lynn? You will forget this or else . . ."

Fear overtook her as blood continued to pour down her face. "Yes, Daddy. I understand," she said through her blood and her tears.

"What did you see?" the voice from the void asked.

Kaely shook her head. "I can't say. Daddy told me to never tell anyone."

"But he's gone now," the voice said.

She blinked several times, trying to see who was talking. Richard's face became clear. "There were bad things there," she said, her voice trembling. "Bad things. Daddy said to forget them." She sobbed. "My face is bleeding. I need help."

"See, you knew the truth," Richard hissed. "All this time. All those women dead, and it's your fault. You killed them." He leaned so close to her that their noses were almost touching. "You killed Bella, and you need to take your own life. It's only fair. You have to pay the price for all the pain you caused." He held up a gun. "It's the only way to bring justice. There's no other choice, Jessie. Do you understand?"

Kaely nodded. “I understand.”

“I’m going to untie you now. Then I want you to pay the price for your sins.”

“I’m sorry, Richard. I’m so sorry. I’ll make it right, I promise.”

Richard’s smile made her feel better, but before he could untie her, the darkness surrounded her, and Kaely passed out.

Forty-Three

Noah and Alex drove up to an old row house. The block had been vacant for years after the city condemned the buildings. Four months earlier, someone using the name Bella Renee Barton had purchased one of the houses with the intent to rehab it. It looked deserted. The boarded-up windows made it impossible to see inside. As Noah pulled his car around to the side of the structure, he saw another vehicle parked in the shadows. A green Ford Explorer. He spoke into the comm set Jeff had given him. "He's here, Jeff," he said. "Park down the block. Hide your vehicles. We need to be as quiet as we can."

"Affirmative," Jeff said. A few seconds later, he pulled over and parked far enough away that his SUV couldn't be seen. All the other vehicles followed his lead. He and Alex got out of the car and waited for Jeff and the SWAT team to meet up with them.

"I believe Richard Barton is inside with Agent Quinn," Jeff told the SWAT leader, who leaned in to listen. Alex stood next to him. "He intends to kill her. Let's get in there, locate them, and then figure out how to breach. I don't want to spook him, but I don't want to give him time to hurt her . . . if he hasn't already."

The SWAT leader nodded. "We'll follow your lead."

"Thanks. Stay behind me." He turned and headed up the broken cement stairs to an ancient door covered in graffiti. Noah pulled on it, and it swung open without making any noise. He breathed a sigh of relief. Once he had the door open all the way, he entered a dirty, trash-filled hallway, the sour smell of urine permeating the air. Obviously, this building had been used by the homeless. If the property wasn't secured before winter came, it would probably fill up again.

Noah checked out several large rooms on the ground floor. They were empty. He motioned to the agents behind him that they'd be going upstairs. The stairs themselves were creaky and broken. He gestured to Jeff, pointing to the stairs, hoping he'd realize that each and every agent needed to step very carefully. Jeff seemed to understand and turned around, passing the message down the line.

When Noah reached the top of the stairs, he pointed at Alex, then motioned to the right side of the hallway. Alex nodded, his weapon in front of him. He began searching the room near him, other agents behind him. Noah looked through the rooms on his side, but again, they were all empty. Had they come here for nothing? Was Kaely here or not?

Alex tapped him on the shoulder and pointed up. That's when Noah saw the small door at the top of the stairs. A dim beam of light bled out from under it. Then he heard something. A voice. A man's voice. It sounded angry. He put his finger to his ear, making sure his comm was working. "I think she's in the attic," he said softly. "Let me go in first and check it out." He motioned to the SWAT team leader. "Wait for my signal." He pointed to Alex. "You stay here. You can't be part of this. Do you understand?"

Alex just looked at him but didn't respond. Noah wanted to read him the riot act, but he didn't have time to deal with him right then.

"This isn't protocol," the SWAT team leader said quietly.

"I know, but I don't want to spook him. I

think my way is best. If things start to go south, come in. Do what you need to do. Just give me a chance first."

The SWAT leader stared at him for a moment but finally nodded. They began their slow ascent up the second set of stairs. Noah's heart beat so hard he was certain everyone in the building could hear it. When he reached the attic door, he put his ear up next to it. Muffled voices. Male *and* female. Kaely was alive. Noah hesitated a moment before holding up his hand toward the agents behind him. He knew this wasn't what SWAT was trained to do, but he was afraid that if they rushed in now, Richard might kill Kaely. Maybe if he thought Noah was the only one here, he'd stay calm. Noah had taken a step closer to the door when Alex reached over and grabbed his arm.

"What if she told him she called me?" he whispered. "If you show up, Barton might realize there are additional agents out here."

"I'm not letting you go in there. I can't. You're not authorized to . . ."

"Then we go in together. I'll tell him I called you. Maybe he'll think there's only two of us. I don't want to freak him out, Noah. We've got to be very careful."

Noah rolled Alex's suggestion over in his mind. He weighed protocol against Kaely's life. He hated to admit it, but Alex was right. If Kaely had mentioned her call to Alex, Barton would be suspicious if Noah showed up without him.

"Okay," he whispered. "But stay behind me. Follow my lead."

"All right. I've got your six."

As Noah reached for the door handle, he realized it might be locked. If it was, their plan was useless. They'd have to break the door down, and their subtle approach went out the window.

As he attempted to turn the knob, Noah was relieved when it moved. He opened the door and walked into a dark room, save for one lone light bulb hanging by a cord from the ceiling. Two chairs faced each other. A man he assumed was Barton sat in one chair, while Kaely sat across from him, a gun in her hand. Her expression was vacant, and she didn't seem to notice he was there. Keeping his weapon trained on Richard, he stepped into the circle of light. Kaely finally looked his way.

"Georgie?" she said. "Is that you?"

"Stop right where you are," Barton said. He swung around in his chair, and Noah saw the gun he had pointed at his chest. "Jessie told me someone might show up. I thought it would be Alex."

"I'm here, Richard," Alex said, stepping around Noah. "I called Noah."

"It's just you two?" Richard asked.

"Yes," Noah said. "We weren't sure our information was correct. We should have called for backup. Believe me, I wish we had now."

"If you'd come in with guns blazing, I would have ended her right away." Richard's voice was too high, and his eyes were wide and wild.

"Georgie?" Kaely said, sobbing. "Is it you? The monster's out. Help me."

"What's wrong with her?" Alex asked. "What did you do?"

Richard smiled oddly. "Lysergic acid diethylamide."

"You gave her LSD?" Noah swallowed hard. "Do you know what it could do to her? She must be terrified."

"*She's* terrified?" Richard said loudly. "Her father terrified men, women, and children for years. And you're worried about her?"

That was when Noah noticed all the newspaper clippings on the wall. Stories about Ed Oliphant. The Raggedy Man. Richard was clearly obsessed.

Alex took a step closer to him. "Richard, we know each other pretty well. Kaely had nothing to do with her father's . . . proclivities. And you know that. You used to tell her that."

"But I was wrong. She knew." He had almost no expression. It was as if Richard was in some kind of trance. "I used to blame myself for not seeing the evil in Ed Oliphant. And when Bella killed herself, I believed I'd failed her. But now I know it wasn't my fault. It was Jessie's. It was completely her fault." He turned to look at Kaely. "And now she's prepared to make things right, aren't you, Jessie?"

As Kaely nodded and stared at the gun in her hand, Noah remembered the last part of the poem. *One last elephant facing final judgment. She was found guilty and given no pity. Jessica Oliphant called it a day. She picked up a gun and blew herself away.* This was the end game. Everything led to this moment. Richard wanted Kaely to kill herself.

"You know she was completely innocent," Alex said soothingly. "She was a victim, just like you. She loves you, Richard. And I think you love her."

"Love her!" Each word was like a bullet fired from a gun, hitting its target. "She saw her father's trophies. His sick pictures. His twisted plans." He shook his head. "She found Ed's *stash.* She could have told someone. Anyone. Ed would have been stopped. If she'd turned him in, Bella might still be alive. I don't love her. I hate her."

"Richard, she was a child," Alex said, his voice lower and more controlled. "You know that. If you think she's guilty, why don't you administer judgment? You could easily shoot her. You have a gun."

Noah bit his lip. Part of him wanted to take over. Stop Alex from saying the wrong thing. But in his gut he believed Alex knew exactly what he was doing. He knew Richard. Noah didn't. Alex was attempting to neutralize Richard. One thing he was certain of was that Alex would do anything to keep Kaely safe. He decided to let him keep going.

"It's her fault," Richard said again. "All of it. I suspected she knew the truth, that her nightmare meant she'd seen something. Bella killed herself. She couldn't face the truth about Ed."

"Then shoot Kaely," Alex said again. "She won't do it herself."

Richard stared down at the gun in his hand, but he didn't point it at Kaely. He just sat there.

As Noah stared at Alex, he saw his head move so slightly, and at first he thought it was his imagination. Then he did it again, and this time his eyes slid toward Kaely. Noah looked over at her. Her eyes were wild, and it was clear she was confused. But as he watched her, she seemed to lock in on him. Her lips began to move although no sound came out. Was she counting?

"One . . . two . . ."

What was she doing? Noah took a step closer.

"Don't move!" Richard screamed. "I'll kill you. I will!" He raised his gun.

"Three!" Kaely yelled. She stood up and charged Richard, knocking him out of his chair. At the same time, Noah rushed him, trying to grab his gun. He heard a gunshot, but he couldn't worry about it. He was too busy wrestling with Richard.

Suddenly Alex was there, and he heard shouts from the SWAT team as they entered the room. Noah kicked the gun out of Richard's reach. Then Alex grabbed Richard and flipped him over. He held his wrists together with one hand and wrapped his other arm around Richard's neck. Noah pulled Richard's hands from Alex's grip and handcuffed him. Once Richard was immobile, he yelled at Alex to remove his arm from Richard's neck.

"Stop it, Alex. You're killing him!" Noah yelled.

Finally, Alex let go and stood. As Richard lay on the floor, whimpering, Noah stood up too. As soon as he did, a wave of dizziness washed over him, and he slumped to the floor.

He watched as Jeff secured Richard's gun. The rest of the SWAT team stood over them, weapons drawn.

He turned to look at Kaely. She was still holding the gun Richard had given her. Noah saw a look on her face he'd never seen before. As he tried to steady himself, Kaely pointed the gun at Richard. Several members of the SWAT team pointed their guns her way and ordered her to put the gun down.

"Don't shoot her," Noah yelled. "She doesn't know what she's doing."

"Kaely, stop," Alex said. He walked over and stood between Kaely and Richard. "Give me the gun, Kaely."

"Georgie?" she whispered. "Is that you? Where am I?"

"It's Alex, not Georgie. You're okay. We're going to get you to the hospital. You'll be fine, do you hear me?"

She nodded, tears running down her face. "I knew you'd come," she whispered. "I knew you'd come. He can't get away with it, Alex. He can't."

"And he won't. But this isn't the way. You know that."

Kaely stared up into Alex's eyes. She slowly lowered the gun and handed it to him. Then she collapsed, and Alex caught her in his arms.

"Call for a couple of ambulances," Alex said to the SWAT commander. "And tell them to hurry."

"Already done," he said.

Noah watched as Alex cradled Kaely's head in his lap. He heard him whisper, "You hang in there, you hear me?" Noah was so focused on Kaely, it took a while for him to realize he'd been shot.

Forty-Four

Kaely opened and closed her eyes several times, trying to make certain the world was normal again. For the most part, the patterns and colors were gone, but furniture in the room wiggled and moved when she looked at it. How long would that last? She turned her head the other way and found Alex sitting in a chair near her bed. His eyes were closed.

"Alex?" she said softly.

Immediately, his eyes shot open. "Are you okay?" he asked. He stood and walked over to her. Kaely almost laughed at his worried expression.

"I was drugged," she said. "It's temporary."

"You were in bad shape when we brought you in," he said. "Then a few hours ago you finally calmed down. You've been sleeping."

Kaely looked toward the window by her bed. "It's morning?"

"Yes. A little after ten o'clock."

Kaely took a deep breath. "I'm so glad to feel almost sane again."

"I'm sure it was terrifying. Especially for someone who likes to be in control."

She nodded. "It was scary, but I knew I'd be okay." She reached out and took his hand in hers. An IV dripped into her other arm. "God was with me, and I knew you'd come."

Alex smiled. "I wasn't the only one who rescued you. I had help from the SWAT team and Noah. Without them, I'm afraid we both might have died."

"Where is Noah?" Kaely asked. "I remember seeing him."

Alex hesitated for a moment. "I have to tell you something about Noah."

Kaely gasped. "Is he . . . is he okay?"

"He was shot, but . . ."

"But he's fine," a familiar voice said from behind them.

Alex let go of Kaely's hand and moved back. Noah maneuvered his wheelchair next to the bed.

"I thought . . . I thought . . ." Her eyes filled with tears.

"I was dead?" Noah said. He scowled at Alex. "Great bedside manner."

"I was getting to it," Alex said.

"Gee, thanks." Noah smiled at Kaely. "Richard shot me, but even though the bullet pierced my vest, it didn't reach my heart. Stung a bit. Bled like crazy."

"I told him it was because he doesn't actually have a heart," Alex said, "but he didn't seem to appreciate that."

Kaely laughed. "Are you sure you're going to be okay?" she asked Noah.

"I promise. I'm doing great."

"He's got a couple of broken ribs," Alex said. "And he's gonna be sore for a while."

"See?" he said to Kaely. "You can't get rid of me that easily."

"I don't want to get rid of you," Kaely said softly. "Thanks, Noah. I don't know what I would have done without you."

"I'm not sure you need much help. What was that move? Counting to three?"

She smiled. "Something Alex and I used in another case. A drugged-out dealer with a knife. I counted to three then hit him. Knocked the knife out of his hand. Alex took him down."

"It was pretty dangerous," Noah said, "but it worked."

"It got you shot," Kaely said. "I'm sorry. If I hadn't been drugged, I probably wouldn't have taken the chance."

Noah shrugged, wincing at the movement.

"Hey, I'll recover, and we got Richard. This minor injury is worth it."

Kaely looked back and forth between him and Alex. "I'm very blessed to have you both in my life." She fixed her gaze on Noah. "What's happened to Richard?"

"He's under arrest. And he's talking. He's admitting to everything. Every killing."

Kaely looked away. She'd trusted someone, and once again she'd been let down. Richard had used information she'd shared with him to create a scenario intended to end her life. After a few seconds, she turned back. "I never suspected him. I didn't read him because . . . well, because I trusted him. It's hard to think you can never relax around anyone. That you always have to be suspicious." She took a deep breath and let it out slowly. "I learned a lesson. I should never trust anyone completely."

"I don't think that's healthy," Noah said. "We all have to trust someone." He paused for a moment before saying, "I trust you."

"Do you?" Kaely asked. "Even though it's obvious I knew about my father, but I didn't tell anyone?"

"Look, I wasn't there for the whole thing," Noah said, "but it seems you saw something when you were a kid. It traumatized you. You weren't trying to hide it on purpose.

Your mind did that by itself. It was fighting to protect you, but the truth kept knocking at you in your nightmares."

"I realize that now," Kaely said, "but still . . ."

"Stop it," Alex said. He reached for her hand again. "God let you see the truth. At least some of those nightmares should stop now. You need to trust Him and quit trying to bury yourself in guilt. You know that's not what He wants. He's trusting you to face this now — without condemnation."

Kaely nodded. "You're right. Thanks." She smiled at him. "You'll do great in your new gig."

Alex's eyebrows shot up. "How do you know what my next gig is?"

"I may not have read Richard correctly, but I know you. I should have realized immediately why you left the Bureau. You're going to the Philippines, aren't you?"

"What's in the Philippines?" Noah asked.

"My parents. They're missionaries there. They've wanted me to join them for a long time, and I finally realized it's what I want too. What I'm called to do." He looked down at Noah. "You can see why I didn't want to tell my SAC the reason I needed a leave of absence. He wouldn't have understood."

Noah wasn't sure he did either, but he didn't say anything. Obviously, Kaely and Alex had this religious stuff in common.

"I have a question," Noah said. "And not a *special* question."

Alex's mouth dropped open. "Oh no. You got three questions too?"

Noah nodded. "I'm only through question two."

Alex frowned. "Hey, I don't think I ever used my third question."

"That's because you learned to trust me," Kaely said. "You didn't need to ask your third question." She cast a quick glance at Noah.

"I plan to use mine someday," Noah said, grinning. "But maybe not for a while."

"So what's your *not special* question?" Alex asked.

Noah hesitated a moment. Then he decided to spit it out. "You called Alex to back you up with Richard. Why didn't you call me?"

"It wasn't because I didn't trust you, Noah. Alex knew Richard. I felt he would be more helpful in that particular situation. Besides, you would have called for backup. I didn't want that."

"Why?"

She sighed. "Believe it or not, I had to

know for certain it was Richard. And if it was, I didn't want him to die. I felt if it was just Alex and me, we could talk him down. Get him to surrender." She hesitated and sought his eyes. "It's the truth."

"You still care about him?" Noah asked. "After everything he's done?"

Kaely nodded. "It's hard to stop loving someone. It will take some time for me to really understand what happened. I mean, I realize Richard pushed back his anger about Bella for years, but it never left. Then when he found out . . . well, he discovered something disturbing about her. The past made itself known. It screamed for attention, and Richard listened. He had to blame someone. He couldn't blame Bella, so he picked me."

"I'm not an expert," Noah said, "but you're the only person in his life still connected to your father. You were the closest he could get to the person he really hates."

Kaely gave him a small, sad smile. "And you say you're not a profiler."

Noah chuckled. "And I stand by that." He frowned at her. "How did you figure out Richard was our UNSUB?"

"I didn't until last night. Richard came over for supper. He mentioned the second letter to the newspaper, but I hadn't told him about it, and of course, the letter hadn't been printed yet."

"Believe it or not, it's in the paper today," Alex said. "I guess a bomb going off and killing the editor doesn't stop the news from going out."

"I'm really sorry about Jerry. And surprised. Why him?"

Alex shook his head. "We'll have plenty of time to try to figure out why Richard did what he did and to try to understand the choices he made."

"There will be a lot of stories in the media for a while," Noah said.

Kaely exhaled softly. "I hope the Bureau won't decide to transfer me again," Kaely said. "I like it here in St. Louis."

Noah shook his head. "That won't happen. Solomon is behind you, even if Reinhardt isn't." He grunted. "For a hot second, we thought he was our UNSUB."

"Reinhardt?" Kaely said. "Why in the world would you think that?"

"We found out he got here three days before the first killing. Then last night he disappeared."

"What really happened?" Alex asked.

"Reinhardt came to town to do a training session with the local police," Noah explained. "That's how he knew what was going on and made the decision to stay. He wasn't trying to hide anything. He just didn't give Solomon details about his trip. Solomon assumed he'd flown in after the letter and the murder in the park."

"Where was he last night?" Kaely asked.

Noah laughed. "He didn't really disappear. He dropped his phone in a puddle. We couldn't get through to him for a while. He thought his phone would dry out and work again. When it didn't, he called in on another phone to let us know what was happening. For a while there, I thought we were going to have to arrest him." He shook his head. "I wasn't looking forward to it."

"He dropped his phone in a puddle," Alex said, clearly amused. "Seems Mr. BAU is just as human as the rest of us."

Kaely grinned. "Not sure he'd admit to that."

"I think you're right."

Noah heard the door swing open behind him. A nurse came into the room. "Sorry to interrupt, but Agent Quinn has a visitor. Is it okay if I let him in?"

Kaely nodded. "The more the merrier. Who is it?"

"He says he's your brother."

Forty-Five

The look on Kaely's face made Noah catch his breath. "I'll tell him to leave," he said.

"No. Remember, it was Richard who said Jason was angry with me. I can't trust that's true now." She nodded at the nurse. "Would you let him in, please?"

The nurse turned and walked out the door. Kaely looked back and forth between Noah and Alex. "Don't go, okay?"

"We won't," Alex said.

When the door opened again, Noah turned to see a man with reddish blond hair and dark eyes like his sister. Noah recognized him from his driver's license photo. He was dressed in jeans, boots, and a leather coat.

"Jessie?" he said when he saw Kaely. "Is that you?"

He didn't seem threatening at all. In fact, he seemed emotional.

"Jason?"

Was the quaver in Kaely's voice fear, or was she glad to see her brother?

"Hi, Jessie." As Jason neared the bed, Alex stepped closer to Kaely. Despite his injuries, Noah was ready to jump up and tackle Jason if he made one wrong move.

"Are you okay?" Jason asked.

"I'm fine. I'll be out of here soon."

Kaely's eyes filled with tears, and she held out her hand. Jason grabbed it. "I read you were being stalked by a serial killer. I had to come and make sure you were safe."

"You left Durango two weeks ago," Noah said. "The story only came out last week."

Jason's eyebrows shot up. "You've been tracking me?"

"Don't get angry, Jason," Kaely said. "Richard tried to convince me you were the man we were looking for."

"Richard?" Jason looked puzzled. "Why would he do that? I haven't talked to him since we left Des Moines."

Kaely nodded. "I realize that now, but we had to find you. Had to know for certain you weren't our UNSUB."

Jason finally smiled. "I like it when you talk FBI."

Kaely laughed.

"You didn't answer my question," Noah said, unwilling to trust Jason yet.

"I left two weeks ago because I went to see our mother. I had something to tell her." He smiled at Kaely. "I met someone, sis. A wonderful woman." He paused a moment. "A Christian. To say my life has changed is an understatement. I go to church now, and . . . I'm getting married. I want to introduce Audrey to my family, but first I need to make sure I still have one."

"Oh, Jason. I've prayed and prayed for you. And of course you have me. You always did. You always will."

Jason leaned in closer to his sister. "You prayed? My logical, analytical sister prays?"

Kaely smiled. "Yeah, your logical, analytical sister figured out that God made sense. Seems we've been traveling a similar path."

"Wow." Jason shook his head slowly. "I shouldn't be surprised, but I am constantly amazed by what God can do."

"Like healing a family," Alex said quietly.

"Yes," Kaely repeated. "Like healing a family."

Jason took his hand from Kaely's and held it out to Alex. "Jason Oliphant."

"Glad to meet you, Jason. I'm Alex Cartwright. I used to work with your sister. Now we're just very good friends."

"I'm sorry," Kaely said. "I'm so happy to see you I've completely forgotten my manners." She gestured toward Noah. "And this is Noah Hunter, a fellow agent. We worked The Elephant case together."

"Looks like you didn't make it out unscathed," Jason said as he approached Noah with his hand out.

"Just a temporary inconvenience," Noah said. "Worth it to stop a murderer."

"And who did your killer turn out to be?" Jason asked.

Noah shook Jason's hand and cast a quick look at Kaely. Shouldn't she be the one to tell her brother the truth about their old family friend?

"Jason," she said softly. "It was Richard."

Jason turned pale. "Richard? How can that be?"

"It's a long story better kept for another time." Kaely frowned at him. "How long will you be in town?"

"I can stay for a while." Although it was clear the news about Richard had shaken him, Jason took his sister's hand again. "The whole week . . . if you want me to. I just bought the auto detail shop where I've been working, so I don't really need permission to take time off. I should get back sometime next week though. Have to make sure things don't fall apart while I'm gone."

Tears sprung to Kaely's eyes. "Oh, Jason.

I would love to spend time with you. Where are you staying?"

"A hotel downtown."

"You could stay with me. Sleep on my couch."

Jason grinned. "Now that beats anything the Marriott can offer. I'd be thrilled to bunk at your place."

"Good." Kaely looked at Alex and Noah. "I should be out of here by tomorrow. Let's all have dinner together."

"I can't, Kaely," Alex said. "I'm leaving this afternoon for Detroit. I need to officially resign and pack for the Philippines." He walked to the other side of the bed and leaned over to kiss her on the cheek. "In fact, I need to get going. I'll miss you, but I'll keep in touch. Just don't get in trouble and make me come back."

Tears washed down Kaely's face as she gazed at Alex. "I'll do my best," she said softly.

Alex took a step back. "Noah, why don't you walk me out? Or I'll walk. You roll."

"Funny," Noah said. "Sure." He nodded at Kaely. "Be right back."

She nodded at him, clearly too emotional to say anything. When Alex reached the door, he hesitated and looked back at Kaely.

Noah could see uncertainty in his expression.

"You promised me that if I asked you to leave, you would," Kaely said gently. "It's that time. I want you to go."

Alex nodded and pulled the door open, holding it for Noah so he could navigate his wheelchair through. Noah paused in the hallway as Alex turned around again and smiled at Kaely. "I won't say what I want to," Alex said, his voice strained. "But you know."

"Yeah, I know," she replied, her voice shaking. "And back atcha."

Alex let the door close and came out into the hall with Noah. After walking a few yards, he stopped and turned around. "I just wanted to tell you that I feel released to leave because . . . because of you." He gave Noah a small smile. "I know you've got her back. I'm not worried about her anymore."

"I'm glad," Noah said. "I . . . I want to ask you something."

"Why didn't I die on that swing?"

"Yeah. You shouldn't have lived. Frankly, it seems almost impossible that you did."

Alex smiled. "With God nothing is impossible, Noah. He has plans for me. He kept me alive." He laughed. "I can see you don't believe that now, but I predict you will someday."

"Well, I'm not so sure about that, but you never have to be concerned about Kaely. I'll look after her. Frankly, working with her is the best thing that's ever happened to me."

"Trust me, I understand." Alex looked around. He pointed to a nearby waiting room. "Let's go in there for a few minutes. I want to talk to you about something."

Noah followed him into the deserted waiting room. Alex sat down in one of the chairs near the door, and Noah pushed his wheelchair next to him. He had half a mind to get out and sit in a regular chair, but his doctor had warned him that his stitches could open up and that would cost him more time in the hospital. Something he certainly didn't want.

Alex stared at his hands for a while, not saying anything. He was making Noah a little nervous. What was this about?

"I'm going to tell you something," he said finally. "Something that could cost me my friendship with Kaely if you tell her. But I'm concerned. I think you should know."

"What are you talking about?" Noah asked.

"Kaely's technique . . . do you know about it?"

"Yeah."

The muscles in Alex's jaw tightened. "She told me the other night that the UNSUBs are starting to talk out of turn. That when she speaks to them, they are answering back. And she hasn't given them permission."

Noah was alarmed. "That doesn't sound good."

"I don't think it is. Kaely laughed at me when I told her it worried me. She told me it was just her own subconscious reacting to her . . . process."

"And you don't believe that?"

Alex shrugged. "I don't know what to believe. But here's something else you should know."

"Yeah?"

"It's about Georgie."

"What about her?" Noah said. "Sounds like she's the only friend Kaely has left. Except us and Solomon."

Alex shook his head. "I'm not sure her friendship is beneficial."

"I don't get it."

Alex's eyes met his. "Noah, Georgie isn't real. She doesn't exist."

Noah could hardly believe his ears. "Isn't real?" he repeated. "She . . . she made her up?"

"Not completely," Alex said. "Georgie was

Kaely's best friend when she was a kid. When Ed was arrested, Georgie's parents wouldn't let her see Kaely anymore. Kaely said she needed someone to talk to. Someone besides Richard. So she invented Georgie. She was there whenever Kaely wanted someone to talk to." He shook his head. "Kaely knows she's not real. She says she's her other side — her normal side. Bouncing things off her helps Kaely to clear her mind."

Noah shook his head. "I don't know. It doesn't sound . . . healthy."

"I agree. When I was here, I got her to promise to wean herself off Georgie. But when I left . . ."

"What do you want me to do?"

"Nothing. And don't ever tell her I told you. But when the day comes that she shares the truth about Georgie — and I'm sure she will — I wanted you to be prepared." He sighed. "She needs real friends, Noah, not imaginary ones. Invisible UNSUBs shouldn't be talking back to her. And now she's lost Richard. I'm worried about her." He leaned toward Noah. "You have to help her. You have to keep her grounded."

Noah thought about how much he'd changed in the short time since he'd started working with Kaely. He nodded at Alex. "I will. I'll do whatever it takes to keep her safe in the field . . . and personally."

"Just be careful," Alex said. "Don't make my mistake. Give her your mind, your loyalty, your life. But keep your heart to yourself. If you don't . . ."

"I get it," Noah said, interrupting him. "I'll be okay."

"I hope so. Because if you don't guard your heart, you could get it broken. I should know." Alex held his hand out and Noah shook it. "Good-bye, Noah."

"Good-bye, Alex."

Noah watched as Alex got up and walked down the hall. For some reason, he felt a great sense of relief. He turned his wheelchair around and headed back to Kaely's hospital room, Alex's words of warning ringing in his ears. He'd meant his reassurances to Alex, but a voice in his head kept asking him if it was too late to protect his heart from Kaely Quinn.

Forty-Six

Solomon walked quickly toward Kaely's hospital room. Ever since he'd had his heart attack, he hated hospitals. The antiseptic smell made his stomach churn. When he finally found the right room, he pushed the door open and walked in. He found Noah sitting in a wheelchair not far from her bed, and another man he didn't know was holding her hand.

"Solomon," Kaely said. "You didn't need to come down here."

"Don't be silly," he said, sounding gruffer than he meant to. "You're my agent. This is where I should be." Seeing her in that hospital bed and knowing what she'd been through had shaken him, but he didn't need her to know that.

"Solomon, this is my brother, Jason," Kaely said, gesturing toward the man holding her hand.

Solomon approached the bed and shook

hands with Kaely's brother. "Glad to meet you, Jason. I'm sure your being here is a blessing to your sister."

"It's a blessing to both of us," Jason said.

"Jason, this is my boss, Special Agent in Charge Solomon Slattery," Kaely said.

"Solomon's fine. My title is too long. I always feel as if someone much more impressive should be attached to it."

Jason laughed. "I'm sure that's not true, but I'm happy to call you Solomon."

"So, how are you feeling?" Solomon asked Kaely.

"Much better. Hopefully, I can go home soon."

"Good, but I want you to take a couple of weeks off. And no arguing."

Kaely looked up at her brother. "No argument from me. I want to spend some time with Jason."

"Well, that's a first," Solomon said. "Kaely Quinn willing to put something before her job." He looked over at Noah. "You too. You need time to heal. Don't come back until you're one hundred percent. Two weeks sounds about right."

"Let me get this straight. She's coming off a high, and I got shot. But we both get two weeks? Did you happen to notice I'm in a wheelchair?"

Solomon forced back a smile. "Okay. Three weeks."

Noah and Kaely laughed.

"Actually, three weeks sounds great," Noah said. "Frankly, I'm tired. Chasing after Richard Barton was exhausting."

"Seems I was right about the poisoning threat," Kaely said. "Richard threw that in just to sidetrack us. It worked. I thank God he didn't implement it."

"I agree."

"I missed the reference to fire, Solomon," Kaely said. "I'm sorry. I should have seriously considered the Unabomber case."

"Don't be ridiculous," Solomon said. "None of us got that. I think Acosta's fate was sealed from the beginning. I don't think any of us could have saved him."

Kaely shook her head. "I just can't figure out why he picked Acosta. He doesn't fit the other victims — people I don't know or someone I care about. Acosta was a thorn in my side."

Noah cleared his throat. "I think I might know why," he said. "And yes, I cleared my throat because this is difficult to say, but I think you need to hear it."

Solomon frowned at his agent. "I'd like to hear it too. Go ahead, Noah."

Noah eyed Kaely carefully. "Kaely, do you

know how we found you?"

"I guess not," she said. "Alex was supposed to follow me, but he told me he lost sight of my car because of the weather and an accident on the road." She looked confused. "How did you locate me?"

"We looked for any property in Richard's name, but the building where he took you was in Bella's name. Not too hard to figure out. And we also traced the phone Richard used to send you the text message supposedly from Alex."

"But that doesn't make sense," she said, uncertainty written on her face. "Richard knows better than that. He's listened to me talk about tracking criminals. Those are huge mistakes."

"I see where you're going with this," Solomon said to Noah. "You think he did it on purpose. That he didn't really want to kill Kaely."

"It's the only thing that makes sense," Noah said.

Kaely snorted. "That's ridiculous. He tried to get me to shoot myself. . . ." Her voice trailed off.

"You're starting to see it," Noah said. "He wanted you to shoot yourself because he couldn't do it. He had plenty of opportunity. Alex knew. He encouraged Richard to kill you, but he wouldn't. Alex knew Richard couldn't hurt you."

"But he did fire his weapon," Kaely said. "He shot you."

"Because I charged him. I think it was an accident."

"But . . ."

"Kaely," Solomon said, "you asked why Jerry Acosta was a target. Why would Richard take out the man who's caused you so much heartache? Who has been hounding you for years?"

Kaely didn't respond. She just stared at the wall.

"Somewhere inside, he still cares about you, Kaely," Noah said. "He took out Acosta for you. And he didn't really want you to die. He just wanted someone to pay for his wife's death."

"I think they're right, sis," Jason said. "Richard was always there for us when we were kids. I think his concern was real."

"Innocent people are dead," Kaely said harshly. "No matter how he feels about me, he's a monster."

"And you catch monsters," Solomon said. "If he isn't executed, he'll never leave prison. Don't worry about him. Just concentrate on you." He stood. "I'll see you in two weeks. If you have any questions while you're off, address them to Ron. I won't be in the office."

He chuckled at the shocked look on his agents' faces. "Yeah, you heard right. I'm taking Joyce on a cruise. She needs it . . . and I do too."

"I'm so glad," Kaely said with enthusiasm. "Have a wonderful time."

"I think I will." Solomon smiled at his agents. "Great work, you two. I'm proud of you." He pointed at Kaely. "When we're both back, you and I are going to talk about not calling for backup when you went after Richard. And it will be a very serious talk. Do you understand?"

She nodded. "I understand."

He looked at Noah. "Maybe you could talk to her about protocol?"

Noah grinned. "Sure, why not? If you really think it will help."

"No, I don't, but try anyway."

"What about Alex?" Kaely asked. "Will he be in any trouble?"

"With who?" Solomon asked. "He's quit the Bureau and is on his way to the Philippines."

"But he . . ."

Solomon held up his hand. "His SAC gave him permission to help us with our case. It may have come a little late, but I don't think anyone will complain." He pointed at Noah. "I understand that Alex isn't easy to control, but in the future, a lead agent can't let something like this happen. Understand?"

Noah nodded. "Yes, sir."

Solomon stood up and turned his attention to Jason. "It was good to meet you. I hope you and your sister will take this opportunity and do something great with it."

"Thank you," Jason said. "We will."

"Good." Solomon walked over to the door. "I'll call and check on you two before I leave," he said to Kaely and Noah. He gulped back the lump in his throat.

"Thanks for everything, Solomon," Kaely said.

"My privilege. My extreme privilege." He hurried out the door before his emotions overcame him. Solomon stopped in the hallway and took out his phone. When his wife answered, he said, "I'm on my way home. Are you packed yet?" Listening to the joy in her voice made him smile. "I love you, Joyce. See you soon." Solomon hung up and headed out of the hospital.

On Wednesday morning, Kaely unlocked the door to her condo and walked inside, happy to finally be home. Jason had dropped her off but was coming back later this afternoon after he packed and checked out of the Marriott. She could hardly wait to spend time with him. Noah was doing better and would be going home tomorrow. She and Jason planned to get together with Noah a few times during their time off, if Noah felt up to it.

She went into her kitchen and opened the refrigerator door. The remnants of her Chinese dinner with Richard filled one shelf. Without thinking, she grabbed every last container and threw them in the trash. She didn't want anything from him. She'd definitely have to go to the store before Jason arrived.

As she closed the door, she realized it had been two days since she'd been home. Mr. Hoover should have been fed by now. She sighed loudly when he suddenly meowed. She turned around to smile at him.

"Hey, there. You know what? I think I'm getting closer and closer to having a real cat. What do you think about that?"

Mr. Hoover meowed one more time and then disappeared.

ACKNOWLEDGMENTS

This book couldn't have been written without the help of Supervisory Special Agent Drucilla L. Wells (retired), Federal Bureau of Investigation (Behavioral Analysis Unit). I'm amazed at the patience she showed toward this writer. I'm so thankful for her, and she is truly a gift from God. Don't give up on me, Dru. We have more books to write together.

Big thanks to Lynette Eason for allowing me to borrow her "FBI buddy." You're the best, Lynette. I owe you big time!

Thank you to Mark Bogner, the weather guy from Wichita. You've always been available when I had "atmospheric" questions. You might know a lot about things like clouds and air pressure, but you're one of the most "down to earth" and humble people I've ever known.

Thank you to Officer Darin Hickey with the Training and Community Affairs Division in Cape Girardeau, Missouri, for always being available to answer my questions. Thank you so much for your service.

Thanks to my assistant, Zac Weikal. What would I do without you? You run my website, send out my newsletters, and promote my books. And sometimes you push this reticent writer to step out of her comfort zone. I truly appreciate you.

How can I thank my daughter-in-law, Shaen Layle (Mehl) for all the help she's given me? If I searched the world for the perfect wife for my beloved son, Danny, I couldn't find anyone better. And now we get to write together? What a blessing!

Thank you to my incredible husband, Norman, who supports me, takes care of me, and loves me.

Thank you to my awesome son, Danny, who has always believed in me. I've written a lot of books, but my greatest creation will always be you.

As always, my thanks to my editors. Raela

Schoenherr, you always tell me the truth. Even when I don't want to hear it. You make me better. And thanks to Jennifer Veilleux, who has worked so hard to make this book a success.

To my Inner Circle and my dear friends: Mary Gessner, Shirley Blanchard, Cheryl Baranski, Tammy Lagoski (who has a relative who shows up in *Mind Games*!), Lynne Young, Karla Hanns, Liz Dent, Rhonda Gayle Nash-Hall, Breeze Henke, Michelle Prince Morgan, Bonnie Traher, Deanna Dick, Zac Weikal, and JoJo Sutis. Thank you for hanging in there with me even though I was writing something a little different when I first joined this group. Love you guys!

My thanks to all the wonderful readers out there who buy and read my books. Without readers, there are no authors. Thank you for all the nice emails and notes you've sent through the years. I pray that every person who reads this will remember that they are loved by God. Completely and forever. Your name is engraved on your Father's hand. You are special. And nothing is impossible in Him.

ABOUT THE AUTHOR

Nancy Mehl is the author of more than thirty books, including the ROAD TO KINGDOM, FINDING SANCTUARY, and DEFENDERS OF JUSTICE series. She received the ACFW Mystery Book of the Year Award in 2009. Nancy has a background in social work and is a member of ACFW. She writes from her home in Missouri, where she lives with her husband, Norman, and their puggle, Watson. To learn more, visit NancyMehl.com.

The employees of Thorndike Press hope you have enjoyed this Large Print book. All our Thorndike, Wheeler, and Kennebec Large Print titles are designed for easy reading, and all our books are made to last. Other Thorndike Press Large Print books are available at your library, through selected bookstores, or directly from us.

For information about titles, please call:
(800) 223-1244

or visit our website at:
gale.com/thorndike

To share your comments, please write:
Publisher
Thorndike Press
10 Water St., Suite 310
Waterville, ME 04901